D1391540

VIRAGO
MODERN CLASSICS

THE MAGIC TOYSHOP

'This crazy world whirled about her, men and women dwarfed by toys and puppets, where even the birds were mechanical and the few human figures went masked . . . She was in the night again, and the doll was herself.'

One night Melanie walks through the garden in her mother's wedding dress. The next morning her world is shattered. Forced to leave her rural home, she is sent to London to live with relatives she has never met: gentle Aunt Margaret, mute since her wedding day; and her brothers, Francie and Finn. Brooding over all is Uncle Philip, who loves only the puppets he creates in his workshop, which are life-size – and uncannily life-like.

'The boldest of English women writers'
Lorna Sage

'Her writing is pyrotechnic – fuelled with ideas, packed with images and spangling the night sky with her starry language'
Observer

THE WRITER

Angela Carter (1940–1992) was born in Eastbourne and brought up in south Yorkshire. She read literature at Bristol University before spending two years in Japan, and went on to become one of Britain's most original writers. Carter wrote her first novel, *Shadow Dance*, in 1965. *Several Perceptions* won the Somerset Maugham Prize in 1968 and *The Magic Toyshop* won the John Llewellyn Rhys Prize in 1969. Angela Carther's death at age fifty-one 'robbed the English literary scene of one of its most vivacious and compelling voices' (*Independent*).

THE DESIGNER

Jacqueline Groag (1903–1986) studied in Vienna during the early 1920s. She was known mainly as a freelance textile designer and book illustrator, producing designs for The Wiener Werkstatte during the 1930s before emigrating to France to escape the Nazi invasion. In France she designed fabrics for Lanvin and Schiaparelli. In 1939, fleeing the Nazi invasion again, Groag moved to England. Here she gained connections with many textile manufacturing and wholesale firms including Liberty's, Heal & Sons, and several book publishers.

By Angela Carter

Fiction

SHADOW DANCE

THE MAGIC TOYSHOP

SEVERAL PERCEPTIONS

HEROES AND VILLAINS

LOVE

THE INFERNAL DESIRE MACHINES OF DOCTOR HOFFMAN

FIREWORKS

THE PASSION OF NEW EVE

THE BLOODY CHAMBER

NIGHTS AT THE CIRCUS

BLACK VENUS

WISE CHILDREN

AMERICAN GHOSTS AND OLD WORLD WONDERS

Non-fiction

THE SADEIAN WOMAN: AN EXERCISE IN CULTURAL HISTORY

NOTHING SACRED

THE VIRAGO BOOK OF FAIRYTALES (EDITOR)

EXPLETIVES DELETED

THE MAGIC
TOYSHOP

ANGELA CARTER

INTRODUCED BY CARMEN CALLIL

VIRAGO

This hardback edition published in 2008 by Virago Press
Reprinted 2008

Published by Virago Press in 1981

First published by W. Heinemann Ltd 1967

Cover design by Jacqueline Groag supplied
by the American Textile History Museum

A CIP catalogue record for this book
is available from the British Library

ISBN 978-1-84408-523-1

Typeset in Goudy by M Rules
Printed and bound in Great Britain by
Clays Ltd, St Ives plc

Virago Press
An imprint of
Little, Brown Book Group
100 Victoria Embankment
London EC4Y 0DY

A Hachette Livre UK Company
www.hachettelivre.co.uk

www.virago.co.uk

INTRODUCTION

Angela Carter died in 1992, from lung cancer. She was fifty-one. For a good part of her latter years she was one of my closest friends, and for most of that time I was also her publisher. Her photograph sits on the mantle in my bedroom and her sketches are still on my walls; one of them, of sweet peas and marigolds, hangs above my desk and gazes upon every word that I write. There was very little Angie could not do: she drew very well, and loved colour, bold colour, so that everything she created – houses, etchings, writing (and her clothes) – had something of the rainbow about them. Angie was particularly keen on every shade of yellow, and as much purple as could be added to anything. Orange also played a large part in her life.

But these talents were mere coda to what she could do with language, with words, which, after her husband and son, were the joy of her life. It was more than words, actually. The ideas behind the words she chose with such care and enthusiasm were just as important to her. She was such a believer, such a curious, cynical, wicked, robustly unsentimental believer.

What did she believe in? When Angie died, I spoke about her at her funeral at Putney Vale on 19th February 1992.

'Pleasure has always had a bad press in Britain. I'm all for pleasure, too. I wish there was more of it around. I also like to argue. A day without an argument is like an egg without salt,' wrote Angie.

And then I went on to say:

There are going to be many such saltless days now for those of us who loved Angie. What will we miss? We'll miss her passionate interest in all of us, her irony, her exotic pleasure in everything, her advice, her fabulous imagination, her subversive irreverence, her anger. Who is there to talk about politics now that she is gone? Her long telephone calls: what phone bills! What profit for British Telecom! How gratifying it was when one's news, gossip or opinions were received with that knowing cackle.

(Such was our mutual addiction to these conversations that in 1987, when she was on one of her constant travels to foreign parts – Angela loved abroad – I sent her a telegram: 'Angie, when are you coming home? You are away too much and I have gossip one thousand miles long and no address to write to you.')

And then: her vocabulary, her cooking, her physical mannerisms, her jokes, her travels, the quality of her voice, her writing, her kindness and her compassion; the sheer originality of every single bit of her. She was the oracle and guide we all consulted, a listener whose eloquent silences kept us hanging on every word she quietly and wickedly uttered.

I first met Angela Carter in 1972, at a book launch party of the 1970s kind. Her memory of it was that my first words were 'Don't you *adore* cabbage?'; mine that she told me that her husband had thrown a typewriter at her the night before: did I recommend that she should leave him? She was thirty-one when I met her and had already written five novels. I had just founded Virago. Angela went on to become one of the first writers I commissioned. Commission, however, is the wrong word to use for publishing Angela Carter. She wrote what she wanted to, and to get Virago off the ground, she chose to write *The Sadeian Woman*, a study of women, sexuality and power, which both outraged and alarmed some of the feminists of the time. Angela was a fervent feminist and a determined social-ist, but she was a ribald, irreverent and very often a topsy-turvy version of each: and she put up with politically correct nonsense from no one except herself. She wrote to me in 1973:

> Herewith is the Sade book for Virago, who I hope is a healthy child and screaming already. Many apologies for the delay – moving was one thing, and I've been trying to work, which means I go into a kind of self-enclosed capsule, from the centre of which the outside world (when I perceive it) and, also, time, appear to be com-pounded of porridge. (I don't like porridge either).

Because Virago was in its infancy she took a peppercorn advance of £400 for this book. Angela was fond of money and the good things it buys, but she never thought the world of it. Over the next twenty years, she continued to produce this and that for Virago. Loyalty was an absolute cornerstone of her personality, and she felt it for all who worked at Virago over the years. As she lay dying in Brompton Hospital, she was fiddling about with a manuscript on her bed: the *Virago Book of Fairy Tales* – 'I'm just finishing this off for the girls'.

For a complicated and formidably original human being, Angie proved to be the simplest person to publish. Everything pleased her. Everything received her attention, from endpapers to the identity of her reviewers. Editorially, of course, there was little to do. She couldn't spell, but apart from that, every word she wrote was chosen with precision, to present with *that* word, and no other, the imagination or opinion she wished to convey. Courtesy was the root of it: Angela was a truly courteous woman. It came from her tremendous interest in, and microscopic observation of, the world about her: she knew what people were worth.

She knew what *she* was worth too. In her later years she became famous herself, the only female in that early gaggle of writers who were, in the 1980s, considered to be Britain's finest – Ian McEwan, Julian Barnes, Martin Amis, and of course, Salman Rushdie. Recognition was slow to come to her; she knew in her bones that her gender had something to do with that. It made her angry, as injustice always did, but that was not the feminism she espoused; hers was of the laughing, ironic and get-on-with-it kind.

Nothing escaped her razor-sharp mind. She was no compromiser and did not cut her purse to fit any pig's ear, but her immense curiosity meant that she took a vast pleasure in everything life had to offer. So while she despised many of the histrionics indulged in by the *glitterati* (mostly male, but neither did she spare such female versions as there were in those days), she was never averse to dabbling her toes in their glamorous pools: good copy for hour-long telephone dismemberment afterwards.

Angela Carter, no narrow Anglophile, was a great traveller and loved America, Japan, Australia, Italy, France. But she was rooted in Britain; in its literature, food, its politics. She was a true child of the last war and the age of Austerity which followed it, and she gave thanks every day of her life to the post-war Welfare State for the good things it gave her. She was an irredeemably radical political animal. Her last years were spent in Thatcher's Britain: 'We're going to hell in a hand-basket' were her words on those years. In this, as in much else, she was the prime representative of a particular British personality which runs a gamut from Shakespeare to Tom Paine to Charles Dickens. She was spared New Labour, Tony Blair, Iraq, George Bush and much else, but she has left behind such a body of work that her views on each require no imagination. More, the language she luxuriated in to express disgust and disdain remain a bible for anyone today who might be lost for words to attack the status quo.

Though she lived in the twentieth century, in fact she belonged to the twenty-first in almost every way. She was fascinated by men, women, children and the beasts of field and sky, but her concentration was on uprooting assumptions about how women live and love, celebrating how they decorate and indulge themselves, and how they hunger for sex. Challenging authority, she stuck a pin into any available literary or cultural balloon, rewriting and reinterpreting fairy tales and myths so that little girls were no longer eaten by wandering wolves, but were given a decent pair of gnashers to do the chewing themselves.

She was the great celebrator of the vulgarian as heroine, and raised her irreverent female creations high, using the fairy tale and the theatrical and music hall images she loved so much. Angie loved the movies, too, everything about them. Popular culture fascinated her. She preceded Madonna and Kylie Minogue, but she prepared us for their arrival. You see them in her heroines as they fly out of her novels and short stories, cursing and sweating, exotic or bawdy, making jokes, using every beautiful word in the English dictionary in magical and exquisite ways, to tell the world to move over, and make way for women.

In that way, she was a seer – an itinerant Pied Piper who travelled whenever she could, doing what she loved to do: teach. She was the Johnny Appleseed of English literature: all over the world are literary incendiary bombs planted by Angela, and in Britain, young writers whom she encouraged.

Virago published *The Sadeian Woman* in 1979. Immediately after that I delved into Angela's suitcases of journalism and in 1982 Virago published a selection, *Nothing Sacred*. Her 'advertisement' for that (Angie never liked to use the word 'synopsis', an insufficiently ebullient word for what was, after all, to become a book) sums up the varied interests of her magnificent magpie mind: 'South London; Venice; Padstow; D. H. Lawrence as closet Queen; Red Indians; Health Foods; Underwear; Teddy Bears; Male Nudes.' By this time the Virago Modern Classics list had been launched and Angela, phenomenally well read, was as interested, as critical, and as supportive of that fiction list as she was of everything else

Virago did. She read novels for me and became passionate about some of the writers on that list – Margaret Atwood, Christina Stead, Eudora Welty, Elizabeth Taylor, Elizabeth Jolley.

By 1981, she had reacquired the rights to some of her earlier novels. Virago was to publish five of her works of fiction in the Classics list, but the first novel we chose was her second, *The Magic Toyshop*, a perfect introduction to her work. You will laugh on the first page, you will be disturbed by the end of the first chapter, you will soon be transported into mysterious and fascinating places. In her day – and since – Angela Carter's writing has often been categorised as magic realism. Angela herself scorned this description, considering herself a stern realist, and as you follow the story of Melanie in *The Magic Toyshop*, you will see how right she was. You will know what it is like have the body and longings of a young girl, set loose upon a dangerous world. Melanie's adventures, at once charming and unsettling, introduce you to the audacious imagination and fabulous sense of wonder and fun of a great writer. Only the person she was could have produced a novel like *The Magic Toyshop*. You are about to encounter the vibrant and conversational ghost of Angela Carter.

Carmen Callil, 2007

1

The summer she was fifteen, Melanie discovered she was made of flesh and blood. O, my America, my new found land. She embarked on a tranced voyage, exploring the whole of herself, clambering her own mountain ranges, penetrating the moist richness of her secret valleys, a physiological Cortez, da Gama or Mungo Park. For hours she stared at herself, naked, in the mirror of her wardrobe; she would follow with her finger the elegant structure of her rib-cage, where the heart fluttered under the flesh like a bird under a blanket, and she would draw down the long line from breast-bone to navel (which was a mysterious cavern or grotto), and she would rasp her palms against her bud-wing shoulderblades. And then she would writhe about, clasping herself, laughing, sometimes doing cartwheels and handstands out of sheer exhilaration at the supple surprise of herself now she was no longer a little girl.

She also posed in attitudes, holding things. Pre-Raphaelite, she combed out her long, black hair to stream straight down from a centre parting and thoughtfully regarded herself as she held a tiger-lily from the garden under her chin, her knees pressed close together. A la Toulouse-Lautrec, she dragged her hair sluttishly across her face and sat down in a chair with her legs apart and a bowl of water and a towel at her feet. She always felt particularly wicked when she posed for Lautrec, although she made up fantasies in which she lived in his time (she had been a chorus girl or a model and fed a sparrow with crumbs from her Paris attic window). In these fantasies, she helped him and loved him because she was sorry for him, since he was a dwarf and a genius.

She was too thin for a Titian or a Renoir but she contrived a pale, smug Cranach Venus with a bit of net curtain wound round her head and the necklace of cultured pearls they gave her when she was confirmed at her throat. After she read *Lady Chatterley's Lover*, she secretly picked forget-me-nots and stuck them in her pubic hair.

Further, she used the net curtain as raw material for a series of nightgowns suitable for her wedding night which she designed upon herself. She gift-wrapped herself for a phantom bridegroom taking a shower and cleaning his teeth in an extra-dimensional bathroom-of-the-future in honeymoon Cannes. Or Venice. Or Miami Beach. She conjured him so intensely to leap the spacetime barrier between them that she could almost feel his breath on her cheek and his voice husking 'darling'.

In readiness for him, she revealed a long, marbly white leg up to the thigh (forgetting the fantasy in sudden absorption in the mirrored play of muscle as she flexed her leg again and again); then, pulling the net tight, she examined the swathed shape of her small, hard breasts. Their size disappointed her but she supposed they would do.

All this went on behind a locked door in her pastel, inno-
cent bedroom, with Edward Bear (swollen stomach concealing
striped pyjamas) beadily regarding her from the pillow and
Lorna Doone splayed out face down in the dust under the bed.
This is what Melanie did the summer she was fifteen, besides
helping with the washing-up and watching her little sister to
see she did not kill herself at play in the garden.

Mrs Rundle thought Melanie was studying in her room.
She said Melanie ought to get out more into the fresh air and
would grow peaked. Melanie said she got plenty of fresh air
when she ran errands for Mrs Rundle and, besides, she studied
with her window open. Mrs Rundle was content when she
heard this and said no more.

Mrs Rundle was fat, old and ugly and had never, in fact,
been married. She adopted the married form by deed poll
on her fiftieth birthday as her present to herself. She
thought 'Mrs' gave a woman a touch of personal dignity as
she grew older. Besides, she had always wanted to be married. In old age, memory and imagination merge; Mrs
Rundle's mental demarcations were already beginning to
blur. She would sit, sometimes, in her warm fireside chair,
at the private time when the children were all in bed,
dreamily inventing the habits and behaviour of the husband she had never enjoyed until his very face formed
wispily in the steam from her bed-time cup of tea and she
greeted him familiarly.

She had hairy moles and immense false teeth. She spoke
with an old-world, never-never land stateliness, like a duchess
in a Whitehall farce. She was the housekeeper. She had
brought her cat with her; she was very much at home. She
looked after Melanie, Jonathon and Victoria while Mummy

and Daddy were in America. Mummy was keeping Daddy company. Daddy was on a lecture tour.

'A lecher tour!' crowed Victoria, who was five, beating her spoon upon the table.

'Eat up your bread pudding, dear,' said Mrs Rundle. They ate a lot of bread pudding under Mrs Rundle's regime. She did bread pudding plain and fancy, with or without currants or sultanas or both; and she performed a number of variations on the basic bread-pudding recipe, utilising marmalade, dates, figs, blackcurrant jam and stewed apples. She showed extraordinary virtuosity. Sometimes they had it cold, for tea.

Melanie grew to fear the bread pudding. She was afraid that if she ate too much of it she would grow fat and nobody would ever love her and she would die virgin. A gargantuan Melanie, bloated as a drowned corpse on bread pudding, recurred in her dreams and she would wake in a sweat of terror. She pushed the fatal bread pudding around her plate with her spoon and slyly shovelled most of her helping onto Jon's plate when Mrs Rundle's broad back was turned. Jonathon ate steadily. Jonathon ate largely out of pure absence of mind.

Jonathon ate like a blind force of nature, clearing through mounds of food like a tank through the side of a house. He ate until there was no more to eat; then stopped, put knife and fork or spoon and fork together neatly, wiped his mouth with his handkerchief and went away to make model boats. The summer Melanie was fifteen, Jonathon was twelve and absorbed in the making of model boats.

He was small, snub-nosed and fair, a grey-flannel-and-school-cap boy, with a healed scab, always, just at the flaking off point on one knee or the other. He made model boats from construction kits, scrupulously painting, assembling and rigging them and then placing them on shelves and mantel-pieces up and down the house, where he could stare at them in passing. He made models only of sailing ships.

He made a model of the three-masted barque, H.M.S. *Beagle*; also of H.M.S. *Bounty*; of H.M.S. *Victory* and of H.M.S. *Thermopylae*. His hands, that summer, were always tacky with glue. His eyes had a far-away stare in them as if he saw not the real world, but the blue seas and coconut islands where his boats, once launched, imaginatively and forever sailed. A mental Flying Dutchman, Jonathon roved uncharted seas under a swan-spread of canvas, his feet on swaying, salt-drenched boards, never treading dry land at all. He walked with a faintly discernible nautical roll but nobody ever noticed.

And nobody ever noticed that he did not see them because his eyes were concealed by glasses with round, thick, bottle lenses. In the things of this world, he was extremely short-sighted. With his glasses and his school cap and the scabs on his knees, he looked the sort of small boy who makes one immediately think of Norman and Henry Bones, the boy detectives. Misled by his appearance, his parents loaded his bookcase with Biggles books, which gathered dust unopened.

Early in the summer, Melanie stole six untouched Biggles books from his room, smuggled them to a town on a cheap day excursion and sold them at a secondhand bookshop in order to buy a set of false eyelashes with the proceeds. But the false eyelashes made her weep painful tears when she tried to fix them in place and then they refused to stay put but riffled through her fingers onto the dressing-table like baleful, hairy caterpillars with a life of their sinister own. Mutely, they accused her – thief! thief! Treacherous, they were the wages of

5

sin. Melanie burned them guiltily in her rarely used bedroom hearth. It was obvious to her that they could not be worn because she had stolen to get the money to buy them. She had a well-developed sense of guilt, that summer.

Victoria had no sense of guilt. She had no sense at all. She was a round, golden pigeon who cooed. She rolled in the sun and tore butterflies into little pieces when she could catch them. Victoria was a lily of the field, neither toiling nor spinning, but not beautiful. Mrs Rundle sang old songs to her, sang how the harbour lights told me you were leaving and that roses were blooming in Picardy but there was never a rose like you; and Victoria chuckled on her knee and grabbed at Mrs Rundle's cat with her cube-shaped fist. Mrs Rundle's cat was an obese, nose-in-the-air Tom. Seated, it was the size and shape of a fur coffee table, a round one. Perhaps Mrs Rundle fed it on scraps of bread pudding.

It sat on Mrs Rundle's indoor slippers (which were yellow felt with red pom-poms) and Mrs Rundle sang to Victoria and knitted.

'What are you knitting?' asked Victoria.

'A cardigan.'

'Cardingan,' perverted Victoria with satisfaction.

'Why is it black, Mrs Rundle?' asked Melanie, come to get orange juice with ice-cubes from the refrigerator, padding on summer-naked feet.

'At my age,' said Mrs Rundle with a sigh, 'there is always someone to wear black for. If not immediately, then sooner than later.' The vowel in later came out immensely elongated, as if steamrollered flat – leeeeeeter. 'You'll catch your death, dear, with bare feet on a stone floor.'

The ice cubes shivered in Melanie's hand.

'Have you known many dead people?' she asked.

'Sufficient,' said Mrs Rundle, beginning to cast off.

'I find death inconceivable,' said Melanie slowly, fumbling for the right word.

'That is only natural at your age.'

'Sing!' commanded Victoria, beating her lollipop paws on Mrs Rundle's black silk knee. Mrs Rundle obediently lifted up her voice.

Melanie thought of death as a room like a cellar, in which one was locked up and no light at all.

'What will happen to me before I die?' she thought. 'Well, I shall grow up. And get married. I hope I get married. Oh, how awful if I don't get married. I wish I was forty and it was all over and I knew what was going to happen to me.'

She stuck moon-daisies in her long hair and looked at herself in her mirror as if she were a photograph in her own grown-up photograph album. 'Myself at fifteen.' And, following, the pictures of her children in Brownie uniforms and Red Indian outfits, and pet dogs, and summer-snapped future holidays. Buckets and spades. Sand in the shoes. Torquay? Would it be Torquay? Bournemouth (the Chine)? Scarborough-is-so-bracing? And never, for example, Venice? And the pet dogs, would they be Yorkshire terriers or corgis; or noble, hawk-nosed Afghan hounds or a pair of white greyhounds on a golden chain?

She said to the daisy girl with her big, brown eyes: 'I will not have it plain. No. Fancy. It must be fancy.' She meant her future. A moon-daisy dropped to the floor, down from her hair, like a faintly derisive sign from heaven.

Meanwhile, they lived in a house in the country, with a bedroom each and several to spare, and a Shetland pony in a field, and an apple tree that held the moon in its twiggy fingers up outside Melanie's window so that she could see it when she lay in her bed, which was a single divan with a Dunlopillo mattress and a white quilted headboard. She slept between striped sheets.

The house was red-brick, with Edwardian gables, standing by itself in an acre or two of its own grounds; it smelled of lavender furniture polish and money. Melanie had grown up with the smell of money and did not recognise the way it permeated the air she breathed but she knew she was lucky to have a silver-backed hairbrush, a transistor radio of her own, and a jacket and skirt of stiff, satisfying, raw silk made by her mother's dressmaker in which to go to church on Sundays.

Their father liked them all to go to church on Sundays. He read the lesson, sometimes, when he was at home. Born in Salford, it pleased him to play gently at squire now he need never think of Salford again. That summer, they went to church with Mrs Rundle, who was devout. She took with her her own bulging, black prayerbook which scattered old dried pressed flowers and bits of fern if she picked it up carelessly. Victoria sat on the floor of the pew, chasing idly the desiccated greenery drifting from Mrs Rundle's prayerbook and cooing. Sometimes she cooed quite loudly.

'Is Victoria retarded?' wondered Melanie. 'Will I have to stay at home and help Mummy look after her and never have a life of my own?'

Victoria, like Mrs Rochester, a dreadful secret in the back bedroom, beaming vacantly, playing with kiddibricks, simple constructional toys and wooden jig-saw puzzles, pushing her indecent baby face against the banisters to coo at unnerved guests.

Jonathon's favourite hymn was 'Eternal Father, Strong to Save'. Whenever the vicar, a pale man who fished and made pale jokes about fishers of men, came to keep the eye on them all which he had promised their father, Jonathon would grip the hem of his cassock fiercely and request that 'Eternal Father, Strong to Save' should be sung the next Sunday.

'We'll see,' the vicar would say, ill at ease beneath the intense glare of Jonathon's spectacles.

All Sunday breakfast and best-dressing time, Jonathon quivered with suppressed anticipation. But, more often than not, the hymn was not sung. Hope faded the moment he saw the hymn numbers posted in the wooden slots on the wall. Then Jonathon climbed aboard the tea clipper *Cutty Sark* or H.M.S. *Bounty* and cast off with a fresh breeze swelling the sails, and steered out across the blue, blue sea, nursing his hurt. The vicar had betrayed him. Gag him with a marlin spike. To the mizzentopmast, keep him there all day – naked, during the long tropic day. Give him a taste of the cat.

Melanie prayed: 'Please God, let me get married. Or, let me have sex.' She had given up believing in God when she was thirteen. One morning, she woke up and He wasn't there. She went to church to please her father and she wished on wishbones as well as on her knees. Mrs Rundle prayed, astonishingly: 'Please, God, let me remember that I was married as if I had really married.' For she knew she could not fool God by virtue of the deed poll. 'Or at least,' she continued, 'let me remember that I had sex.' Only she phrased it less bluntly. Mrs Rundle became abstracted from time to time during the service as she wondered how the roast beef and potatoes left at home in the oven were getting on. But she always apologised when she returned in mind to God.

Neither Jonathon nor Victoria prayed, having nothing to pray for. Victoria tore the fringes off the hassocks and ate them.

Melanie was fifteen years old, beautiful and had never even been out with a boy, when, for example, Juliet had been married and dead of love at fourteen. She felt that she was growing old. Cupping her bare breasts, which were tipped as pinkly as the twitching noses of white rabbits, she thought: 'Physically, I have probably reached my peak and can do nothing but deteriorate from now on. Or, perhaps, mature.' But she did not want to think she might not be already perfect.

One night, Melanie could not sleep. It was late in the summer and the red, swollen moon winked in the apple tree and kept her awake. The bed was hot. She itched. She turned and twisted and thumped her pillow. Her skin prickled with wakefulness and her nerves were as raw as if a hundred knives were squeaking across a hundred plates in concert. At last, she could bear it no longer and got up.

The house was heavy with sleep but Melanie was wide awake. She felt strangely excited to be up and about when they all slept; she imagined a trail of zeds . . . zzzzz . . . issuing from their three sleeping mouths like bees and buzzing dreamily around the house. She wandered idly into her parents' empty room. Shoes under the bed waited patiently for her mother's returning feet, an empty tobacco tin pined on the bedside table for her father to come back and throw it away. The room was lit completely by the moon; the white crochet cover on the low, wide bed glowed in the moonlight with a pregnant luminosity. Her parents slept in this bed, which was generous and luxurious as a film star's.

Leaning over the wicker heart which formed the bedstock,

Melanie tried to imagine her parents making love. This seemed a very daring thing to think of on such a hot night. She tried hard to picture their embraces in this bed but her mother always seemed to be wearing her black, going-to-town suit, and Daddy had on the hairy tweed jacket with leather elbow-patches which, together with his pipe, was his trade mark. His pipe would be tucked into the breast pocket while they did it. Melanie tried but could not imagine her parents' nakedness. When she thought of her mother and father, their clothes seemed part of their bodies, like hair or toenails.

Her mother, in particular, was an emphatically clothed woman, clothed all over, never without stockings whatever the weather, always gloved and hatted, ready for some outing. A wide-brimmed brown velvet hat with a black ribbon rose at the side superimposed itself on Melanie's picture of her mother being made love to. Melanie remembered that, when she was a little girl and her mother cuddled her, the embraces were always thickly muffled in cloth – wool, cotton or linen, according to the season of the year. Her mother must have been born dressed, perhaps in an elegant, well-fitting caul selected from a feature in a glossy magazine, 'What the well-dressed embryo is wearing this year.' And Daddy – Daddy was always the same; tweed and tobacco, nothing but tweed and tobacco and type-writer ribbon. Of these elements, he was compounded.

Her parents' wedding photograph hung over the mantel-piece, where the familiar things seemed exotic and curious in the light of the moon. The French gilt clock, for instance, which told her parents' time and had stopped at five minutes to three on the day after they left for America. Nobody had bothered to wind it up again. Next to the clock was a Mexican pottery duck, bright, gay and daft, its blue back splotched with yellow flowers. Her mother had bought it after seeing its photograph in a Sunday colour supplement. Melanie wandered over to the mantelpiece, picked up the pottery duck and put it down again, and raised her eyes to the wedding photograph.

On her mother's wedding day, she had had an epiphany of clothing. So extravagantly, wholeheartedly had she dressed herself that her flying hems quite obscured Melanie's father. One could only see his shy grin, misted over with blown tulle, and Melanie could not tell whether, as she suspected, he was wearing the leather-patched tweed jacket even on his wedding day, because he could not take it off. But her mother exploded in a pyrotechnic display of satin and lace, dressed as for a medieval banquet.

Cut low in front to show a love-token locket nestling in the hollow of her throat, her white satin dress had scooping sleeves, wide as the wings of swans, and it flowed out from a tiny waist into a great, white train, arranged around in front of her for the photograph so that the dress appeared as if reflected in a pool of itself. A wreath of artificial roses was pressed low down on her forehead and a fountain of tulle sprang up and around it and spouted in foam past her waist. She carried a bunch of white roses in her arms, cradled like a baby. Her smile was soppy and ecstatic and young and touching.

She was surrounded by relations of whom they had seen less since Daddy had done so well with the novel and then the biography and then the film and so on. Aunt Gertrude, too tight perm, awkward feet in too tight shoes, grasping a shiny, patent leather handbag like the week's groceries. Melanie remembered the Ashes of Violet flavoured kisses of her Aunt

Gertrude from the few family Christmases when Grandfather (scowling at the camera as if he expected it to gobble his soul) was alive. Good-bye, Grandfather. Good-bye, Auntie Gertrude. And good-bye brilliantined Uncle Harry with Auntie Rose on his arm. Rouged Auntie Rose. The round patches of rouge came out black in the photograph. She might have been a sweep they asked along for luck. Good-bye, Uncle Philip.

Unlike the rest, Uncle Philip did not smile at the camera. He might have strayed into the picture from another group, an Elks' solemn reunion or the grand funeral of a member of the ancient and honourable order of Buffaloes, or, even, from a gathering of veterans of the American Civil War. He wore a flat-topped, curly-brimmed, black hat such as Mississippi gamblers wear in Western films and a black bootlace tie in a crazy bow. His suit was black, his trousers tight, his jacket long. But the final effect was not of elegance. Under the black hat, his hair seemed to be white, or, at least, very fair. He had a walrus moustache which concealed his mouth. It was impossible to guess his age. However, he seemed old rather than young. He was tall and of a medium build. His hands were clasped before him on the silver knob of an ebony cane. His expression was quite blank; too blank, even, to seem bored. Mother's only brother. Her only relative living, for all the others were father's family. And he could not even raise a smile at his sister's wedding. It seemed churlish of him.

Melanie had never seen Uncle Philip. Once, when she was a little girl, he sent her a jack-in-the-box. He was a toymaker. When she opened the jack-in-the-box, a grotesque caricature of her own face leered from the head that leapt out at her. That year, her parents had sent him one of their printed

Christmas cards showing themselves and Melanie (Jonathon not yet born) sitting smiling at the window of the little mews cottage they had recently bought, almost in Chelsea. Her father was beginning to make a name and money. And, in return, came this horrid toy. The jack-in-the-box frightened Melanie very much indeed. She had nightmares about it regularly into the New Year and, intermittently, until Easter. Her mother threw the jack-in-the-box away. Her parents agreed the gift was thoughtless and in bad taste. No cards were sent to Uncle Philip after that. The tenuous contact was lost for good.

Photographs are chunks of time you can hold in your hand, this picture a piece of her mother's best and most beautiful time. Her smiling and youthful mother was as if stabbed through the middle by the camera and caught for ever under glass, like a butterfly in an exhibition case; Melanie, looking at the photograph, thought that Uncle Philip had no place in this fragment of her mother's happy time. He was a colour which clashed; or, rather, a patch of no colour at all. He occupied a quite different time. He looked as if he had met an ancient mariner on the way to the wedding and been catapulted into a dimension where white roses and confetti did not matter any more.

'Well,' thought Melanie, 'I don't suppose I shall ever see him.'

She examined the wedding dress more closely. It seemed a strange way to dress up just in order to lose your virginity. She wondered if her parents had sexual intercourse before they were married. She felt she was really growing up if she had started to speculate about this. Daddy must have been a bit of a Bohemian, in spite of his family and, besides, was living in a flat by himself. A Bloomsbury bedsitter, coffee brewing on a gas-ring, talk about free love, Lawrence, dark gods. Had he already sacrificed his smiling bride to the dark gods? And, if so, would she still be smiling, since it was her mother? And would she have dressed herself in virginal white? What about the letters in the women's magazines which Melanie borrowed secretly from Mrs Rundle?

'My boy friend says he will leave me unless I let him love me to the full but I want to be honestly married in white.'

Symbolic and virtuous white. White satin shows every mark, white tulle crumples at the touch of a finger, white roses shower petals at a breath. Virtue is fragile. It was a marvellous wedding-dress. Did she, Melanie wondered for a moment, wear it on the wedding night?

Her mother was a woman of sentiment. In a trunk starred with faded stickers from foreign places, under a piece of Indian embroidery thrown over it to conceal it prettily, there lay the wedding-dress, all treasured up, swathed in blue tissue to keep the satin white. What did she keep it for? Would she be laid out in it or wear it up to heaven? But in heaven was no marriage nor giving in marriage.

Melanie frowned in the moonlight, wearing her prosaic striped pyjamas which she had outgrown that summer so that the legs came half-way up her calves. She fingered a few scent bottles on her mother's dressing-table. There was a china tree for rings (but the rings were all on her mother's fingers in America, being shown the Empire State Building, the Grand Canyon and Disneyland); and there was a pin-tray in china to match, with two pins and a broken shirt button in it. There was also a framed photograph of Victoria holding a fluffy toy dog, patently a photographer's prop, which Victoria, equally patently, was considering tearing up. It was the sort of picture, thought Melanie, which only a mother would find endearing. She wondered if she herself would be blind to the unattractiveness of her children, if they proved to be unattractive. Absently she dabbed stale Chanel behind her ears and at once smelled so like her mother that she glanced at herself in the mirror to make sure she was still Melanie.

Her face was all mooney. Her hair was night-time screwed up in a top-knot and she pulled it free so that it fell down her back. She tried her hair in various styles, over her face, scraped-back ballerina, all bunches round on one side asymmetrically, while she considered the locked-away wedding-dress.

'Would it fit me?'

All the time, while she wondered, she watched herself; and abstractedly she unbuttoned the top of her pyjamas and practised a few poses in case she ever wanted to be a model-girl or a cabaret dancer. Her mother's dressing-table mirror was wider, although shorter, than her own. But all the time, she was thinking: 'Shall I? Shan't I?' She opened a drawer and found in a corner a face-powder-caked penny.

'Heads it is,' she said to the shadows. Heads it was. She took a deep breath and began to heave the trunk away from the wall in order to get at its brass clasps. She felt wicked, like a grave-robber, but the coin had fallen and the die was cast. The lid creaked open. A great deal of loose tissue paper packed in the top rose up, lazily rustling after so many undisturbed years, and hovered a few inches in the air, momentarily levitated, an emanation. She brushed it away.

The wreath came first, padded with paper. Artificial roses and a few sprigs of lily of the valley that could not be seen in the photograph, with, here and there, a pearl, to simulate dew.

Some of the petals of the roses were bent and disarranged; one rose was squashed entirely, like a dada exhibit. Melanie straightened them all carefully and turned the wreath round and round in her hand. A bridal wreath. And laid it on the bed.

She unfolded acres of tulle, enough for an entire Gothic Parnassus of Cranach Venuses to wind round their heads. Melanie was trapped, a mackerel in a net; the veil blew up around her, blinding her eyes and filling her nostrils. She turned this way and that but only entangled herself still more. She wrestled with it, fought it and finally overcame it, losing patience with it and piling it anyhow on the bed, beside the wreath. It was time for the dress.

The dress was very heavy. The sliding satin had a sheen on it like that on the silver teapot which never went out of the drawing-room cabinet except to be polished. All the moonlight in the room focused on its rich and mysterious folds. Melanie tore off her pyjamas and clambered into the dress. It was very cold to the touch. It slithered over her, cold as a slow hosing with ice-water, and she shivered and caught her breath.

It was too big. Her mother had married in a buxom bloom of puppy-fat. Two skinny Melanies could have worn the dress between them for a Siamese-twin bridal. Melanie remembered reading of the marriage of a pair of Siamese twins. They would have needed a very big bed. A quadruple bed.

She was bitterly disappointed that the dress was too big. She weltered and rolled in white satin. She kicked the hem before her, back to the dressing-table, to find the pins and pin herself up. But she saw in the mirror that it did not matter if the dress was too big.

17

Her face under the streaming black hair was blanched and transfigured by the cast-up shimmer of the dress, which skimmed the very edge of her breast in the manner of the dresses of Elizabethan virgins. She moved in a rich tent which curiously emphasised her own slenderness and illuminated her like a candelabrum. She knew she could not cope with the veil but she reached for the wreath and set it straight on her head. The little pearls gleamed like eyes, or the tears of fishes, which they are said to be. But her mother's pearls were artificial. Nevertheless, they gleamed.

'And am I as beautiful as that?' she thought, startled, under the pearls and flowers.

She opened her mother's wardrobe and inspected herself in the long mirror. She was still a beautiful girl. She went back to her own room and looked at herself again in her own mirror to see if that said different but, again, she was beautiful. Moonlight, white satin, roses. A bride. Whose bride? But she was, tonight, sufficient for herself in her own glory and did not need a groom.

'Look at me!' she said to the apple tree as it fattened its placid fruit in the country silence of the night.

'Look at *me*!' she cried passionately to the pumpkin moon, as it smiled, jovial and round-faced as a child's idea of itself.

A fresh little grass-scented wind blew through the open window and stroked her neck, stirring her hair. Under the moon, the country spread out like a foreign and enchanted land, where the corn was orient and immortal wheat, neither sown nor reaped, terra incognita, untrodden by the foot of man, untouched by his hand. Virgin.

'I shall go down into the garden. Into the night.'

Quick down the stairs, huddling her skirts around her,

oops – mind the creaking one. She tugged breathless at the front door bolts, breaking a fingernail. Quietly, gently, or down would come Mrs Rundle, brandishing the poker she kept beside the bed to deal with burglars in the night. The night. Melanie let herself into the night and it snuffed out her daytime self at once, between two of its dark fingers.

The flowers cupped in the garden with a midnight, unguessable sweetness, and the grass rippled and murmured in a small voice that was an intensification of silence. The stillness was like the end of the world. She was alone. In her carapace of white satin, she was the last, the only woman. She trembled with exaltation under the deep, blue, high arc of sky.

Such a round moon. Trees laden to the plimsoll-line with a dreaming cargo of birds. The dewy grass licked her feet like the wet tongues of small, friendly beasts; the grass seemed longer and more clinging than during the day. Her dress trailed behind her; she left a glinting track in her wake. The still air was miraculously clear. Shadowed objects – a branch, a flower, stood out with a dark precision, as if seen through water. She walked on slow, silent feet through the subaqueous night. She breathed tremulously through her mouth, tasting black wine.

The lilac bushes stirred. A small, furry, night animal scuttled across the lawn in front of her and vanished with a scrabbling noise into a pile of grass cuttings; the creature, whatever it was, had no more corporeal substance than wind-blown leaves.

'I never thought the night would be like this,' said Melanie aloud, in a tiny voice.

She shook with ecstasy. Why? How? Beyond herself, she did not know or care. Great banks of cloud reared and dissolved in the heavens and here and there shone a star. The world, which was only this garden, was as empty as the sky, endless as eternity.

At primary school, in scripture lessons, the teacher described eternity. Miss Brown, who lisped and wore glasses and smelled of lemon soap, twirled chalk and talked about eternity ambitiously to the children, when they asked her. Eternity, she said, was like space in that it went on and on and on with God somewhere in it, like sixpence in a plum pudding (thought Melanie when she was seven) jostled by galaxies for raisins and lonely, maybe, for the company of other sixpences. How lonely God must be, thought Melanie when she was seven. When she was fifteen, she stood lost in eternity wearing a crazy dress, watching the immense sky.

Which was too big for her, as the dress had been. She was too young for it. The loneliness seized her by the throat and suddenly she could not bear it. She panicked. She was lost in this alien loneliness and terror crashed into the garden, and she was defenceless against it, drunk as she was on black wine.

Sobbing, she broke into a sudden run, stumbling over her skirts. Too much, too soon. She had to get back to the front door and closed-in, cosy, indoors darkness and the smell of human beings. Branches, menacing, tore her hair and thrashed her face. The grass wove itself into ankle-turning traps for her feet. The garden turned against Melanie when she became afraid of it.

The white front-door step was sanctuary. She sank down on it. Mrs Rundle scrubbed and scoured the step once a week, swept it once a day with her familiar, work-hardened, homely hands. Melanie laid her throbbing cheek against the cool stone and it smeared honest, shop-bought scouring powder on her face like a caste mark. But the door was shut. It had swung to behind her. She had no key. She was locked out. She had locked herself out.

She almost despaired when she realised she could not go through the door. And, besides, she had cut her feet when she ran on the gravel path, not noticing at the time; but now she saw they were bruised and bleeding and that there were little flecks of blood, black in the moonlight, on the hem of her mother's dress. But the worst thing was sitting outside the house and not being able to get in. She clutched the stone for comfort.

'I must pull myself together. What shall I do now?'

She had left her own window open. She could, perhaps, climb the apple tree and scramble into her own bedroom at last and slam down the window on the deserts of vast eternity outside. But she would have to leave the refuge of the step and venture out once more. Yet either the apple tree or wait here till morning. Until Mrs Rundle came down to get the breakfast. And she would have to explain to Mrs Rundle how she came to be locked out of the house all night in her mother's wedding dress.

She had climbed the apple tree when she was eight and again when she was twelve. And now that she was fifteen? But it was the apple tree or nothing, even though she must walk round to the back of the house, whatever lurked there. Whatever monsters. Whatever huge, still, waiting things with soft, gaping mouths, whose flesh was the same substance as the night.

She knew they were there, waiting for her to trip up and tumble. They shifted in the nebulous space beyond the corners of her eyes. She tried to look straight ahead of her, so she did not call them into her sight by accident. She kept as close

21

to the house as she could, trekking through flower beds carelessly; the house was some protection. Her blood throbbed in her ears; the noise it made could have been the raucous breathing of the monsters around her. In the silence of this night, no horror from film or comic book or nightmare seemed too outlandish to be believed.

'Don't be foolish,' she said to herself, 'there is nothing there. Nothing.' But 'nothing' clanged inside her head and she was afraid of the echoes. In this fear, she arrived at last at her stairway, her own tree, her friend, whose knobby old branches were thick with fruit. But this fruit, tonight, when she was so scared, seemed sinister poison apples, as if even her playmate tree had turned against her and there was no comfort in it.

In her tree-climbing days, the ascent would have taken only a few minutes. But she had given up climbing when she started to grow her hair and stopped wearing shorts every day during the summer holidays. Since she was thirteen, when her periods began, she had felt she was pregnant with herself, bearing the slowly ripening embryo of Melanie-grown-up inside herself for a gestation time the length of which she was not precisely aware. And, during this time, to climb a tree might provoke a miscarriage and she would remain forever stranded in childhood, a crop-haired tomboy. But needs must when the devil drives.

'How can I climb the tree in this dress, though?'

Hobbled in yards of satin which would rip and tear and tangle irreparably as she struggled for hand and footholds. She would mesh in the branches unable to move up or down. They would have to bring men with ladders and ropes from the farm to free her in the morning, dead or alive. Don't be silly. Alive. Alive to experience the indignity of it all. So she must take off her dress and climb stark naked in the treacherous and deceitful night. There was nothing else she could do.

She became aware of an area of deeper black on a low branch, a coalesced focus of dark, like one of the monsters of her overwrought imagination, which stirred. The beginnings of a scream swelled in her throat. Green eyes flashed and the blackness mewed. She shook her head with relief. It was Mrs Rundle's cat. She had company. She rubbed its ears for it and it throbbed and rattled with purring, a domestic sound, unexpected and reassuring. It was as if someone had lit a small fire for her. As long as the cat kept purring, Melanie had the courage to slip out of her dress. She pulled her hair around her, to protect herself for the night, drawing towards its end at the end of summer, had grown cold.

She parcelled up the dress and stuck it in the fork of the tree. She could carry it up with her and put it away again in the trunk and no one would know it had been worn if they did not see the blood on the hem, and there was only a little blood. The cat put its head on one side and turned its sequin regard on the parcel; it stretched out its paddy paw and stroked the dress. Its paw was tipped with curved, cunning meat hooks. It had a cruel stroke. There was a ripping sound.

'Oh, God,' said Melanie aloud. The cat had made a long tear. She struck at it; it leapt from the tree, thudded to the lawn and vanished. She was alone again and the moon was beginning to slide down the sky. Soon it would set and a perfect darkness would obliterate her. She prayed: 'Please, God, let me get safe back to my own bed again.' Also, she crossed her fingers.

She was horribly conscious of her own exposed nakedness. She felt a new and final kind of nakedness, as if she had taken even her own skin off and now stood clothed in nothing, nude in the ultimate nudity of the skeleton. She was almost surprised to see the flesh of her fingers; her very hands might have been discarded like gloves, leaving only the bones.

A shower of apples fell down around her as she tested the first branch. But it was strong enough to hold her. She took a deep breath and swung up. The bark scraped and furrowed her shins and thighs and stomach as she threw herself into the gnarled arms of the tree.

She had to scrabble painfully for every foothold and handhold. Once a branch broke with a groan under the trusting sole of her foot and she hung in agony by her hands, strung up between earth and heaven, kicking blindly for a safe, solid thing in a world all shifting leaves and shadows. Apples tumbled continually as she moved, and the waning moon blinked between leaves that thrust leathery hands spitefully into her eyes and into her gasping mouth. In an alien element, she fought for each panting breath. The little twigs tore her cheeks and soft breasts. She seemed to be wrestling with the tree. She ran with sweat. And there was the dress to drag behind her, like Christian's burden.

She did not know how long she struggled upwards but at last she saw her window-ledge above her head, a vision of the promised land. But it was high over the last firm branches and somehow she had to swing herself and the dress perilously up to it. Thank God, the window was wide open on Edward Bear and *Lorna Doone* and silver-backed hair-brushes. Swaying, bracing herself, biting her lips, she rose up in a foam of leaves.

After two false starts when, dizzied and trembling, she almost precipitated herself out of the tree to the inhospitable ground below, she flung up the dress. It opened out, flapping white wings in her face, settling like a giant albatross in the window frame for a quivering moment and then toppled forward out of sight. And she flung herself up after the dress, crashing into her room face down on the floor.

She was bruised and filthy and she bled from a hundred little cuts. She lay on her creamy Indian carpet, sobbing with relief to feel the solid floor under her at last. When she could get up, she limped to the window and shook her fist at the moon. Clutching Edward Bear, she burrowed under the blankets to the heart of the bed and went to sleep at once.

In the morning, she saw that the dress was in ribbons.

She laid it out. It eclipsed her own narrow bed but it was rags. The tree had completed the work the cat started. The skirt hung in three detached panels and the scored and tattered sleeves hung to the bodice by a few threads only. Besides, the dress was filthy, streaked with green from the tree and her own red blood. She had bled far more than she realised. She fingered the dress, stiff with horror.

And what of the wreath? She had forgotten the wreath, must still have had it on her head as she ascended the tree. But it was nowhere in the room. She went to the window. The wreath hung on a high, top branch among apples too high to be picked. It was like a white bird's nest. The pearls caught the fresh morning sunshine. And there the wreath must stay, unless they called in the fire brigade.

Toast and bacon smells floated up from the kitchen. Life went on.

'Oh, you fool!' said Melanie savagely to herself in the mirror.

Her hair was larded with apple leaves. She brushed and combed them onto the floor, wrenching out long strands of hair in her fury. It did her good to feel the pain. She was chastened and humiliated, a foolish child who, sooner or later, would have to confess to the moonlight adventure that had ended so disastrously.

She took the ruins of the dress back to the chest, squashed them in anyhow and crammed all down under heaping tissue paper. When her mother came home, then she would tell her, privately. And perhaps nobody would notice the wreath in the meantime. For it was very high up in the tree and Mrs Rundle was short-sighted and Jonathon was nearly blind and Victoria never looked up.

'Can I have Melanie's nice bacon?' demanded Victoria. And Jonathon ate her slices of toast. Melanie could not eat for the weight of guilt and shame which seemed to have settled on her stomach. When the table was cleared, she went to her room and got out her schoolbooks as if to do schoolwork was a propitiation. She had neglected *Lorna Doone* all summer; now she took copious notes from it.

Mrs Rundle and Victoria went to the village shop and Jonathon went with them, to buy a new construction kit. The empty house boomed and reverberated around Melanie; she sensed the strange not-being of a houseful of deserted rooms and the back of her neck twitched when she heard chance thumpings and creakings. It was a sunny morning and the apples on the tree gleamed with health. An apple a day keeps the doctor away. The wasps would be busy already, burrowing into the trove of windfalls at the foot of the tree. She hated wasps. She could hardly bear to think of the wasps gorging themselves under her window.

At half past eleven, in the drowsy middle of the hot morning, there came a tremendous knocking at the door, so loud and unexpected that her pen-hand jarred in a blot in her note-book. She went downstairs. Mrs Rundle's cat was ponderously chasing flies in the hall. It was a witness of her folly; it had had a paw in last night's destruction. She kicked at it as she went past and it spat at her.

There was a messenger boy with a telegram in his hand at the door. As soon as she saw him, she knew what the telegram contained, as if the words were printed on his forehead. The morning blacked out for a second. When it was morning again, the boy was still there, waiting for his tip. There was sixpence change from the milk bill on the hallstand, which was lucky as Melanie had no money on her. The cat sat on the third stair and blinked. The boy went away. She heard the exhaust of his motorcycle in the distance.

'It is my fault,' she told the cat. Her voice wavered like waterweed. 'It is my fault because I wore her dress. If I hadn't spoiled her dress, everything would be all right. Oh, Mummy!'

Her stomach contracted. She went upstairs to the lavatory and vomited. She clutched the unopened telegram in her hand all the time. When she looked at it, she vomited again. She went into her bedroom. She met herself in the mirror, white face, black hair. The girl who killed her mother. She picked up the hairbrush and flung it at her reflected face. The mirror shattered. Behind the mirror was nothing but the bare wood of her wardrobe.

She was disappointed; she wanted to see her mirror, still, and the room reflected in the mirror, still, but herself gone, smashed. She trod over the broken glass to the window and looked out at the wedding wreath on the tree.

'I shall go and get it and put it away. I must. Then she might come back.'

But she knew that if she climbed onto the window-ledge, she would surely fall. And, besides, how could the dead return?

'Oh Mummy!'

She went into her parents' bedroom to look at them on their wedding-day. The wedding-dress was gone and the woman was gone and the man was gone, the man standing diffidently a little behind his bride, squinting because the sun was in his eyes.

'Oh, Mummy! Oh, Daddy!'

The tears began to stream down her face. She took the photograph, carefully removed it from its frame, holding the telegram between her teeth as she did so, and then tore up the photograph and threw the snowflake fragments into the fireplace. Then she broke the frame in pieces. After that, she began to wreck the room.

She pulled open drawers and cupboards and tipped out the contents in heaps, attacking them with her strong hands. She dug into boxes and jars of cosmetics and perfume, daubing herself and the furniture and the walls. She dragged mattress and pillows from the bed and punched them and kicked them until springs twanged through the brocade mattress cover and the pillows burst in a fine haze of down. The telegram was still clenched between her teeth, gradually darkening with saliva. She neither saw nor heard anything but wrecked like an automaton. Feathers stuck in the tears and grease on her cheeks.

Mrs Rundle came home with Victoria, both eating ice-cream cornets because of the heat. Mrs Rundle set the ready-peeled potatoes to boil and laid the table. Jonathon brought his new box home in his arms. He had bought a kit for the *Cutty Sark*. Behind his glasses, his eyes were luminous with excitement.

'Dinner's nearly ready, Jonathon,' said Mrs Rundle comfortably.

He sat down obediently at table with the box across his knees; it was precious and he would not let it go. Victoria played with paper bags from the shopping. The meal was served and the two children began to eat. Mrs Rundle wondered where Melanie was. She would need her dinner, having not eaten breakfast. Jonathon and Victoria ate hungrily; Mrs Rundle did not want to disturb them.

'Melanie!' called Mrs Rundle from the foot of the stairs.

No reply.

Was the girl in her room, perhaps fallen asleep over her books? Wheezing a little from the stairs, Mrs Rundle found the room empty and broken mirror-glass all over the floor. She looked at the mess and sighed.

'She broke her mirror accidentally and is hiding because she dare not tell,' Mrs Rundle said sagely to herself.

On the landing, to her surprise, she heard a low wailing. She followed the unexpected sound. She found Melanie sitting cross-legged on a pile of ripped-up nightdresses. There was an oppressive stench of Chanel No. 5 from a litter of broken bottles. Melanie sat with her face screwed up. Covered with lipstick and mascara, her face was a formalised mask of crimson and black and from her open mouth issued a wordless stream of dismay. Mrs Rundle had seen a good many things in her time and took things in her stride.

She had to force Melanie's hot, tense fingers apart to take the telegram from her. Melanie took no notice of Mrs Rundle at all. Mrs Rundle got out her reading glasses from her apron pocket, polished them and read the telegram. She shook her head slowly. She put her arms round Melanie but Melanie was unbending as wood, and wailing. So she left her alone and stumped heavily downstairs.

'Jonathon,' said Mrs Rundle, 'run for the doctor. Your sister's been taken bad.'

'I haven't had my pudding yet,' said Jonathon reasonably.

'It'll keep hot in the oven.'

'I want my pudding NOW!' clamoured Victoria, for she could see that, today, for a treat, it was apple pie. Mrs Rundle cut her a thick wedge and poured custard over. They had better eat while they could. She ate her own pie slowly, cere-moniously, as if it were funeral baked meats. She knew from experience that a full stomach is a help in times of trouble. Then she gave her cat a saucer of potatoes mixed with gravy.

'You and I will be looking for new quarters, soon, Pussy,' she told it. It purred as it ate and waved its tail.

2

Melanie swam like a blind, earless fish in a sea of sedation, where there was no time or memory but only dreams. Summer changed to autumn before she surfaced and lay palely on her bed, remembering. When she was strong enough, she went out one early morning and buried the wedding-dress decently under the apple-tree. Her breast felt hollow, as if it were her heart she had buried; but she could move and speak, still.

'You must be a little mother to them,' said Mrs Rundle. Mrs Rundle sewed black armbands to their coats, even Victoria's. Mrs Rundle's coat was black already; she was always prepared for mortality to strike. She was disappointed, even aggrieved, that the remains would not be brought home for a funeral. Since there were no remains to speak of. But even so.

Melanie started wearing her hair in stiff plaits, in the manner of a squaw. She plaited her hair so tightly that it hurt her, straining hair and flesh until it felt as though the white seam down the back of her head might split and the brains gush out. It was a penance. She chewed at the spiky end of a plait and kicked at a kitchen chair-leg. Through the open door into the hall drifted the murmuring voices of the auctioneer's men.

Everything was to be sold. There was no money left. Daddy hadn't saved any money because he thought he could always make more. In a vacuum, the children existed from day to day. There was still food for them to eat and Mrs Rundle was still there. She was a fixed point. Melanie stayed beside her, now, helping her about the house. She did not like to be alone. The mirror was broken and she hated the casual glimpses she got of her face as she cleaned her teeth or when she passed the hall-stand. But Mrs Rundle, the mother-hen, was looking for a new post and the house was to be sold over their heads, and the furniture, too.

'A little mother,' repeated Melanie. She must be a mother to Jonathon and Victoria. Yet Jonathon and Victoria hardly seemed to feel the lack of a mother. They had their own private worlds. Jonathon pressed on with his new model. Victoria babbled like a brook, chasing motes in the sunbeams. Neither referred to their parents or seemed to realise that their present life was coming to an end – Victoria too young, Jonathon too preoccupied. When prospective buyers came to look at the house, which happened more and more frequently, they stayed out of the way until they had gone.

'The burden is all mine,' said Melanie.

Mrs Rundle knitted a knee-sock. For Jonathon, a parting-gift. She was turning the heel.

'They told me to tell you,' she said. 'The lawyers did. Since I am close. I have been waiting my time.'

'What is this?'

'You are to go to your Uncle Philip.'

Melanie's eyes grew wide.

'Your Uncle Philip will take the three. And it is not right for a family to be separated.' She sniffed emphatically.

'But we have never known him. He was Mummy's only brother and they drifted apart.' She dredged the name from a chance remark in the remote past. 'The name was Flower. Mummy was a Miss Flower.'

'The lawyer says he is a perfect gentleman.'

'Where does he live?'

'In London, where he has always lived.'

'So we shall go to London.'

'It will be nice, and you growing up. All London for you. Theatres. Dances.' From magazines and novels she recollected: 'Soirées.'

'How does he make a living? He used to be a toymaker.'

'And still is. He is married. There will be a woman's guidance.'

'I didn't know he was married.'

'These days,' disapproved Mrs Rundle, 'there is such a lack of contact within families! Fancy not knowing about your uncle's wife! She is, after all, your aunt!' Her steel needles flashed.

'It will all be new and strange.'

'That is life,' said Mrs Rundle. 'I shall miss you all and often think of the baby, growing up into a little girl. And you, into a young lady.'

Melanie bent her head and the plaits swung over her face. 'You have been so kind.'

'I shall help with the packing, of course.'

'When' – she gulped – 'when do we go?'

'Soon.'

October, crisp, misty, golden October, when the light is

sweet and heavy. They stood on the step and waited for the taxi with black bands on their arms and suitcases in their hands, forlorn passengers from a wrecked ship, clutching a few haphazardly salvaged possessions and staring in dismay at the choppy sea to which they must commit themselves.

'I may never see this house again!' thought Melanie. It was an enormous moment, this good-bye to the old home; so enormous she could hardly grasp it, could feel only a vague regret. The rose wreath still hung in the apple tree, a little weather-beaten, already.

Mrs Rundle kissed them wetly one after the other. She, too, was leaving the house that day. She wore her good, black, cloth coat and her neatly darned cloth gloves and her sturdy, serviceable laced-up shoes. Her cat slept in a basket beside her trunk. Her new employer would pick her up by car. Their relationship was at an end. She belonged to another house, other people.

'Oh, dear,' said Melanie, suddenly. 'School.' The sight of the trunk reminded her. She had not thought of it till now. But she and Jonathon should be back at school and Victoria starting at the village junior and mixed infants democratically this term.

'Your Uncle Philip will see to all that,' said Mrs Rundle. 'Mind you look after them on the journey and buy them sweets and comic books for the train.' She dug amongst the bottles of aspirin and loose hairpins and tubes of digestive mints in her whale-backed black simulated leather handbag. 'Take this.' A pound note for a good-bye present.

Then the taxi came for them. Did the taxi-driver, the ticket-collector at the station, the other passengers standing on the platform – did they sense the difference about the children and, seeing the black armbands, nod sadly, knowingly, and smile in encouragement and sympathy? Melanie thought they did and froze at the first breath of pity, summoning all her resources to act coolly.

A little mother.

'I am responsible,' she thought as they sat in the train and Victoria pulled up seat cushions to see what lay beneath them and Jonathon studied a diagram of the rigging on a schooner. 'I am no longer a free agent.'

A black bucket of misery tipped itself up over Melanie's head. Part of herself, she thought, was killed, a tender, budding part; the daisy-crowned young girl who would stay behind to haunt the old house, to appear in mirrors where the new owner expected the reflection of his own face, to flash whitely on dark nights out of the prickly core of the apple tree. An amputee, she could not yet accustom herself to what was lost and gone, lost as her parents scattered in fragments over the Nevada desert. A routine internal flight. An unscheduled squall. An engine fault. Two Britons are among the dead. We regret to announce the death of a distinguished man of letters. And his wife.

Mummy.

No, Mother. Now she was dead, give her the honourable name, 'Mother.' Mother and Father are dead and we are orphans. There was, also, an honourable ring about the word 'orphans'. Melanie had never even known an orphan before and now here she was, an orphan herself. Like Jane Eyre. But with a brother and sister whom she must look after for they had nothing left but her.

'London! London!' cried Victoria every time the train, a slow, halting, bucolic train, drew to a standstill, either at a drowsy country station where cow parsley foamed along the line or simply nowhere, among the fields, to have a little rest.

'They won't know us at the station, in London,' said Jonathon suddenly. 'We have never seen one another.'

'They will easily recognise three children travelling alone,' said Melanie.

The train was a kind of purgatory, a waiting time, between the known and completed past and the unguessable future which had not yet begun. It was a long journey. Jonathon stared from the window at a landscape which was not the one Melanie saw. Victoria, at last, went to sleep and did not see the slow beginnings of London nor wake when the train finally halted at the arched and echoing terminus. Melanie was stiff, aching and covered in smuts. She felt oddly cold and sick but bit her lip staunchly and gathered their cases together.

'Jonathon,' she said, 'you must carry Victoria.'

He considered this, holding a special parcel of his own.

'I would rather carry the model I am working on, in case it gets injured,' he said reasonably. She realised there was no use arguing with him.

'I'll carry her, then, and we'll get a porter.'

Victoria was a great, heavy lump of a child and Melanie's arms cracked under the weight of her. Buffeted helplessly by the crowd, Melanie peered around the platform. There were no porters to be had. And where was Uncle Philip?

Then her attention was caught by two young men who leant against a hoarding, drinking tea from cardboard cups with unhurried, slow, rustic movements. Their stillness attracted her. They created their own environment around them. Although behind them was a six-foot-high beer-bottle, with the red-lettered statement 'A Man's Drink!' across it,

36

they superimposed upon it a silent and rocky country where there was always a wind blowing with a touch of rain on it and few birds sang. They were hard but gentle men. They were country people in a sense that Melanie was not, although she had just come from the green fields and they might have lived in London all their lives. They were brothers.

Obviously brothers, although startlingly dissimilar – two different garments cut, at one time, from the same cloth. The younger was nineteen or so, just a few inches taller than Melanie, with longish, bright red hair hanging over the collar of a dark blue, rather military looking jacket with shoulder flaps and brass buttons. He wore washed-out, balding corduroy trousers wrinkled with their own tightness. His clothes had the look of strays from a parish poor-box. His face was that of Simple Ivan in a folk-tale, high cheek-bones, slanting eyes. There was a slight cast in the right eye, so that his glance was disturbing and oblique. He breathed through his slack-lipped mouth, which was a flower for rosiness. He grinned at nothing or a secret joke. He moved with a supple and extraordinary grace, raising his cup to his mouth with a flashing, poetic gesture.

His companion was the same man grown older and turned to stone. Taller, wider in the shoulder, clumsily assembled, with a craggy, impassive face. A bruising-looking man in a navy-blue, pin-striped suit with trousers frayed at the turn-ups and a beige and brown shirt of the sort that is supposed not to show the dirt. His brown and blue tie was speared with a tie-pin in the shape of a harp. He had a half-smoked, stubbed-out, hand-rolled cigarette, disintegrating into rags of paper and shreds of tobacco, stuck behind his ear.

They drank their tea and did not talk to each other. They

kept quite still, although all the commotion of the station swirled around them. They inhabited their silence and gave nothing away.

When the younger one finished his tea, he tossed the cup over the hoarding with a lyrical, curving, discus-thrower swing and wiped his mouth with the back of his hand. He seemed to be inspecting the train, raking the length of it with a slow, sweeping, lop-sided gaze. His eyes were a curious grey green. His Atlantic-coloured regard went over Melanie like a wave; she submerged in it. She would have been soaked if it had been water. He touched the other man's arm; at once he dropped his cup and they came towards her. And if one moved like the wind in branches, the other's motion was a tower falling, a frightening, uncoordinated progression in which he seemed to crash forward uncontrollably at each stride, jerking himself stiffly upright and swaying for a moment on his heels before the next toppling step. The boy smiled and stretched out hands of welcome; the other did not smile. Melanie knew they were coming for her and started.

She was dismayed to see these strangers accosting her when she expected to see an old man in a cowboy hat with a black and white photograph face. Half-remembered Sunday newspaper stories about men who haunted main-line London railway stations to procure young girls for immoral purposes ran through her mind. But the boy said: 'You'll be Melanie.'

So they knew her name and it was all right. She saw his mouth moving; he was still talking but a train was blowing its whistle and drowned his voice, which was extremely soft.

'I'm Melanie,' she said. 'Yes.'

'Let me take the child off you, Melanie.' He spoke with a faint but recognisable Irish lilt. She had to bend close to hear what he said. She surrendered Victoria gladly and flexed her strained arms.

Jonathon came from the train with a porter behind him loaded with their gear.

'He came right into the carriage from the corridor and said, "I expect you need a hand, sir,"' Jonathon explained. And added, wondering: 'He called me "sir"! Golly!'

'This is Jonathon,' said Melanie. 'And Victoria is the baby.'

'My name is Finn,' said the boy. 'And this is Francie. Finn and Francie Jowle. Pleased to meet you.'

With disconcerting formality, the brothers shook hands with both Melanie and Jonathon, though Finn had to juggle dangerously with Victoria to do so.

'But who are you?' asked Melanie.

'Your Aunt Margaret is our sister,' said Finn. 'In a way, we're uncles.' He grinned, a loose and vulpine grin, drawing his lips back over his teeth, which were yellow and crooked.

'But you're Irish!'

'There is no law, that I know, to prevent it,' said Finn, so gently she was ashamed. Victoria stirred in his arms. He spoke to her and she dug her face into his navy blue breast and slept again, more deeply. It was a cast-off fireman's jacket he was wearing. Melanie experienced a jolt of surprise. They went to the taxi rank in a disorderly procession.

'It is a very long way, for a taxi, but your uncle gave Francie the money and insisted,' said Finn. 'He would not,' he added, 'trust *me* with the money, you understand.' He grinned again.

'I had a pound. But I bought milk and nut chocolate with it.'

'A whole pound went on chocolate?'

'And magazines. For the journey. One called *Sea Breezes* for

Jonathon and the *Beano* annual for Victoria. You see, they had to be amused.'

'Nevertheless, it is a lot,' he said.

Melanie was squashed next to him, Francie silent and monolithic beside her, Jonathon on the tip-up seat in front of them. London slid past but Melanie did not look at it.

'Jowle?' she asked tentatively.

'Jowle.'

'It doesn't,' she said, 'sound much like an Irish name.'

'Perhaps not. But there it is.'

Then there was silence and then Melanie began to smell the men. She was puzzled for some moments as to the source of the smell, so little did she expect the brothers would be so dirty. Crushed as she was close to them, their smell filled her nostrils until she almost choked with it. And also with horror, for she had never sat close to men who smelt before. A ferocious, unwashed, animal reek came from them both; in addition, Finn stank of paint and turps on top of the poverty-stricken, slum smell. And Francie's collar, she saw, was rimmed with dirt and his neck was filthy. She could not see Finn's neck for the hair.

All her fifteen combed and scrubbed years rose up in an endless vista of baths and shampoos and clean underwear; a cortege of full baths in which she had washed herself, a slithering file of bars of soap which she had rubbed to nothing against her flesh. She tried to invoke the memory of sudsy hot water to protect her against their smell but it was no help. Surely the taxi-ride would never end and she be out in the fresh air. The clock ticked up shillings inexorably. Jonathon watched it, for a while, with admiration, as if appreciating its impudence in charging them so much.

'Is it very far, still?' Melanie asked in a congested, small voice.

'Still farther,' said Finn abstractedly. What was he thinking about? His profile was wild and eccentric, a beaky nose, eyes now hooded beneath heavy lids.

'Still farther,' he repeated.

'It is beginning to get dark,' she said, for light drained from the streets and Jonathon's face wavered and dissolved in the pool of dark inside the taxi.

'And will get darker,' responded Finn. His voice suddenly warmed. There was a certain ritual quality in this exchange, as though Melanie had stumbled on the secret sequence of words that would lead her safe over the sword-edge bridge into the Castle of Corbenic. Francie turned his head, rearranging his tightly buttoned mouth into the archaic smile of an early Greek terracotta statuette. A whiff of staleness came from his disturbed jacket.

'And you know,' said Finn, 'about your auntie?'

'Well, yes. Margaret. Your sister.'

'But did they tell you—' he stopped. The two brothers exchanged an equivocal glance in the gloom; their eyes flashed whitely to one another.

'She's dumb,' said Francie, the first time he had spoken. His voice was flat and harsh. He began to hum a tune, dissociating himself, rolling a cigarette with easy movements. He did not need to see his hands in order to roll himself a cigarette.

'Dumb?' said Melanie querulously.

'Not a word can she speak,' said Finn. 'Ah, they should have told you. It is a terrible affliction; it came to her on her wedding day, like a curse. Her silence.'

Francie paused in rolling his cigarette and frowned as if his brother had said too much; but Melanie did not notice. The new aunt had been a shadow in her mind, a wispy appendage of the toymaking uncle. Now she had a substance because she had a characteristic. Dumbness.

'How awful!' she said, shocked.

'We're very close, the three of us,' said Francie. 'It is right for brothers and sisters to be close.' His tobacco had a richly herbal smell, as though it was good for you.

'She's a gran' cook,' said Finn, offering this apparently in compensation. 'Such pastry!'

'Does she make bread pudding often?' asked Jonathon.

'Rarely,' said Finn, after a moment's thought.

'Oh, good,' said Jonathon. So he must have noticed and, in the end, resented, Mrs Rundle's endless bread puddings.

The taxi climbed through gaunt, grey streets with, here and there, ragged October trees dropping sad leaves into a deepening, sheep-white and shaggy mist. Melancholy, down-on-its-luck South London.

'We are nearly home,' said Finn and Melanie suddenly could not help but sob. Finn put his hand on her knee and said softly: 'We, too, have lived here, on and off, since our parents died.'

'Then we are all orphans!'

'In the same boat, yes.'

'Boat,' echoed Jonathon raptly.

They reached a wedge-shaped open space on a high hill with, in the centre, a focus, a whimsical public lavatory ornately trimmed with rococo Victorian wrought ironwork and, drooping over it, a weary sycamore tree with white patches on its trunk, like a skin disease. There were a number of shops, all brightly lighted now. A fruitshop, with artificial grass banked greenly in the windows and mounds of glowing oranges, trapped little winter suns; groping, mottled hands of bananas; giant crinkly green roses which turned out to be savoy cabbages when you looked more closely; buds of black-currant cordial which were red cabbages, to be cooked in spices and vinegar. A butcher's shop, where a blue-aproned, grizzle-headed man in a bloodstained straw boater reached between two swinging carcasses of lamb for sausages from a marble slab. A sweetshop with crackers and sweets done in reindeer and holly Christmas packs and a crepe paper Santa Claus in the window, already, jostling the Roman candles, fairy fountains and whizz-bangs for November 5.

More shops. A junk-shop, where a withered, pale woman sat and knitted by a paraffin stove among broken old things – pitchers, candlesticks, a few books, a sagging chair, a limping table, a chipped enamel bread-bin full of cracked saucers. A new furniture shop with a three-piece suite in uncut moquette in the window next to a cocktail cabinet shiny as toffee. All the shops were in the lower parts of tall, old houses and had curly, old-fashioned lettering on them, but for the furniture shop, which winked in faulty neon:

'Everything for the 'ome.'

'Here will do,' said Finn to the taxi-driver outside the public lavatory. Francie paid him from a thick but grimy roll of notes.

'But where is Uncle's house?' asked Melanie.

'His shop. We live over the shop. Over there.'

Between a failed, boarded-up jeweller's and a grocer's dis-playing a windowful of sunshine cornflakes was a dark cavern of a shop, so dimly lit one did not at first notice it as it bowed its head under the tenement above. In the cave could be seen the vague outlines of a rocking horse and the sharper scarlet of its flaring nostrils, and stiff-limbed puppets, dressed in rich, sombre colours, dangling from their strings; but the brown varnish of the horse and the plums and purples of the puppets made such a murk together that very little could be seen.

Over the doorway was a sign, 'TOYS PHILIP FLOWER NOVELTIES', in dark red on a chocolate ground. Stuck in the door, under a card on which was written 'Open' in an italic hand, was a smaller visiting card reading: 'Francis K. Jowle. Fiddle. Reels and jigs, etc. A breath of Auld Ireland. Generally available. Moderate fees.' And a shamrock and the pencilled message, 'Enquire within.'

Finn pushed at the door, which stuck momentarily on a thick doormat as if unwilling to let them in. A bell jangled angrily above them and a bright pink parakeet, on a perch by the counter, flew up and screeched defiantly. But it was held by a chain on its leg and soon subsided, fluttering. There was a long counter of polished reddish-brown wood and, behind it, shelves piled with cardboard box upon cardboard box and many coloured, oddly shaped parcels. But the light was as murky as that in the window, which was separated from the interior by a dusty, maroon velvet curtain. There was nobody in the shop but the parakeet. On the counter lay a writing-pad and a felt-tipped pen.

'Of course,' thought Melanie. 'So that Aunt Margaret can sell things to people by writing the prices down, she being dumb.'

The word 'dumb' tolled like a bell in her mind.

'We call the bird "Joey",' said Finn. 'He minds the shop, in a manner of speaking.'

'No sale,' snapped the parakeet. Victoria raised her sleepy

head and wondered at it. Finn still carried her with no sign of fatigue. He must be strong, for all his lightness.

A door opened and a light so bright and sudden it hurt their eyes spilled through from the back. Aunt Margaret. The light shining through her roughly heaped haycock of hair made it blaze so you might have thought you could warm your hands at it. She was a red woman, redder, even, than Finn and Francie. Her eyebrows were red as if thickly marked above her eyes with red ink but her face was colourless, no blood at all showing in cheeks or narrow lips. She was painfully thin. The high, family cheek-bones stuck up gaunt and stark and her narrow shoulders jutted through the fabric of her sweater like bony wings.

Like Mrs Rundle, she wore black – a shapeless sweater and draggled skirt, black stockings (one with a big potato in the heel), trodden down black shoes that slapped the floor sharply as she moved. She smiled a nervous, hungry sort of smile, opening her arms to welcome them as Finn had done. Finn put Victoria in her arms and she sighed and cuddled the baby with the convulsive, unpractised hug of a woman who, against her desire, has had no children. Melanie wondered how old she was but there was no way of telling; she could have been any age between twenty-five and forty.

'Go along into the back with your aunt,' said Finn to Melanie and Jonathon. 'Francie and I will take your things up to your rooms.'

In the little back parlour, a coal fire, rendered more fierce by the confines of the small, black-leaded grate, thrust yellow flames up the chimney. An electric kettle, plugged into the wall, steamed on a tin tray, surrounded by waiting cups. In the corner was a large gilt cage containing a number of stuffed

45

birds with glossy black plumage, yellow beaks and sharp little eyes; they were disconcertingly lifelike and for a moment Melanie thought they were real. There was a single, sagging, comfortable, leather-covered armchair of great age, with a crochet anti-macassar slipping down the back of it, and a number of cane-seated, straight-backed chairs. Nailed to the wall was a large blackboard with a compartment for chalk attached to it. On the blackboard was written: 'Greetings to Melanie, Jonathon and Victoria,' in white chalk, surrounded with decorative blue scrolls. Melanie felt a lump in her throat; it was a touching and whole-hearted welcome.

Aunt Margaret picked up chalk and wrote: 'Take off your coats and be comfortable. I am minding the shop so we must stay downstairs for a while.' Melanie noticed the woman's index finger was stiffly grained with chalk dust. She would have been a talkative woman if she could. Then she settled Victoria in the big chair and set about making tea. There were also big cream buns from a paper-bag, two each for the children.

'Our last meal was breakfast,' said Jonathon. 'Sausages and bacon. Of course, that was at home.'

'We were at home,' said Victoria. There was cream and jam smeared on her cheek. 'No home, now,' said Victoria. Her mouth opened in a round O of woe on an undulating panorama of partially masticated cream bun. Aunt Margaret seized her chalk again, rubbed the board clean with the ham of her hand and scrawled rapidly: 'Here is your home, now!'

'She can't read,' said Melanie. Victoria wailed. Aunt Margaret glanced round for something with which to distract her and darted to the corner where the cage was. She pulled a lever at the base of the cage. All the birds began to hop up and down and twitter, opening and shutting their beaks. Instantly entranced, Victoria beamed; before their eyes, her miserable O spread out into a Happy Sambo melon-wedge grin. She beat her hands together. The birds hopped and sang for perhaps two minutes; then the mechanism began to run down and the birds hopped more and more slowly and heavily, the twittering drew itself out in gasps. They were growing exhausted. Victoria drooped again. Aunt Margaret pulled the lever once more and the birds perked up and began to jump, brisk as ever.

'How extraordinary!' said Melanie.

The woman darted to the blackboard and told her: 'Your uncle made that.'

'He must be very clever.'

'It is on order. It has been paid for. Really, I shouldn't play it.' Her white forehead screwed up with worry.

Aunt Margaret was bird-like herself, in her hither-and-thither movements and a certain gesture she had of nodding her head like a sparrow picking up crumbs. A black bird with a red crest and no song to sing. The parakeet in the shop, hearing the sweet, mechanical noise, set up a loud jabbering: vehement, meaningless syllables as though incoherent with anger because he thought the toys were mocking him. The house was still full of birds.

The brothers came for their tea, smiling at their sister. They did not need words to communicate with her. She caressed Finn's tumbled hair lightly and put her cheek against Francie's lapel. They loved one another and did not care who knew it. Their love was almost palpable in the small room, warm as the fire, strong and soothing as sweet tea. And Melanie, seeing them, felt bitterly lonely and unloved. But Finn came and sat beside her and gave her another cream bun, which she accepted gladly as a token of friendship, although she did not want it.

'But you mustn't spoil your supper,' he said, 'for it's rabbit pie. And if ever a woman could make a rabbit pie, it's our Maggie. Isn't that so, Francie?'

Francie smiled his archaic smile and Aunt Margaret laughed soundlessly.

'Rabbit pie, we shall have, leaving the bones for the dog,' said Finn reflectively.

'Ooh, is there a doggie?' cried Victoria, bounding up and down.

'She always wanted a dog but Mum – Mother wouldn't let her have one. She said all children wanted dogs and then didn't look after them. Or cats, they wanted.'

'Well, Victoria has part shares in a dog now, at least,' said Finn.

They all had more tea. Jonathon took no interest in the room or the company. He sat with his eyes fixed on great breakers rolling on a coral atoll somewhere in the immense Pacific. A bottle swept up to his feet and rolled in a rock pool. He smashed it open. There was a message in it. He read it with surprise. It prompted a question. From a long way away, he asked: 'When shall we see our uncle?'

'Tomorrow,' said Finn readily. 'He was called away unexpectedly today, which is why Francie and I came to meet you, instead of him.'

Why was Finn the only one who talked? Well, Aunt Margaret could not and Francie would not. It was Finn who showed their rooms to Melanie and Jonathon. Jonathon had a high, airy attic, freshly whitewashed, with a little iron bed with a cover made of knitted squares sewn together like a refugee blanket. The window, hooded in the roof, had a view of a great, curving valley, full of lights, a ravishing, night-blooming city flower-bed.

'In daytime, you can see St Paul's,' offered Finn.

'It is almost,' said Jonathon, 'like a crow's nest. On a ship. Only, with a bed.'

In his excitement, he took off his glasses and polished them on his pocket handkerchief, which was no longer clean. Will we have clean handkerchiefs here, every day, as a matter of course, wondered Melanie apprehensively. Jonathon's eyes, unprotected, blinked on and off, unused to open air. He began to unpack his things at once. He loved his room. They left him. Now Melanie was alone with Finn.

She and Victoria were to sleep one storey below Jonathon in a long, low room papered with fat, crimson roses. There was a shiny brass bed for Melanie with a round-bellied white chamber pot underneath it. Dust layered the bottom of the chamber pot; it had not been used for a long time and was probably meant for show. Melanie made a vow never to use it herself. There was a moth-ball smelling cupboard for their clothes. There was a chest-of-drawers painted pale blue with flowers cut from seed-packets glued onto it for decoration. There was a reproduction of 'The light of the World' in a bamboo frame over the mantelpiece. There was no mirror in the room. The electric light bulb hung in a spherical Japanese lantern, blue, with a green cuttlefish curling round it, so that the light was cold and garish. On the window-sill was a potted geranium, still in pink flower. The curtains were blue and white gingham. Melanie looked out of the window and saw, far below, a tiny, walled, city jungle of a garden, all tangled bushes in the dark.

'Excuse me,' she said, and opened her case to retrieve Edward Bear. She felt better when he lay on her pillow. She had lived with Edward Bear for ten years. Finn lit a cigarette and lolled against the chest-of-drawers, which shifted under his weight. She wished he would go away.

'That's a fine bear,' he said conversationally. His voice was scarcely louder than the faint London hum of traffic far away that came through the window.

'It is something from the old days,' she said, digging her hands in Edward Bear's yielding fur.

'But aren't you too grown-up for furry toys, Melanie?'

'I'm fifteen. That is, sixteen in January.'

'January. Well, you're a fine grown girl for fifteen.' He was grinning again, slackly. His squinting eyes slithered and shifted like mercury on a plate. She could see the pointed tip of his tongue between his teeth. He tapped his cigarette ash on the floor. The curl of his wrist was a chord of music, perfect, resolved. Melanie suddenly found it difficult to breathe.

It was as if he had put on the quality of maleness like a flamboyant cloak. He was a tawny lion poised for the kill – and was she the prey? She remembered the lover made up out of books and poems she had dreamed of all summer; he crumpled like the paper he was made of before this insolent, off-hand, terrifying maleness, filling the room with its reek. She hated it. But she could not take her eyes off him.

'You've lovely hair,' he said. 'Lovely. Black as Guinness. Black as an Ethiopian's armpit.'

She thought that he was stretching out his lordly paw and playing idly with her, and he in his absurd fireman's jacket.

'Why do you do up your hair in those tortured plaits, now, Melanie? Why?'

'Because,' she said.

'You know that's no answer. You're spoiling your pretty looks, pet. Come here.'

She did not move. He ground out his cigarette on the window-ledge and laughed.

'Come here,' he said again, softly.

So she went.

He put his hands on her shoulders and inspected her face closely; nodded as if he approved of it and began to unfasten her hair. Burning, she held her breath. She had never been so close to a young man before. The smell of paint fought with his body smell and won; it was almost overpowering. He shook out her hair for her, took his own comb from his pocket (a gap-toothed, black comb, threaded with red hairs) and combed it out. He concentrated. He had, she saw, stopped playing with her. The atmosphere around him changed, grew less charged, grew ordinary. He was simply doing her hair, fluffing it out like a real hairdresser. For secret reasons she acknowledged but did not understand, she felt bitterly offended.

'Now you look pretty,' he said approvingly, running the palm of his hand over her head to give it a final shine. 'We can have supper, now, and you'll be the belle of the ball.'

They ate at a round mahogany table with a stiff white cloth in a dining-room containing much heavy furniture. There was hardly room to move for large chairs and cupboards. Damp stained the walls, which had, long ago, been papered brownly with a pattern of leaves. A distorting witch-ball the size of a football stood in a wooden fruit bowl on the sideboard, in the middle of a mute congregation of bottles of tomato ketchup, salad cream, H.P. Sauce, Daddies Favourite sauce and Okay fruit sauce, all with dried dribbles running down their sides. Aunt Margaret carried in an oblong, golden pie from the kitchen, steaming and savoury. Francie spoke a strange grace.

'Flesh to flesh. Amen.'

Then they ate and the dog lay under the table. It put its wet nose on each of their knees in turn, for titbits. It was a white bull-terrier with pink eyes.

'Has the dog a name?' asked Melanie.

'Sometimes,' said Finn. 'It is an old dog.'

It was as good as a ballet to watch Finn eat but Francie mopped gravy with bread and chewed bones from his fingers. He was also a noisy eater, as if providing an orchestral accompaniment for his brother. The food was abundant and delicious. There was both white bread and brown bread, yellow curls of the best butter, two kinds of jam (strawberry and apricot) on the table and currant cake on the sideboard ready for when they had dealt with the pie.

Aunt Margaret poured fresh tea from a brown earthenware, Sunday-school treat pot that was so heavy she had to lift it with both hands. They drank their tea very dark and all put much sugar into it. Aunt Margaret presided over the table with placid contentment, urging them to eat with eloquent movements of the eyes and hands. The children ate hungrily, relaxing over the meal; she must, thought Melanie, be nice if she cooks so well.

When the pie finally changed places with the cake on the sideboard and they all had second cups of tea, the dog, judging it would get no more scraps, came from under the table, stood on three legs to scratch its left ear, shook itself and clawed the door, whining. Finn opened the door and the dog went out, wagging its tail.

'It takes itself for a little walk at night. Round the block. A quick pee. A sniff at all the corners to see what's new. Home. Bed.'

'How does it get back in?' asked Melanie. It seemed a very self-sufficient dog.

'The back door is never shut and there is an alley at the end of the garden. It just comes in.'

'But what if people, strangers, burglars, for example, get into the house, if you leave the door open, always?'

'We keep a welcome for all,' said Francie in his voice which creaked through lack of use.

There was a blackboard in the dining-room, also. Aunt Margaret wrote on it now: 'The baby ought to be in bed.' And Jonathon wanted to work on his model in his room. There was a general scraping-back of chairs. Melanie offered to help with the washing-up but Aunt Margaret shook her head. No chores on her first night. So Melanie would unpack a few things and go to bed early, herself. She was shaking with weariness and she was a little scared of these new people, especially of the men.

Aunt Margaret came to the girls' bedroom and unhandily undressed Victoria, although she could perfectly well undress herself. The dumb woman brooded over the child with a naked, maternal expression on her face which Melanie found both embarrassing and touching. She found that Margaret carried everywhere with her a writing pad and a felt-tipped pen. When she pinched Victoria's cushiony thigh (Victoria writhing and screaming with pleasure), she scribbled on the pad for Melanie to read: 'What a fine, plump little girl!'

'Yes,' said Melanie. 'Everyone says so.'

'Is it five she is?' wrote Aunt Margaret with a trace of brogue.

'Five years and four months.'

Aunt Margaret tucked up Victoria and hung over the cot for a long minute as though she would have liked to sing her a lullaby. Her red hair was piled up on top of her head in a rough knob; she shed hairpins like the White Queen. One or two clattered into the cot. Victoria sighed and shut her eyes. Hairpins fell like steel rain.

'How beautiful to watch a small child sleeping!'

'Yes,' said Melanie. 'I suppose it is.' She did not want to carry on a lengthy conversation with this garrulous dumb woman; she wanted to go to bed and hug Edward Bear. Aunt Margaret's curly, black handwriting skipped and hopped on the paper because Melanie's eyes were so tired.

Aunt Margaret swiftly bent down and kissed Victoria's already slumbering forehead. Then she kissed Melanie good-night on the cheek, taking her in a stiff, Dutch-doll embrace; her arms were two hinged sticks, her mouth cool, dry and papery, her kiss inhibited, tight-lipped but somehow desperate, making an anguished plea for affection. She darted off straight after that, leaving Melanie fingering her cheek in surprise.

Once she was in bed with Edward Bear, the light out, the night shut safe outside behind the drawn curtains, Melanie cried a little because she was not tucked into her bed with the satin headboard and the striped coverlet. But her new sheets smelled of lavender and there was a comforting stone hot-water-bottle at the foot of the bed, wrapped up in part of an old blanket so that it would not bruise her toes, and Victoria's gentle breathing was drowsy as the humming of bees, and she slept, with the tears drying on her cheeks.

But the texture of her sleep was light and shimmering and when she opened her eyes again much later, it did not seem as though she had slept at all. Yet the darkness in the room had deepened and the water-bottle had cooled. She turned luxuriantly on her side, yawning, the brass bed groaning under her, and, not quite awake, thought that she heard music. A distant radio playing; but surely, it was too late for the radio. Or the wind, perhaps, singing in telegraph wires. But that was a country noise and she was in London, in her uncle's house. She lifted up her head to listen to the music.

Drifting through the house was the faint noise of a violin and also of another instrument, a pipe or a flute. They were playing together as close as one single instrument which sounded like fiddle and flute at the same time. They leapt up and down the scale like mountain goats, dancing to their own pulsing rhythm. Dance music for some intricate, introspective, self-contained dancer. Music in the house. Francis K. Jowle, fiddle. But who played the flute? Was it Finn?

The tune finished. It did not so much reach a conclusion as slow down and dribble into silence, as though the players had got bored with the melody and let it slip through their fingers carelessly. There was a pause. Then Francie began to play by himself, slowly, tenderly.

Melanie sat up straight in bed. She felt he was drawing his bow across her heartstrings. Her pillow tumbled to the floor unnoticed, and so did Edward Bear. But she gripped her hands together to help herself bear the wailing glory of the music which was a lament for all lost and gone, loved things, an expression of a grief she had thought too deep to express. She tingled with the pity of it all.

The music pulled her out of her bed. She wanted to know

the source of it. Rising, she thrust her feet into her shoes, felt her way to the door, opened it and followed her clue down the stairs. Two storeys below her room, the kitchen lay across the landing from the dining-room. All the lights still burned. The music was coming from the closed door. It grew louder every moment. She knelt down and put her eye to the keyhole, to see what she could see.

The first thing she saw was the white dog, back from its stroll, seated on a rag rug in front of a two-bar electric fire, beating its tail leisurely yet rhythmically ... thump ... thumppp ... in time to the slow, pulsing beat of the air on the fiddle. It was a sensitive and musical dog. This sight brought her immediately down from her high, tragic pinnacle and made it seem all somehow cosier, as she thought she was sharing this music with such a wise and friendly dog.

Melanie shifted her position a little and Aunt Margaret moved into the focus of the keyhole. She sat or perched on an upright chair smiling like an angel just dropped from the skies. Her hair was loose and hung on her shoulders, a burning bush. Melanie guessed Finn had unpinned it. Her face was skim milk, a bluish white, against her flaming hair. She held an ebony flute with silver keys on her lap and she caressed it absently as she listened to Francie.

Melanie moved again and saw Francie, like a statue of a fiddler, with only his hands alive. His fiddle, with a white dandruff of rosin underneath the strings, was wedged under his chin. His fingers on the strings hovered like butterflies over a flowerbed on a day of hot summer. His face was harsh, grave and dignified.

The slow air ended and Melanie sighed. Aunt Margaret put her hands on Francie's; he lowered his fiddle impassively. They looked at each other, exchanging some meaning without words. Then Aunt Margaret put the flute sideways to her lips, eagerly, as though she were thirsty for it. Another dancing tune. The dog's tail speeded up till it seemed to thump out a quick cloud of dust from the rag rug. Francie grinned, and joined in with her after the first few phrases. His bow flashed and flickered. This time, Melanie heard an odd, clicking noise and shifted again, to see what it was.

Finn playing spoons. Melanie had never seen anyone playing spoons before. The back-to-back pair of dessert spoons riffled through his fingers, producing an intricate, staccato percussion which he was, however, unable to keep up for more than a few minutes together; then he would get his fingers tangled up and the spoons would clang to a halt and he would shake his head furiously and begin all over again. Finn played spoons badly, even Melanie could see that. He had taken off his fireman's jacket and was wearing only a high-necked, short-sleeved singlet of yellowed wool, badly stained beneath the arms. Disgusted with his own incompetence, he dropped the spoons on the table and stood up. The musicians glanced at him expectantly. He came into the centre of the floor. Melanie slewed round on her knees to watch him. He began to dance.

He fulfilled all the promise of his physical grace, although his was a stylised kind of dancing and there was nothing flamboyant about it. His facial expression never changed. His body hung strangely limp, his arms dangled loosely by his sides; all his personality seemed concentrated in his fleet, dextrous feet, which moved in a complex and various sequence. Not a note of music was without its corresponding motion of his eloquent and lively feet. The others watched him as they played,

Francie giving little grunts of encouragement, Aunt Margaret nodding her head. Her eyes were stars.

And this was how the red people passed their time and amused themselves when they thought nobody was watching.

3

Now, who has planted this thick hedge of crimson roses in all this dark, green, luxuriant foliage with, oh, what cruel thorns?

Melanie opened her eyes and saw thorns among roses, as if she woke from a hundred years' night, *la belle au bois dormant*, imprisoned in a century's steadily burgeoning garden. But it was only her new wallpaper, which was printed with roses, though she had not before noticed the thorns. And familiar Edward Bear lay on her pillow and Victoria slept on her stomach in her cot six feet away, behind white painted bars. Grey, uncertain light leaked in through the curtains. The tip of Melanie's nose was frozen with cold.

She put her face in Edward Bear's belly, for warmth. The fur smelled peppery. She remembered yesterday. 'The Last Meal in the Old Home', like a Pre-Raphaelite painting, the three orphans and the grieving servant seated in melancholy around the old table, using the old knives and forks they would never use again. What would become of the knives and forks, who would want to buy them? They are stainless steel flotsam swishing around the uncaring beaches of other people's lives.

They would probably be thrown away. They sat at a table covered with a checked tablecloth and tiles clicked underfoot (Mummy brought back the tiles from Spain), and there was a big, brick fireplace with horse-brasses and copper pans and the boiler in the middle for the central heating, where there should have been a huge fire. But never mind. Such a lovely, old-fashioned kitchen. Her mother had once been photographed in the kitchen in a frilly apron, mixing a cake. The photographs were printed in a series of features about celebrities' wives and who they were and how they coped. It was a lovely kitchen. Their last meal in it should have been a kind of sacrament. But Victoria had greased herself like an Eskimo with sausage fat, being too young for sentiment. Well, goodbye to all that.

They had come to London and eaten rabbit pie and the day ended inappropriately with music and dancing. Finn dancing in his stained vest and Francie playing the fiddle like the devil himself, who had been a fiddler, and the dumb aunt in a cape of fiery hair whistling along a flute. Or had she dreamed it? But, if so, why? And if she had not dreamed it, how had she got back to bed? Had Finn carried her? She pictured herself in her graceless flannel pyjamas clutched to Finn's narrow young breast, she limp as a bolster with a black wig on it. Finn looked like a satyr. Maybe his legs were hairy under the worn-out trousers, coarse-pelted goat legs and neat, cloven hooves. Only he was too dirty for a satyr, who would probably wash frequently in mountain streams.

'Finn looks untrustworthy,' she thought. His eyes were so shifting, so leering and slippery; the slight cast made one unsure of the direction of his gaze. And his ugly, noisy way of breathing through his mouth. He reminded her of a clothes-peg-selling or paper-flower-hawking gipsy, who would raid the henhouse or seduce the maids or steal the washing from the line or all three together. He disturbed her, but not pleasantly. Still, he was young and she had been afraid the house would be full of only old people.

The light looked tremulous and early. She would have liked to sleep again but found she could not and so she had to get up. The cold struck through her pyjamas. She was accustomed to central heating. She would have to buy some new, thick pyjamas for the winter which was just beginning, if there was any money. But – the thought upset her – would there be any spare money, any pocket-money, for her own small, personal needs, shampoos and stockings and perhaps a little face-cream, that sort of thing? There was no way of telling. She belted her raincoat over her pyjamas. Her old candlewick cotton dressing-gown had finally shrunk to uselessness just before her parents went away. In the rush of their departure, there had been no time to buy her a new one. 'We'll bring you a really super one back from America,' promised her mother.

She had to find her own way to the bathroom and was pleased with herself for so quickly remembering that it lay at the end of the passage. She felt less of a stranger once she knew where the bathroom was. Too tired to wash the night before, she had not used it. Now, feeling the train grubbiness all over her, she thought she might have a bath. It would be good to roll in hot water all over.

But water ran cold in the bathroom basin. She held her hand under the flow for a long time but the water grew no warmer. Incredulously, she had to accept the fact that there was no hot water in the bathroom neither to bath in nor to wash her face with. She had not realised there were still houses where there was no hot-water system or that a relative of hers might live in one. Neither was there proper toilet soap. Squatting toad-like in a blue and white china soap-dish with a Greek key design was a worn cake of common household soap, coarse-textured and yellow and marked with dirty thumbprints from careless usage, which stung her face and probably corroded it. She could feel her skin, corroding. Cold water and washing soap, this was how it was to be. There was a crack in the deep, old-fashioned wash-basin and a long, red hair was fixed in the crack and floated out in the water as the basin filled. The towel was on a roller; it fell off, towel and roller, both, when she tried to dry her hands. The towel was striped and not quite clean and slimy and harsh to the touch at the same time. Four frayed toothbrushes, pink, green, blue and yellow, were stuck in a plastic rack which had got itself caked up with toothpaste. On a smeared glass shelf, a full set of false teeth grinned faceless, like a disappeared Cheshire cat, from a cloudy tumbler. The plastic gums were hectically coloured a sunset pink. Melanie thought they must belong to Uncle Philip. He had come back, then.

The lavatory had most of the works of the cistern showing. When she tugged the chain (which had a pottery handle bluntly instructing her to 'PULL' on it), there was a raucous, metallic clanking fit to wake the whole house, but not a trickle of water came down to flush the bowl. She tried again. This time a few, reluctant drops spattered the millpond surface but did not disturb it. She gave up. There was, she observed, no toilet paper next to the lavatory; but, hanging from a loop of string, a number of sheets of the *Daily Mirror* roughly ripped into squares. There was a copy of the *Irish Independent* thrust down behind the lavatory pipe. Someone must have been reading it during an attack of constipation.

The bathroom was painted a dark green half-way up the walls and, above that, cream. It was a narrow, high room with unsuitable, stately proportions to the tall window, which was glazed with frosted glass and half-covered by a torn, plastic curtain with Disney fish on it. There was no mirror in the bathroom, not even a shaving one. Over the bath, which stood on four, clawed, brass feet and contained a puddle of grit-flecked water in which floated a small plastic submarine from a packet of cereal, was a large geyser, the exposed metal of which had turned green with the years.

Melanie washed as quickly as she could. The bathroom depressed her very much. 'The Last Wash at the Old Home'. Not a genre picture at all, but a photograph from an advertising book on bathrooms. Porcelain gleamed pink and the soft, fluffy towels and the toilet paper were pink to match. Steaming water gushed plentifully from the dolphin shaped taps and jars of bath essence and toilet water and after-shave glowed like jewellery; and the low lavatory tactfully flushed with no noise at all. It was a temple to cleanness. Mother loved nice bathrooms. She thought bathrooms were terribly important.

'Don't,' said Melanie sternly to herself, 'cry because of the state of their bathroom.'

But all the same, it was hard. She forced herself not to think of the old bathroom and, by extension, of her mother. Now, though, she perceived that many things which she had taken for granted in her life, simple, cosy, homely things, were, in fact, great luxuries. No wonder there was no inheritance for the children and they must scrape themselves with newspaper and redden their pampered fingers in icy water now that the goose who laid the golden eggs was dead.

The bedroom seemed already known and safe. She put on her black trousers and her chocolate-brown sweater because they were at the top of the first suitcase she opened and she would have worn them at home on a cool autumn day when there was mist on the hills and woodsmoke in the lanes and . . . She looked out of the window. The morning was damp, though not rainy, the grey day just beginning.

There were a few leaves left on the straggly garden bushes, hanging all crumpled and lifeless. Bare patches of dun-coloured earth showed through the scanty garden-plot grass. Creepers grew on the walls; deciduous, they stretched out their bare stems in a complicated network like barbed wire. There was a narrow alley with dustbins in it at the bottom of the garden and, beyond that, the rude and unkempt backsides of a row of tenement houses with blind, curtained windows and washing (long pants, vests, sheets, shirts) limp in the windless air, strung out on high lines running from pulleys at far-up windows. Tin baths, like giant snails, stuck half-way up the walls as if resting in a trip to the top. A new territory lay here, in which she must live.

Victoria turned over in her sleep and cooed at a dream. She was peachy and downy and sweet with baby sleep, a blue ribbon in her hair, which was dark and curly. What would Victoria become, here? Would she grow up into a street urchin, plimsolls, no socks, grimy tee shirt, with a London accent grating on a nicely-brought-up ear? And Jonathon, in his cabin under the eaves? And what of herself, of Melanie?

The house was entirely quiet. Melanie decided to adventure downstairs to the kitchen, where she had not been. She wanted to learn the new domestic geography as soon as she could, to find out what lay behind all the doors and how to light the stove and whereabouts the dog slept. To make herself at home. She had to make herself at home, somehow. She could not bear to feel such a stranger, so alien, and somehow so insecure in her own personality, as if she found herself hard to recognise in these new surroundings. She crept down the lino-covered stairs.

The kitchen was quite dark because the blinds were drawn. There was a smell of stale cigarette smoke and some unwashed cups were stacked neatly in the sink, but the room was ferociously clean. It was quite a big room. There was a built-in dresser, painted dark brown, loaded with crockery, a flour jar, a bread-bin. There was a larder you could walk into. Melanie experimentally walked into it and pulled the door to on herself in a cool smell of cheese and mildew. What did they eat? Tins of things; they seemed particularly fond of tinned peaches, there was a whole stack of tins of peaches. Tinned beans, tinned sardines. Aunt Margaret must buy tins in bulk. There were a number of cake tins and Melanie opened one and found last night's currant cake. She took a ready-cut slice of it and ate it. It made her feel more at home, already, to steal something from the larder. She went back into the kitchen, scattering crumbs.

There was a long table of scrubbed pine with a tablecloth (splashed with russet chrysanthemums, the sort of tablecloth you see through the windows of other people's houses as you walk by at teatime) folded back to cover crockery set out ready for breakfast, perhaps to keep mice from dirtying the cups.

It was a brown room, like the shop and the passages, which were all painted a thick, dark brown. The kitchen wallpaper was old and brown and shiny and streaky with grease. There was another blackboard on the wall and on it the legend: 'Arrived on time. Fast asleep.' Uncle Philip must have come back so late at night or early in the morning that only Aunt Margaret was still awake. Melanie tried to reconstruct his return, Aunt Margaret making tea, he asking after the new-comers and she telling him in her own way. He wore his Mississippi gambler's outfit. But she could not visualise his face clearly.

The room was full of other people's unknown lives. A scorchmark on the cloth that had its own secret history, mysterious unopened mail behind a small plaster model of an Alsatian dog on the mantelpiece (which was a modern, ugly mantelpiece made of beige tiles). The fireplace itself was obviously never used; there was a fan of newspaper where the sticks and coal should be. Over it hung an extraordinary painting. She opened the curtains more widely to get light to see it.

It was a portrait of the white bull-terrier, executed with incredible precision. Every white hair seemed visible on the pink, painted skin, as if brushed in separately, and you could see the grainy texture of the nose. The bull-terrier sat squatly full-face on a spiky tuft of grass. It had a wicker, flower-girl basket of pinks and daisies in its mouth. Drops of dew trembled on the flowers. The dog's eyes glittered unnaturally because they were made of pieces of coloured glass stuck onto the canvas. Behind him was a rocky shore and a sea with many white-capped rollers in parallel lines, under an ominous, bruise-coloured, storm-laden sky with a streaky, orange sunset. The dog commanded the entire room. There was something official about it, as if it were a guard-dog or sentinel, on the

66

constant *qui vive* behind its glass eyes, taking turn and turn about with the real housedog, and the basket of flowers was stuck in its mouth in an attempt to disarm, an accessory borrowed to lend it a harmless look. There was no sign of the real dog but for a baking dish full of fresh water on the floor by the sink. He was evidently off-duty.

Beside the portrait was a carved cuckoo clock with green ivy and purple grapes growing around a green front door. As Melanie inspected the dog, the front door flew open with a whirring sound that startled her very much. The bird emerged, bowed and cuckooed seven times. It was a real cuckoo, stuffed, with the sounding mechanism trapped, somehow, in its feathered breast. There was a grotesque inventiveness, a deliberate eccentricity in the idea of the cuckoo clock that Melanie had never encountered. The bird backed into its house and the door slammed shut. She hoped the clock would break down so that she would not have to see the bird again; she did not like it. She felt withered and diminished. Nothing was ordinary, nothing was expected, except for her two black legs and the black plaits on each side of her head.

Perhaps she could make tea. The gas stove was commonplace enough, although very old, standing on four straight legs. She filled the big, black kettle and set it over the burner. Tea would be nice. Should she take tea to her aunt and uncle in bed? Would that start their relationship well? But she did not know which of the many doors of the hallway was that of their bedroom. Or tea to Francie and Finn, Finn asleep with red hair on a white pillow like bread and marmalade? She felt a curious quiver in the pit of her stomach to think of Finn, a half-frightened, half-pleasurable sensation. But she did not know where the young men slept, either.

There was a tin tea-caddy decorated with neo-Chinese, kimono'd figures in a garden, on a shelf beside the stove. She measured tea into the Whitsun treat pot, one, two, three, and half-filled it, judging the proportions by rule of thumb. Then there were footsteps on the stairs. She stood quite still, with the tea-pot lid in her hand, fragrant steam rising in her face. The footsteps went down, past the kitchen, into the shop; she thought they might vanish altogether but they shortly returned, accompanied by a padding, clicking sound, paws on linoleum. Finn, carrying five bottles of milk and followed by the dog, came into the kitchen. Melanie relaxed and put the lid on the pot at last.

'Hello,' she said.

'You're early about the house,' he said without surprise. There was still sleep-dirt in his gummed-up eyes and his hair was knotted and tangled, not combed this morning. He yawned hugely, so hugely she noticed a decaying molar.

'Would you like some tea? I hope it was all right. I mean, to make tea.'

'Oh, yes, at this time of day. Lashings of tea, I'd like; and three sugars.'

She wondered what he meant by 'at this time of day'. Would she not be allowed to make tea at other times? He was, she saw, partially dressed. He wore his cord trousers but his feet were bare and an unbuttoned pyjama jacket revealed fleeting glimpses of a snow-white breast. He turned on the electric fire and knelt before it, holding out his hands to the reddening bars. Melanie turned her eyes from his nakedness and handed him tea, which he drank thankfully. The dog, after lapping a little water, went and sat down heavily beside him, eyes turned up at the portrait of

68

itself thoughtfully, perhaps making a critical assessment of it. Or mutely communing with it. Finn groped for cigarettes in his pyjama pocket. Melanie burned her mouth on scalding tea. The cups were cheap willow pattern, but this was homely.

'Drop more?' he asked, passing his cup. How could he drink his tea so hot, so quickly. 'Nothing like a cup of tea to wake you up.'

Beside him, Melanie was acutely conscious of her clumsy hands and the long legs she could not arrange elegantly, no matter how hard she tried. But at least she did not squint and his cast seemed more noticeable than ever in the morning, as if sleeping refreshed it.

'You've tied up your hair again,' he said casually.

'It is more practical,' she said, blushing a little.

'Ah, well,' he shrugged, rubbing his eyes to get the sleep out of them. Then he looked Melanie up and down. Then he said violently: 'No, you can't wear them!'

'What?'

'Trousers. One of your Uncle Philip's ways. He can't abide a woman in trousers. He won't have a woman in the shop if she's got trousers on her and he sees her. He shouts her out into the street for a harlot. Ah, it's dreadful, sometimes. Do you realise you're a walking affront to him, Melanie?'

'I know he's back,' she said. 'I saw his false teeth in the bathroom.'

'Melanie, will you slip up and put on a skirt? Or he'll turn you out!'

Bewildered, she looked down at herself. She was covered. She was proper. He must be joking.

'Please!' He beseeched. He implored.

'Well . . .' she said. Although it seemed odd. 'I suppose you know him better than I.'

'Yes. I do. I know him very well.'

She lingered with her hand on the door-knob.

'Is there anything else like that I ought to know about him?'

'No make-up, mind. And only speak when you're spoken to. He likes, you know, silent women.'

She looked at the blackboard.

'Yes,' she said.

He rose choreographically and refilled his cup for the third time. His breast rose up from the pyjama top like the prow of a boat cresting a wave. His flesh was white velvet with a sub-dued sheen on it and his nipples were bright pink, pink as the parakeet, but he filled the room with his smell of sweat and sleep and she wished he did not breathe through his mouth. She noticed the soles of his feet, black and grainy with dirt.

'Hurry up and change your trousers, Melanie.'

She went and took a grey pleated skirt from her case and zipped herself into it. It was a schoolgirl skirt and very inno-cent. On impulse, she unplaited her hair and shook it out. It rustled round her ears as it had done before she went into mourning. Victoria showed no sign of waking. When she got back to the kitchen, Finn was reading an old newspaper, seated on the table and eating dry chunks of bread gouged from a loaf in the crumb of which his fingers had left grey prints. The dog growled and worried over a chopped mound of horsemeat in an earthenware bowl with 'Dog' on it.

'That's better,' said Finn approvingly, and did he notice her hair as well? 'Have some bread.' So they ate bread together while he read the paper. The cuckoo cried the half-hour. Melanie jumped.

'Your uncle made that clock.'

'Gosh!'

'You don't know half the things he can make, Melanie.'

'Once, he gave me a jack-in-a-box he had made. But it frightened me.'

'But you surely know about the dolls and hobby horses and baby houses and all?'

'No,' she said.

'He is a master,' said Finn. 'There is no one like him, for art or craft. He's a genius in his own way and he knows it.' He considered. 'Would you like to see a little of the work? For now is the time. Before the house wakes up. The only time for seeing it.'

'Why is that?'

'Ah, it's his way. He doesn't like to be inspected. Especially the theatre. He likes, above all, to keep the theatre to himself.'

'Theatre? What kind of theatre?'

'For the puppets and their plays. But no one knows about the puppets. They're not for sale. They are his hobby.'

There were traces of egg-yolk, dried, down his front, and his cuffs were grey and tattered. And his teeth, like Francie's, were yellow from smoking. He lit a new cigarette. Sweet Afton, with a picture of Robert Burns on the packet. The dog, its breakfast finished, lay down, sighing, on the rag rug. The fire coloured its flanks orange.

'Who painted the dog's picture?'

'I did.'

'It – it's very like.'

'A dog is a dog,' he said and shrugged. 'I paint his puppets and his scenery and his toys. Some toys, that is.'

'Is that all you do?'

71

'I learn the craft. I'm your uncle's apprentice, Melanie.' He leapt off the table. 'You might as well come and see.'

She did not quite like the way he kept calling her by her name; there was a humorous inflection on the three liquid syllables as though he found the name funny. But she was curious and went after him. The dog opened a lazy eye to watch them safe out. Finn padded with a squishy noise on his bare and filthy feet. And his toe-nails were long and curved, like the horns of a goat, reminding Melanie of the cloven hooves she thought he might have had. His toe-nails looked as if a knife would blunt on them and could not have been cut for months, possibly years. He opened the door to the shop on the ground floor. The shop gloomed behind its blinds and the parakeet drowsed.

'We'll look at one or two of the public things first, though,' said Finn and switched on the light. 'Good Joey,' he said to the parakeet as it chattered into wakefulness.

'Your uncle works both wood and a little metal,' he said. His soft voice had no expression in it. 'What do you think of this?'

He took a cardboard box and from it drew a toy consisting of two monkeys with bright brown fur and boot-button eyes. One monkey wore a pin-striped suit, beautifully made in miniature, and the other a black dress, just as finely made. The male monkey held a tin fiddle, the female a tin flute. They stood on a tin dais enamelled red. Melanie felt a twinge of discomfort. Smiling blandly, Finn turned a key. The furry arms moved. Tin bow drew across strings, tin flute moved against furred mouth. From a musical box in the base issued a thin, clear parody of last night's music and the monkeys tapped their feet.

'A jig,' said Finn. '"The Rocky Road to Dublin". And I wish I was treading it now.'

Melanie watched the monkeys in silence. At last the mechanism ground to a halt. The parakeet screamed: 'No sale! No sale!'

'It is a good line,' said Finn. 'Popular. There is also a dancing monkey with bells on its ankles. Bells.'

'I heard music in the night.'

'It was I who carried you to your bed. We didn't find you till late, and you were curled up on the landing, outside the kitchen door. It was very touching, finding you like that.'

'I wondered how I got to bed.'

'Do not,' said Finn, dismissing the previous night, 'treat your uncle lightly. However, he also does romantic work. Lyrical.' From another box he took a large rose.

'A white rose,' said Melanie and caught her breath.

'What's the matter?'

'Oh – nothing.'

When the key was turned, the stiff petals (stiffened canvas? card? thin shavings of wood?) arched gracefully open to reveal a frilled shepherdess doll no longer than a child's hand. A tiny tinkling started up in the heart of the rose. The shepherdess raised one leg and pirouetted. Then she changed to the other leg. Finally, she curtsied. The petals closed over her head. The tinkling ceased.

'We call that,' said Finn, 'our "Surprise Rose Bowl".' He took a bar of bubble-gum from his pocket, unwrapped it and put it in his mouth. 'Ten guineas. He thinks it's quite beautiful.' He blew a bubble which exploded like a fart.

'It is ingenious,' said Melanie hesitantly, unsure of her own response.

'It is fatuous but it sells,' he said and put it away. 'This is better. This was my idea.'

He showed her a yellow bear with a bow tie round its neck, riding a bicycle. It rode along the counter, ringing the bell of its bicycle at intervals. Its progress was erratic. One particularly violent swerve took it right off the counter and Finn caught it in mid air, upside down, wheels spinning. It was such an odd and witty little toy that Melanie giggled and stretched out her hand for it, to work it herself.

'I am glad you laugh,' said Finn. 'I thought you were trying to give it up. But you can see the shop any time. Let's go downstairs before it gets too late.'

So they went into the basement, a long, white-washed room running the whole length of the house. A window at one end gave onto a coal hole; a little daylight filtered through at an angle from an iron grating in the pavement above. There was a clean, sweet smell of new wood and a tang of fresh paint. Wood shavings crunched underfoot. A carpenter's bench ran along one wall, covered with a wooden-leg factory *Walpurgisnacht* of carved and severed limbs. There was a rainbow-splashed painting bench along the other wall. The walls were hung with jumping-jacks, dancing bears and leaping *Arlecchinos*. And also with partially assembled puppets of all sizes, some almost as tall as Melanie herself; blind-eyed puppets, some armless, some legless, same naked, some clothed, all with a strange liveliness as they dangled unfinished from their hooks. There were masks on the walls, too, all kinds of masks in all kinds of colours – fluorescent pinks and purples splotched with dark blue and gold. Finn put on a mask and turned into Mephistopheles, shaggy eyebrows and moustache, pointed beard on a mottled, red and yellow face set in a snarl.

'Real hair,' he said, tugging his beard. 'We cater for a quality trade.' The room was lit by strips of neon, which cast no shadows.

Red plush curtains swung to the floor from a large, box-like construction at the far end of the room. Finn, masked, advanced and tugged a cord. The curtains swished open, gathering in swags at each side of a small stage, arranged as a grotto in a hushed, expectant woodland, with cardboard rocks. Lying face-downwards in a tangle of strings was a puppet fully five feet high, a *sylphide* in a fountain of white tulle, fallen flat down as if someone had got tired of her in the middle of playing with her, dropped her and wandered off. She had long, black hair down to the waist of her tight satin bodice.

'It is too much,' said Melanie, agitated. 'There is too much.'

'Ah, you've seen hardly anything, yet.'

She could not bear to look at the fallen doll in white satin and tulle.

'I – I don't like the theatre. Please, Finn, close the curtains for me.'

Reluctantly, he pulled the cord again and mercifully the red curtains blanked out the abandoned sylphide.

'You see, the puppet theatre is his heart's darling, in a manner of speaking. Or obsession, rather. You should see the scenes he puts on! And sometimes he lets me pull the strings. That's a great day for me.' His voice curled ironically at the edges.

'There is too much,' she repeated. This crazy world whirled about her, men and women dwarfed by toys and puppets, where even the birds were mechanical and the few human figures went masked and played musical instruments in the small and terrible hours of the night into which again she had been

75

thrust. She was in the night again, and the doll was herself. Her mouth quivered.

Finn saw her distress and his own loose mouth turned down in sympathy, like the moon on its back. To her intense dismay and astonishment, he suddenly hurled down the room in a series of cartwheels; he made a whizzing plaything of his devilish masked self, a fizzing Catherine wheel, flashing arms and legs, landing on his hands before her, his upside-down false face obscured by hair both false and real, tumbling over his *papier-mâché* cheeks.

'Laugh at me,' he said. 'I'm trying to amuse you.'

He kicked his filthy heels in the air.

'I want to go home,' she said hopelessly, bleak as November. She buried her face in her hands. She smelled his closeness, rank and foxy. Slowly he righted himself and took off the mask, although she could not see his face for she was not looking at him.

'The nun brought us,' he said, 'Francie and me, in our stiff best suits and creaking shoes. She came with us from the orphanage back home, two hundred heads in two hundred beds and two hundred broken hearts under two hundred army surplus blankets and the good nuns to look after us. She brought us across the Irish Sea, trusting to God, but God chose her to suffer from the weather and she puked her guts into St George's Channel, poor thing, and Francie crying because he closed our mother's eyes, since there was no one else to do it. And he only fourteen years old, then, and already a wonder on the fiddle; but he couldn't get the feel of her eyelids off his hands. Like water-lily petals, he kept on saying. White and moisty. But dead.'

'Finn, don't go on.' She felt the tears coming. But the tears, surprisingly, were no longer for herself but for Finn and Francie so long ago, especially Francie. Finn opened his arms as if to embrace her but she was still holding the tears in her eyes with her fists. And then came a great booming from overhead. He shrugged, he was always shrugging.

'They are banging the gong for breakfast, we must run. You'll be better after a bite and a sup of something. And it's best not to be late for meals, in this house.'

Blocking the head of the stairway on the kitchen landing was the immense, overwhelming figure of a man. The light was behind him and Melanie could not see his face; besides, Finn walked before her up the stairs. But the man seemed to be holding a round turnip-shaped watch in his hand and glaring at it. He was murmuring to himself. All at once the stair lights came on. The murmur swelled to a roar.

'Three minutes late! And you come dancing up in your stinking rags as if it didn't matter! Do I keep a boarding house for dirty beatniks? Do I? Do I?' And he launched a great, cracking blow at Finn's head so that Finn reeled and staggered, clutching the banisters for support. Swaying, Finn began to laugh.

'Melanie, this is your Uncle Philip!'

But she recognised him already from his photograph, although he had put on so much weight. He ignored her completely, seizing hold of Finn's pyjama jacket and trying to pull it from his back. There was an ugly scuffle, Finn slipping back and forth like an eel, a laughing eel, for he kept on laughing. He ducked under Uncle Philip's arm and grabbed his blue jacket from an antlered rack on the landing, hastily buttoning himself to the neck.

'What the eye doesn't see,' he said breathlessly.

'The porridge is cooling,' said Uncle Philip. 'It is cooling because you are so late. If there's one thing that disgusts me it's cold porridge. Besides you Jowles,' he added. 'Besides you Jowles.'

But he was apparently considerably mollified now that Finn had covered himself up. On the antlered rack, Melanie saw, was a flat-topped, curly-brimmed, black hat such as Mississippi gamblers wear in Western films. With age, it had lost most of its pile and acquired a rich patina like a very old penny. Uncle Philip could only ever have possessed the one hat.

4

All the other meals (except for odd cups of tea and light snacks) were eaten in the dining-room, which, however, never lost a musty and unused smell no matter how often they sat in there. But breakfast was the exception and was always taken in the kitchen, although Melanie never found out why.

In the kitchen, Jonathon and Victoria, ruddy and brilliant with cold water, sat before untasted bowls of porridge. Aunt Margaret must have woken them and organised their washing. Her aunt directed Melanie to sit beside Victoria with a nervous wave of her thin arm. She wore a dirty apron in dark, printed cotton, which went round her back and fastened with thin tapes, pulled awry over her black skirt and sweater, and she appeared flustered. She might have pinned up her hair in her sleep, it was so untidy.

Victoria had on her nice towelling bib with a green frog on it but seemed subdued by the ceremonial atmosphere surrounding the meal: the gong and the shouting; for she was unusually subdued, thank God. Melanie could not have supported a laughing, singing Victoria for breakfast and Uncle

Philip might have struck the baby, which would have been dreadful. The two Jowle brothers sat opposite Melanie and Victoria, like a moral picture contrasting tidiness with slovenliness, for Francie was already painfully neat in his suit and a fresh, green tie, stabbed through, today, with a different tiepin, a small dagger. At the head of the table was a large chair, with arms, on which Uncle Philip ponderously seated himself, presiding magisterially over the platter of cut bread and the marmalade jar, which was in the shape of an orange and sticky on the outside. Aunt Margaret crouched at the table foot, one eye on the kettle to see when it boiled. There was another grace, less strange than Francie's but truncated.

'For what we are about to receive,' said Uncle Philip and left it at that. He took up his spoon. It was a signal. At one accord, they attacked the porridge.

Milk in a brown jug and a choice of sugar or golden syrup still in its green and gilt can. Finn monopolised the golden syrup and made ecclesiastical embroidery with it in his bowl, dreamily, not eating. There was a total silence but for the symphonic range of slurpings and splutterings with which Francie accompanied porridge. Finn continued to make subtle, interwoven, lacy patterns and the other bowls emptied. Time passed. Uncle Philip darted Finn Medusa glances from beneath his bushy brows.

'Finn,' he said at last, awfully.

'Yes, sir?' said Finn briskly, grinning. Why did he grin so much, showing his discoloured teeth?

'Stop playing with your food, damn it!'

'I was only,' said Finn, 'designing.'

'Stop playing with your food or else.'

Aunt Margaret shuddered and closed her eyes. Sighing,

Finn cleared his porridge bowl with astonishing quickness. He might have been spooning it into his pocket, not eating it at all. Under cover of the porridge business, when all his attention was fixed on Finn, Melanie dared look at her uncle at last.

His size still shocked her, when he had been so spare at her mother's wedding. And how old was he? Older than Aunt Margaret, that was certain – far older, but how much older? His hair was elderly but not white. Rather, it was yellowish, like tarnished silver, but silken and glossy, brushed across his forehead from a parting on the left. A lot of hair, cared for with considerable vanity. His shaggy, walrus moustache was deeper coloured, streaky, with irony grey still in it and it was brown and sodden where it dipped into his own, special, pint-size mug which had the word 'Father' executed on it in rosebuds. The moustache made him look like Albert Schweitzer, but not benevolent. The mug was the right size but the wrong design, too pretty, for his large, gnarled hand, rough with scar tissue and discoloured by years of work in paint and wood. Melanie thought she would not like to hold his hand. His eyebrows beetled like those on the Mephistopheles mask and the eyes beneath them were no colour, like a rainy day.

He wore an exceedingly white shirt with a butterfly collar, starched to a gloss like glass, and a shoe-string tie which he might never have taken off since his sister got married. He sat in shirt-sleeved, patriarchal majesty and his spreading, black waistcoat (the shiny back of it cracked in long lines) was strung with an impressive gold watch-chain, of the style favoured by Victorian pit-owners. If there was trouble at the pit, he would never have cared. A comprehensive white linen napkin was tucked under his chin. His authority was stifling. Aunt Margaret, frail as a pressed flower, seemed too cowed by his presence even to look at him. She had only the tiniest portion of porridge, a Baby Bear portion, but she took the longest to eat it, nibbling in tiny crumbs from the edge of the spoon. She had not finished it when Uncle Philip crashed down his own spoon on an empty bowl.

'Finn change plates! Pronto!'

Aunt Margaret, leaving her own food, started up to the stove, taking from the warm oven plate after plate of bacon and fried bread, but Finn stretched at leisure, yawned an artificially exaggerated yawn, his throat a crimson tunnel. Uncle Philip glowered.

'Are you trying to annoy me, young man?'

Finn stacked the plates. Passing behind Uncle Philip's broad back with a leaning tower of dishes in his hand, he performed a swift, small, derisive dance where the old man could not see. No one else spoke or moved. The meal passed through bacon and ended in marmalade and the same oppressive silence in which it began.

They used the willow pattern china, of which there was a great deal, for breakfast, lunch and tea during the week, although there were also some plain, white, ex-army issue mugs in which Finn and Francie occasionally had cocoa and hot milk late at night. On Sundays, there was a whole service, with vegetable dishes and a soup tureen, of a much finer china; plain white with a green band. Aunt Margaret was proud of this. It had belonged to her own mother, once, in Ireland. This china lived in the sideboard in the dining-room and only came into the kitchen to be warmed before a meal and washed up afterwards. Melanie, after a while, began to notch off the weeks in her mind by the appearance of the green-banded china, 'Here comes another Sunday.' And on Monday mornings, she would look at the little bridge on her willow pattern plate and wish she could run across it away from her Uncle Philip's house to where the flowering trees were. But she did not guess this was how it would be on her first morning.

'For what we have received,' said Uncle Philip. He dropped his napkin in his plate and pushed back his chair. 'Finn, get decent and come down at once.'

The door slammed behind him.

The room seemed to grow brighter. Finn, grinning, and Francie lit cigarettes and tilted their chairs back on two legs. Aunt Margaret put the kettle on the stove for the washing-up; there was no hot water in the kitchen, either. The children drew together defensively, the younger ones each catching hold of Melanie's hands, even Jonathon. Victoria sniffed audibly. An agonised expression passed over Aunt Margaret's face.

'His bark is worse than his bite,' she chalked on her blackboard.

As if obeying some obscure stage direction, the dog barked.

'He didn't even ask our names,' said Jonathon, in vague astonishment.

'He knows your names,' pointed out Finn gently.

'Hadn't you better be getting ready?' Melanie asked him.

'First I must wash, mustn't I? And shave?'

' 'E's 'orrible!' gasped Victoria, making her mind up about Uncle Philip in a rush. Her recently acquired aspirates gave way completely under the stress of emotion. Aunt Margaret, full of concern, scooped her up and cuddled her.

'She's not accustomed to sharp voices,' explained Melanie.

'She'll have to learn, then,' said Finn, scratching an armpit.

Melanie was to stay with her aunt in the shop, that day, to learn the prices of things and where things were kept, once the pots were washed. Victoria could stay with them and play by herself. It was a domestic prospect. Jonathon, left to his own devices, asked and obtained permission to go off and work on his ship.

'Jonathon is good with his hands,' said Melanie.

'How pleased your uncle will be,' said Finn, loitering for hot shaving water. 'He can whittle a puppet or two with us.'

'School . . .' she said faintly, drying a fork.

'Ah,' said Finn, 'too late in the term to start school, now.'

Francie, still smoking at the table, laughed like a coffee-grinder whirring, and Aunt Margaret, up to her elbows in suds, turned warningly to him with a finger on her lips.

'Himself can't hear, Maggie,' said Finn, putting his arms around his sister's waist from behind. 'Don't you fret.'

She leaned back against him and he kissed her neck where the red hairs draggled dispiritedly from her chignon. Melanie intruded. She separated herself from their intimacy by putting the forks precisely away in a drawer, where other forks were. Then she dried and put away knives, and spoons, also. She was a wind-up putting-away doll, clicking through its pro-grammed movements. Uncle Philip might have made her over, already. She was without volition of her own.

Outside was a weatherless London morning, a mean monotone, sunless, rainless, a cool nothing. This, she thought, was her own climate. No extremes, ever again. Fear no more the heat o' the sun and all that. She was in limbo and would be for the rest of her life, if you could call it a life, dragging out its weary length with no more great joys or fearful griefs for

84

her, for her blood was running too thin to bear them. And she was only fifteen. It was appalling.

As she put away the cutlery and was so sorry for herself, she found it made things easier if she dramatised them. Or melo-dramatised them. It was easier, for example, to face the fact of Uncle Philip if she saw him as a character in a film, possibly played by Orson Welles. She was sitting in a cinema watching a film. Soon a girl in white would come round selling ice-cream, salted nuts and popcorn. But the flavour of the month was no flavour at all. She tried not to look at the easy, mutual affection of Finn, Francie and the dumb woman.

The night before, these three had blended together as if it was the easiest thing in the world, forming a new, three-headed animal talking comfortably to itself through Francie's hands and Aunt Margaret's lips and fingers and Finn's feet. And Melanie had spied on them through a keyhole, and would never get closer to them than the keyhole in the door behind which they lived. Watching a film was like being a voyeur, living vicariously. They were an entity, the Jowles, warm as wool. She envied them bitterly. 'Make yourself at home.' How could she? It all fell apart, her detachment. Suddenly, she yearned above all things to break into their home movie.

But did she really want to belong to them? For a moment, she ached with longing – then, just as suddenly, revolted against them. They were dirty and common. She hated to use the word 'common', only common people called other people 'common'; her mother taught her that. But it fitted.

'I haven't seen a single book in the house, not one.' And the lorry-drivers' caff line-up of sauce-bottles in the dining-room. And Francie dowsing himself with porridge and (now) meditatively picking his teeth with a used matchstick. And Finn's vile singlet and viler pyjamas. And the only pictures in the house that she had seen were the sentimental, old-fashioned print in her room and Finn's dog over the mantelpiece, which a child might have painted and hung up, to show off. And tea, tea, tea with everything, just when she had begun to appreciate the sophistication of coffee. And the holes in Aunt Margaret's stockings. And no lavatory paper. It was all disgusting. They lived like pigs.

But in spite of all that, they were red and had substance and she, Melanie, was forever grey, a shadow. It was the fault of the wedding-dress night, when she married the shadows and the world ended. All this was taking place in an empty space at the end of the world. She dried cups, saucers and plates on a soaking cloth for there was nothing else for her to do.

Yet how did they manage to stay red and substantial (or, in Aunt Margaret's case, intermittently substantial) when they lived under the weight of Uncle Philip, the Beast of the Apocalypse? How could she, Melanie, have ever guessed that her uncle would be a monster with a voice so loud she was afraid it would bring the roof down and bury them all?

Oh, poor Aunt Margaret, who was so gentle, and yet slept (probably) in the same bed as he, for they were married. He made toys that parodied her innocent amusements and those of her brothers and she trembled when he raised his leonine voice. And she wanted babies, Melanie could see that; but did she want Uncle Philip's babies? Aunt Margaret wanted babies so much, she wanted Victoria for her very own. Then she could have Victoria. Melanie gave up all rights in Victoria on the spot and felt a lessening of tension. A burden had been taken off her.

'I suppose I could run away,' she thought, propping plates upright on the dresser shelves. 'I could get a job and live by myself in a bed-sitting room, like the girls in stories in magazines.'

Brewing Nescafé on her own gas-ring and buying solitary quarter pounds of cheese for herself; and painting one wall geranium red and another cornflower blue and the others white, as she wanted to do at home but her mother would not let her. She thought of her mother, clear and distinct, very small, seen through the wrong end of a telescope, lying in the wreckage on yellow sand wearing her best black suit, with a small, travelling hat, surrounded by the charred fragments of other people's flesh. But it would not have been in the least like that, really. Melanie hung cups on hooks on the dresser; her arm went up and down, up and down. She watched it with mild curiosity; it seemed to have a life of its own.

Later that morning, sitting in the back parlour of the shop, she wrote a promised letter to Mrs Rundle on a sheet torn from her aunt's pad. She chewed the pencil, swallowing splinters; what could she tell Mrs Rundle, who was now (if she had ever been much more than) a stranger, living at a distance, forgetting them, putting them into her past, memories packed with other memories in her bulging handbag?

'Dear Mrs Rundle,
We had a good journey but it was tiring. We hope you had a good journey.'

She thought for a while, then crossed out 'journey' the second time and wrote in 'trip', so as not to repeat herself.

87

This was style, as they had taught her at school. Somehow she suspected she would never be going back to school.

'Victoria and I share a room. Aunt Margaret seems very fond of Victoria, already.'

Victoria, oddly quenched, sat at Aunt Margaret's feet and gazed at the shifting patterns in the fire, singing to herself a wordless, keening song. Why did they not give her toys to play with? There were plenty of toys.

'Aunt Margaret is dumb,' wrote Melanie. And then crossed out 'dumb' and inserted 'sweet' because it occurred to her that Mrs Rundle might have known about this affliction from the lawyers but had not been able to find the words to tell the children about it.

'Uncle Philip is a bit old-fashioned but I am sure we shall all settle down very' – she intensified this – 'very soon.

'I hope you are settling down and the cat is well.'

This was a lie. She did not hope the cat was well. She hoped it was dead. She was convinced the cat was basically evil, but it was Mrs Rundle's beloved if delinquent child and she had to ask after it.

'Best love,

from Melanie, Jonathon and Victoria.'

She sighed as she finished the letter. She would have to find an envelope and buy a stamp (where was the post office?) and post the letter and then a day would pass and then Mrs Rundle would take out her spectacles to read the letter in some new kitchen, with a refrigerator and a stove with automatic oven-control and an eye-level grill and gleaming plastic working surfaces and an electric blender and an electric coffee-mill, probably. They would have fresh-ground coffee in red lacquered pots at Mrs Rundle's new house, Melanie was certain of it. She clung to the picture of Mrs Rundle at home, for she had been a part of her home and the children had moored for a short while in the black harbour of her lap.

The shop-bell rang, the parakeet squawked. She went with her aunt to sell Hallowe'en masks to a small boy in diminutive jeans, with snot caked in his nostrils. There was a tremendous stock of wild and scarey masks. They emptied boxful after boxful on the counter, in front of the small boy – lions, bears, devils, witches (pale green with hair made from real straw). These masks were rather less elaborate than the ones in the workroom. When Melanie said so to her aunt, the older woman scribbled: 'Those are the de luxe models, these are the standards. But, please do not go to the workroom.' She offered the boy a grizzly bear mask with fur fabric ears.

Ecstatic, the boy tried on one mask after another, roaring like a lion or mewing like a cat. He was, perhaps, seven years old and had his money tied up in a corner of his handkerchief. His flat, South London voice seemed coarse and ugly to Melanie and, once again, she hoped Victoria would not pick the accent up. He must have saved up his pocket money for a long time in order to buy one of Uncle Philip's masks. They seemed expensive to her at nineteen shillings and eleven-pence but the small boy loved them.

Striped in a tiger mask, he feinted across the counter at Melanie; she bit off an exclamation. The mask was quintessential tiger, burning bright with phosphorescent paint. It was quite bestial, ferocious. She did not think the masks were nice toys for young children. At last the boy counted out sixpences and pennies onto the counter and picked up his final selection, an elephant mask with moulded plastic tusks of extreme sharpness and a foam-rubber trunk you could raise or lower by pulling a string. It had the face of an elephant in rut, Melanie thought. She invited him to cover it up with a paper bag but he snapped the band round the back of his head and ran off into the street, an elephant ramping above the collar of his jersey, his new trunk bobbing. Smiling, Aunt Margaret put the money away in a drawer which was the till. It was a lovely, warm and unstrained smile.

'It is a pleasure to serve children,' she wrote.

'But exhausting, I expect,' said Melanie.

'The children here are used to me,' wrote Aunt Margaret. Melanie wondered what she thought she had said. Thankfully, she cleared away the horrid masks.

Time passed very slowly. At half past eleven, tea was made in the back parlour. Melanie wondered if she would have to take a tray to the basement but it seemed they had their own gas ring down there and brewed up continually for themselves. But she took tea up to Jonathon and Aunt Margaret showed her how to trap the heat in the cup by putting the saucer on top.

Jonathon's attic was very cold. He was gnawed and pinched with cold; the scabs on his knees showed up a bright purple because of the cold and his nose was red and raw-looking. He scarcely looked up as Melanie came in. The floor was webbed with loops and tangles of black thread and his ship rode proudly on the strips of Turkey carpet and he sat on his heels weaving an intricate cat's cradle of rigging. He was neatly dressed in his grey flannel school suit, as if it was an ordinary day. Shorts and jacket with a badge on the breast and long, grey, wrinkled socks – the clothes he had travelled in. It was a breath of the past. He always blindly put on in the morning the clothes he had taken off the night before, unless others were substituted on the chair beside the bed while he slept.

'Here's a hot drink,' said Melanie.

He did not hear her.

'Jonathon! I've brought you some tea!' She put the cup down on the floor beside him and touched his shoulder. Slowly he stripped the black thread from his fingers, peering at her through his glasses as if wondering who she was. His glasses were dim and smeared. He took them off, breathed on them and polished them clean with his handkerchief, which was now very dirty. His eyes were pink-rimmed and defenceless. He reminded her of a small, vole-like animal, a guinea pig or a mole. He put the spectacles back on and examined her again.

'Oh, it's you,' he said. He looked at the tea in a baffled way.

'Drink it,' she said, 'before it gets cold.'

With frightening tractability, he drank the cup down in three swallows and handed it back to her empty. He waited politely for her to go away, his eyes on his ship. She felt she was intruding; but he was, after all, her brother and she had a right to intrude on him.

'Jonathon,' she said, 'are you all right?'

He considered this, or seemed to be considering this.

'What do you mean?' he asked eventually.

'Are you happy or can you see your way to being happy?'

He sat quite still, his hands on his knees, making no attempt to reply to her, as if to him her question was boring and irrelevant.

'Jonathon, tell me if you are happy or not.' After all, he was her brother and she was anxious for his welfare.

'I want to get on with my ship,' he said. 'Please.'

'Oh,' she said faintly and went away.

She felt lonely and chilled, walking along the long, brown passages, past secret doors, shut tight. Bluebeard's castle. Melanie felt a shudder of dread as she went by every door, in case it opened and something, some clockwork horror rolling hugely on small wheels, some terrifying joke or hideous novelty, emerged to put her courage to the test. And now she was entirely alone, brother and sister both lost to her, Jonathon upstairs, Victoria downstairs and Melanie treading the dangerous route between them, connected to neither.

'If only,' she thought, 'I wasn't so young and inexperienced and dependent.'

Behind the doors (which doors?) slept, at nights, Aunt and Uncle, Francie, Finn. But not now, at this hour; who occupied the rooms in the daytime? Bluebeard's castle, it was, or Mr Fox's manor house with 'Be bold, be bold but not too bold' written up over every lintel and chopped up corpses neatly piled in all the wardrobes and airing cupboards, on top of the sheets and pillowslips. Melanie knew she was unreasonable, that empty rooms and quiet beds lay all around her, but the fright was still there and her scared feet pattered with too loud a noise, waking echoes. On the kitchen landing, the dog sat staunchly at the top of the stairs, blocking her way with its back to her, apparently sunk in thought. It had an uncanny quality of whiteness, like Moby Dick. In the brown house, it glowed. She was very much startled.

She stood behind the dog. It did not move. She was trapped.

'Good dog,' she said experimentally. 'Nice dog, let me by. Please.'

Its tail began to move this way and that with a faint, swishing noise.

'Please,' she said again. It looked over its shoulder at her with twinkling red eyes. She wondered insanely, 'Which dog is it, the real one or the painted one?' At last she stepped over it and went down, half thinking it might snap off her leg in passing. But it stayed stock still. It watched her, unwinking, until she reached the room behind the shop and shut the door on its crimson gaze.

Aunt Margaret was peeling potatoes into a plastic bowl of water on her knees and Victoria was helping with a small but dangerous-looking knife and they were surrounded with puddles. Aunt Margaret looked down at the round top of Victoria's head with warm and tender eyes, her birdy head cocked on one side. Victoria, at least, was integrated.

Soon her aunt went to get the midday dinner, taking Victoria with her, and Melanie was left in charge. There was, she found, a certain satisfaction to be got from standing behind a counter; she had always been a customer, at the receiving end, until now. She played shops for a while. She counted over the money in the till and inspected a roll of invoices. She made doubly sure she knew where the paper bags, the brown wrapping paper, the string and the roll of Sellotape were kept.

She turned over some of the stock. Repelled yet attracted by the ferocious masks, she finally tried on one or two, but there was no mirror where she could see herself, although she felt peculiarly feline or vulpine according to the mask she wore. They even seemed to smell of wild animals. Then she ruffled the parakeet's crest and watched it peck a sunflower seed. It walked sideways on its perch and hunched its shoulders, looking slyly up at her as though it could tell a tale or two, if it chose.

No one came in to buy. The shop was so dark that they let the light burn all day. It was always five o'clock of a winter evening there and all the tempting boxes gave it a night-before-Christmas look, a richly expectant atmosphere of surprise packages. She was happier in the shop than in the house. She was happy to be near a door into the street, where she could see passers-by and know that other lives went on in their placid courses.

She fingered the boxes with a furtive secrecy, like a child rooting among the holly-wrapped parcels hidden away on top of her parents' wardrobe. She took off lids which Finn had left unopened. She held her breath with wonder and delight. She was seven years old again.

There were simple, wooden toys for babies, kept apart on a special run of shelves. These were entrancing. Horses on wheels to pull on a string, red, blue and green horses dappled with black, white and yellow flowers. Rattles shaped like pigs and owls with dried seeds in their hollow bellies. Whistles shaped like variously coloured birds, through whose tails one blew. Melanie put a bird-whistle to her lips, producing a note of intense, piercing sweetness. Wooden tumblers, swinging – allez oop! – head over heels on wooden frames. Wooden models, primitive in design as the very first toys of all, of two men hammering in turn on an anvil.

She began to recognise Finn's idiosyncratic painter's hand, showing itself in the blossoming horses, the queer, saucer-shaped faces of pig and owl, the speckled peacock glory of the birds, the strained, professional grimaces on the faces of the tumblers, the tight-lipped endeavour on the faces of the hammering men. He had paid special attention to the hammerers; they were all decorated with various kinds of facial hair ranging from pencil thin, Ronald Colman moustaches to curly, Ancient Assyrian style full sets of ringlets, and their diminutive, painted jackets were striped, starred, arrowed and dotted at random. Finn seemed to like particularly to paint toys for very young children. Inside a very large, square box was a Noah's Ark. It was a masterpiece.

She set out the pieces one by one on the counter.

Noah stood six inches high, with a white beard to his knees and wading boots of real rubber. The Noahs were a curious family. Mrs Noah was the traditional peg-shape, as if that was the perfect, the only shape for a Mrs Noah and the maker had adopted it with relief after unsuccessfully trying out a hundred new variants of his own which had not done. She had a bun of hair at her nape from which stuck out carved hairpins, thinner than split matchsticks. Her cheeks were round and red and she smiled.

Shem and Ham, however, were greasy Orientals, gaming-house or strip-club proprietors, in pin-striped suits, with black curls and red, smiling mouths disclosing gold teeth. But Japhet (she knew it was Japhet for the name was printed in little letters on his tee-shirt) was nobody but Finn himself, perfect down to the squint, in blue jeans. He had signed himself as a signature on the ark. She remembered him saying: 'We are all in the same boat.' Well, he was in the ark and would presumably survive any deluge.

There were thirty pairs of animals in the body of the ark, ranging from a lion and a lioness almost as big as Noah himself, down to a pair of white mice no bigger than Melanie's little finger-nail. The lions were both crowned, to show they were king and queen. She giggled with sheer delight to handle them all, so little, so pretty, the cats so catlike, the kangaroos (with a baby in the mother's pouch) so expressive of the basically humorous nature of kangaroos. She set all the animals out in a long line, headed by the lions; a circus parade carved from wood and delicately coloured. She found she was thinking small, on the scale of the ark, seeing her own hands huge as those of Gulliver in Lilliput.

The flat-bottomed ark itself had a sea-scape on its side, painted up to the plimsoll-line, a dimensionless vision of the remote deeps full of strawberry-coloured fish and forests of weeds and barnacled rocks with, here and there, a plump mermaid of the kind sailors have tattooed on their arms. Either the mermaid was energetically breasting the waves or she sat on the upturned keel of a drowned vessel and combed out long and improbably yellow hair. The body of the ark was green, with painted heads of animals peering from the portholes. There was a price tag on the mast. Seventy-five guineas.

'Goodness!' she exclaimed.

'It is a fair price for the work,' said Uncle Philip. 'A man must charge a fair price. That's only economics. And kindly put those things away, miss. I don't like people playing with my toys.'

'No sale!' chanted the parakeet.

Uncle Philip left no space in the doorway. He had clipped up his shirtsleeves with steel bracelets above the elbow and was swathed in a coarse apron which had once been white and which covered him from the knot of his tie to his ankles. His pale eyes held no kindness. He scowled. His eyebrows met like an iron bar. Melanie nervously clattered the animals back into the box.

'And you be careful with them things! They're your bread and butter, now.'

And so they were.

Above them, the dinner-gong clanged awfully.

5

'We might as well not be in London at all,' said Melanie. There was nobody in the kitchen but herself and Victoria. 'We might just as well be somewhere else.'

'Like where?' asked Victoria incuriously. With a spoon, she scoured the crumbs from a used jar of raspberry jam. She sat on the floor. Her hair was stuck in spikes with jam. An angry rash of jam surrounded her mouth and her dress was smeared and sticky. She was content. She had grown fatter than ever. She was always clutching a fistful of sweets or biting into a between-meals snack of bread and condensed milk or scraping out bowls in which Aunt Margaret had mixed cake. Aunt Margaret spoiled her and adored her.

'Like where?' asked Victoria, crimson with jam.

'Like anywhere.' But there was no point in talking to Victoria, who had forgotten anywhere else because she lived from day to day.

Melanie had been told they had come to live in a great city but found herself again in a village, a grey one. The isolation of the Flower household on its South Suburban hill-top was complete. Melanie left the house, a basket on her arm and a list in her pocket like a French housewife, only to do the shopping. But she never was given any money for the Flowers had credit at all the shops with which they dealt and Uncle Philip paid the bills quarterly, by cheque. Sometimes the dog went with Melanie and sometimes it stayed at home and sometimes it was busy. It had no lead or chain but trotted quietly beside her. Sometimes Victoria went with her and sometimes Victoria stayed at home but Victoria was never busy. Now that Melanie did the shopping, Aunt Margaret never went out at all.

The people in shops sent their regards to her aunt through Melanie and asked how she was keeping, as they had asked after Melanie's mother and also after Mrs Rundle when Melanie had gone shopping in the village. Tongues solicitously tutted over the black band still stitched to Melanie's sleeve for they all (as they would have in the village) knew of the children's arrival and how they had been orphaned. Aunt Margaret must have covered pad after pad with their scribbled story.

They were kind to her in the shops. The grocer, a hard-faced ex-soldier whose right hand lacked a thumb (Melanie wondered, had he lopped it off on the bacon-slicer? But she never dared ask him, for fear he would tell her) – the grocer treated her to infrequent smiles and would give occasional chocolates to Victoria, who would go back to the toyshop with a heavy brown moustache and sideburns. She was a messy child. The butcher, who was gentle and warm-hearted in spite of the cruel bloodstains on his boater, loaded her basket free with bones for the dog and offered to show her the mysteries of his store room where, shaggy with frost, the sides of meat hung in refrigerated darkness. But this she refused, although she appreciated the gesture.

The woman in the greengrocer's shop would sometimes slip a bunch of violets or a single head of a chrysanthemum that had accidentally snapped into Melanie's hand and this pleased her most of all. She was a dark, tinker-looking woman who talked in a wheedling, laughing, low-pitched whine; her hands were always black with earth from dealing with potatoes. She gave Victoria a banana whenever she saw her and would tell Melanie to help herself from the baskets of nuts. She said 'God bless you' instead of goodbye, and Melanie would leave the greengrocer's feeling reassured and cracking an almond between her teeth. 'I wish Uncle Philip was a greengrocer,' said Victoria, once. 'Or,' she added, 'a sweety man.'

But where was London and the bustle and anonymity of a great city? She could see the lights of it from the upper windows but never got any nearer.

The Flowers were quite private. Nobody visited them in the evenings or dropped in for a chat during the day, except in the way of business – to sell wood to Uncle Philip or to arrange a booking for Francie and his fiddle. No friends, no callers. Life was a charmed quiet. There was no television set, no record player, not even a radio. Uncle Philip loved silence. But Francie had smuggled a tiny transistor radio into the house and on this he furtively listened to Radio Eireann sometimes, when there was music.

After Melanie shopped, she helped her aunt, either serving in their own shop or writing out price tags or performing the endless task of polishing the woodwork of counter and drawers, a Forth Bridge of polishing that was no sooner completed than the messy fingers of small customers meant it must be started again. The change in her way of living was so vast she could scarcely credit it; she would stop, sometimes, with the polishing rag in her hand, under the watchful eye of the para-keet, and say aloud: 'But this can never be me, not really me!' But it was.

In the evenings, after tea was cleared away and washed up and her aunt had tucked Victoria into her cot, Melanie sat in the kitchen and read her own old books. She had been right; there was not a single book in Uncle Philip's house, except for his account book, unless there were some secret ones in the brothers' bedroom. This was possible but, if it were true, she never saw them read anything, although Francie occasionally bought a copy of the *Irish Independent*. This he read in the lavatory, where she had seen it on the first day. He always stored it behind the pipe and when Uncle Philip found it, he would throw it out onto the landing and jump up and down on it. Soon it would reappear behind the pipe, with footmarks on it.

A single case of her own books had survived and it was a haphazard collection, containing *Winnie the Pooh* and the Dr Dolittle books, which she found herself reading nostalgically over and over again. Some of her own childhood seemed trapped in the pages on which she had dribbled chocolate and, years ago, marked specially loved pages with sweetpapers and scraps of hair-ribbon. She never touched the few adult books, mostly school text books, and she hid the copy of *Lorna Doone*, but she clung to the rest as if they were lifebelts.

She read and read and read while her aunt mended the socks of her husband and brothers or sewed innumerable but-tons on their shirts. She also sewed clothes for toys and puppets, tiny dresses and jackets for anthropomorphic bears and monkeys and robes and mantles in silks and velvets for the few puppets they sold in the shop and gowns and breeches for the tall puppets who performed in the theatre. There was a never-ending pile of sewing in her huge, wicker sewing basket, which was of the kind in which snake-charmers keep their snakes. Wave after wave of brilliantly coloured cloth issued from the basket, threatening to engulf her, but she struggled manfully against it, her fingers as fast as light. Melanie thought that at least Uncle Philip could have bought her a sewing machine, so she need not have to stitch the long seams by hand.

Melanie and Aunt Margaret sat in complete silence but for the ponderous ticking of the cuckoo clock and its regular two note interjections. Melanie was still not used to it. It made her start every time it sounded. The tap dripped into the sink. Sometimes the dog scratched at the door to be let in. Sometimes it scratched to be let out. Sometimes it went to sleep on the rag rug before the electric fire and snored quietly, or its paws would twitch as it chased rabbits in its sleep. Aunt Margaret would lift her head from her sewing now and then and smile nervously at Melanie, to show they were friends. Occasionally Finn had an evening off and then he and Melanie played pencil and paper games such as 'Battleships', but usually Uncle Philip needed Finn downstairs to help with the puppets. Uncle Philip worked on his puppets in the evenings, when the toys were put away.

She saw her uncle only at mealtimes but his presence, brooding and oppressive, filled the house. She walked warily as if his colourless eyes were judging and assessing her all the time. She trembled involuntarily when she saw him. She could not link him in her mind with her mother at all, though the two of them had once shared a mother themselves. He seemed of a different texture and substance from her gentle and ineffectual mother; he was hewn or cut out of thunder itself. She sensed his irrational violence in the air about him. Sometimes he fell in a landslide on Finn, clouting him round the head over the dinner table when Finn's insouciant insolence went too far. Often, Finn emerged from the workroom with a bruise on his cheekbone or a swollen eye, the result of a disagreement over some detail of the work in hand. Then Aunt Margaret, moaning, would rub him with ointment in spite of his protests. or stick him with Band-Aid, if the skin was broken. But Finn never seemed to care, taking it all casually in his stride.

Francie, day and night, locked himself in the room he shared with Finn (it was, Melanie discovered, the room next to her own) and played the fiddle continually, except when he was engaged to play it outside, at London Irish clubs, ceilidhs and gatherings. Melanie could hear the liquid trilling echoing faintly on the landing when she went upstairs to the lavatory. On the nights when the tide of sewing ebbed to a low watermark, Aunt Margaret crept up to Francie's room and played her flute with him. She never asked Melanie to come and listen to them and, on these occasions, Melanie, alone with the live dog and the painted one in the kitchen, felt that nobody in all the world cared whether she lived or died.

Jonathon now worked on model ships under the eye of Uncle Philip and was learning how to carve them directly from wood. He spent every minute that was not wasted in eating or sleeping in this pursuit. Even in the evenings, he crafted his ships while Uncle Philip and Finn made puppets until it was half past eight and time for him to go to bed. He would then pass through the kitchen to say an abstracted 'good night' and that was as much as he said to Melanie, nowadays, although he had never said much more.

'Philip is pleased with Jonathon,' chalked Aunt Margaret on a blackboard.

'Oh, good,' said Melanie. But she knew in her heart that, if she had ever had Jonathon, she had lost him for good.

There was no pocket money for any of them. Shampoo came from a communal bottle. Melanie decided to say nothing about new pyjamas for herself until the need became really pressing.

Meanwhile, the remaining leaves fell from the sycamore in the square and were swept into oblivion by the stiff brooms of council employees. The nights drew in earlier and earlier, clothed in sinister cloaks of mist like characters by Edgar Allan Poe. Melanie stood with her face against the cold glass of her window-pane, seeing not the bleak yard and the lights blossoming in the backs of other houses but berries reddening on the hedges around home and fields glinting with frost. Smoke from bonfires of dead leaves caught the throat. She stood, gloved, in the garden, throwing breadcrumbs and bacon rind onto the lawn and watching the hungry birds swoop down. A series of pictures followed one another through her mind. Lamp-lit faces around a table where cold-weather food steamed, hearty stews and puddings running with golden syrup. Her mother fastening Melanie's coat snugly at the neck and tucking in a scarf. The log-fire in the drawing-room and Father puffing his pipe as he rustled *The Times*, Mother reading a novel, Melanie on the fur rug between them buffing her nails and the rain snarling against the windows so that the fireside seemed even cosier.

All rich, strange and remote, as if it had never happened or had happened to another person. Instead, this was reality – this chilly, high, inconvenient house with its threatening vistas of brown paint along which draughts roared like engines. This, she told herself, was the harsh, unloving truth, the black, bitter bread of life; the tenderness of the lavish past was tenuous, insubstantial.

'Eve must have felt like this on the way east out of Eden,' she thought. 'And it was Eve's fault.'

There was a reply to her letter to Mrs Rundle. Mrs Rundle's handwriting was black, round and stately, progressing across the paper with the majesty of an antique Rolls Royce. Mrs Rundle was glad they were well and settling in. Families should get on together, that was only right. She was suited in her new position but she missed the children.

'And I only wish that I was family and so could be of help to you and had some rights to see you. But there, I am not, and have no family at all except my memories. And there is nothing I can do only to remember you in my prayers, which I do every Sunday, and wish you all the very best. And a special kiss to my Victoria, my little girl, but all my love to you all.'

All her love. Trunks and chests and crocks and wardrobes of it, a lifetime's hoarded-up love prodigally distributed at last. But there was nothing she could do, except love them from a distance. She would send them a card at Christmas, with crosses for kisses on it, though Victoria had already forgotten her and she, too, was already forgetting their precise and real selves. Their figures were dissolving in her mind, their features blurring, till they became as subtle and ambiguous as Mr Rundle himself; and, romantically tinged with melancholy because of the death of their parents, they became dream children, good and beautiful. Which dreamed it? Now you see it, now you don't. Was it Mrs Rundle's dream that she was a part of? All the same, Melanie folded the letter and kept it among the knickers and handkerchiefs in her chest of drawers, as a kind of talisman, to remind her the past was real.

Wednesday was half-closing day. Just before she turned the sign on the door round to read 'Closed', a woman came in to look at the toys. She was an expensive woman, all in suede, come by car from north of the river. She represented a type of customer they persistently attracted, whom Uncle Philip especially loathed.

'That sort of person,' he said once, in dry fury, 'brings the Sunday colour supplements.'

'We had a photographer here, once, from a colour supplement,' Finn told Melanie one morning as she exclaimed over a fresh assortment of jumping-jacks (soldiers in red jackets, each sporting a row of meticulously painted medals) that they were too good for children.

'This man wanted to do a photo-feature. Toys for grownups. He said we – your uncle and me – were a unique fusion of folk-art and pop-art. He said, we stick with him and we'd have half London beating on our doors to buy.' Finn pulled the string of a jumping-jack and its arms flailed. 'Then your uncle smashed his camera for him. Two hundred pounds worth of equipment down the back stairs. It took all my Irish blarney to keep us out of court.'

'But why?'

'Philip Flower is his own master. He doesn't want people he despises buying his gear for conversation pieces.'

'I'd like something little and gay,' said the woman, smiling at Melanie from a mouth painted the very palest possible orange. 'Something to make my friends say, "Wherever did you find that?"'

But she had to be served. Melanie covered the counter with toys for her and she ran her suede gloves over the painted surfaces of wood and tin, crying out at intervals: 'Golly! How super!' and finally she bought merely a witch mask. 'Mean bitch,' thought Melanie who was, willy nilly, developing some shop-keeper attitudes. She wrapped up the mask politely although she heard the gong sound and knew she would be late for dinner.

The woman stepped lightly away on her high-heeled, patent leather boots to her basket-work Mini parked beside the public convenience. She was the sort of woman who used to come for the weekend at home, sometimes, with a suitcase full of little black dresses for cocktails and dinner. (Why was there such a difference in the nature of dinner when the meal was served at midday, as at the Flowers?) Melanie could easily have grown up into that sort of woman.

Finn, also late for dinner, came from the workroom and helped Melanie put the disordered stock away. She was never quite at ease with Finn, in spite of playing 'Battleships' with him; his oblique glance sidled around her and he grinned as if he knew secrets about her which he would not share. And she still could not stomach his physical dirtiness, his extraordinary, extravagant, almost passionate dirtiness. He had taken off his paint-stiffened apron but there was blue paint in his hair and his hands were blue, like those of the Jumblies who went to sea in a sieve.

'What shall we do this afternoon?' he asked as casually as if they spent all their Wednesday afternoons together.

'Well,' she said, stalling.

'Would you like to go for a walk?'

'I haven't so much as been outside the square, yet,' she said, longingly. Might they go to London, the golden city?

'Then we'll go for a walk.' He smiled almost sweetly. She was worried because she did not know if the rules of the house permitted her to go out walking with Finn and, besides, they were going to be late for dinner. But Uncle Philip was not seated at the table, scowling at the two empty places; his place was not even set ready. He had gone to look for wood. He needed more wood.

'When the cat's away . . .' said Finn and there was a feeling of holiday. They ate steak pudding with exceptional appetite and, when everything was cleared away, Melanie ran upstairs to comb her hair. She paused with her ribbon in her hand and tossed her hair loose down her back without plaiting it up again, to please Finn, although he was uncouth. From the next room, she heard the plaintive and tentative sound of Francie tuning up.

Aunt Margaret helped Victoria construct a high house from a greasy set of playing cards on the kitchen floor. She smiled up at Melanie, pointing to her raincoat and raising her red eyebrows interrogatively.

'I'm showing Melanie the neighbourhood,' said Finn, clutching his sister's shoulders and rocking her kneeling form to and fro in an embrace which made her laugh soundlessly until she looked like a young girl. The first storeys of the house of cards came tumbling down and Victoria burst into tears.

'Let's go,' said Finn. He wore a black p.v.c. raincoat which creaked as he moved. He, too, had combed his long hair for the outing and had gone to the lengths of scrubbing the blue paint from his fingers. These preparations disturbed her; why had he bothered to make himself beautiful for her?

All the shops were closed and there was a Sunday peace in the little square. The white bull-terrier, about its own business, lurked thoughtfully in the doorway of the secondhand shop, lifting its leg to urinate as they went by.

'Good dog,' said Finn. Three-legged, it wagged its tail but did not follow them, perhaps not wishing to intrude.

There was a bubble-gum machine outside the tobacconists. Finn extracted a packet each.

'I haven't had bubble-gum for years,' she said doubtfully.

'I only eat it to annoy your uncle.'

She unwrapped it and put it in her mouth.

It was a dour afternoon, with few men and women in the streets, which had a pinched, frozen look as if there were not enough fires burning in the houses to keep them snug. Privet hedges drooped with the weary strain of keeping in green leaf at the turn of the year when all the other trees had thrown down their leaves in surrender. They walked through sad places where small coloured children sat on doorsteps, too depressed and apathetic to play games, and stared after them with huge black eyes in which the tropic sun was extinguished. Now and then they passed a baby wailing outside a peeling front door in a battered pram. Overflowing dustbins festered in areas and neglected front gardens. Ranks of curdy milk bottles waited for a milkman who never came.

'This part of South London has seen better days,' said Finn, through a mouthful of bubble-gum.

'Yes,' said Melanie, who was not enjoying her walk so far.

It was a high and windy suburb. The square, its shabby focus, topped a steep hill and these streets ran sharply down;

once stately and solid streets, fat with money and leisure, full of homes for a secure middle class with parlours in which its bustled daughters could play 'The Last Rose Of Summer' and 'Believe me if all those Endearing Young Charms' politely on rosewood pianos antlered with candlesticks; and roast-beef coloured dining-rooms where the gentlemen mellowed over rich, after-dinner port and mahogany reflected ox-roasting coal fires tended by black flocks of housemaids. And, now, crumbling in decay, over-laden with a desolate burden of humanity, the houses had the look of queuing for a great knacker's yard, of eagerly embracing the extinction of their former grandeur, of offering themselves to ruin with an abandonment almost luxurious. Yet there were still trees, planted in the good, old days, and one could see a great deal of sky. It was an airy, almost woodsy, unhappy place. With hardly any traffic.

'You lived in the country, of course.'

'But I remember living in Chelsea. That is, a little.'

'Ah,' said Finn. 'This is not like Chelsea.'

'No,' she said. She kicked a tin which lay on the pavement. It had once held pineapple rings, if its label was to be believed. It rattled along the road, waking a baroque concerto of echoes from rotting red-brick gables, and somewhere, in a front-room shrouded with dirty net curtains, a baby began to cry.

'Where are we going?' she asked.

'To the park.'

'Park?'

'All that there is left of the National Exposition of 1852, Melanie. They held it here, in a pleasant village outside London, and ran up to a hundred excursion trains a day out to it. They built this vast Gothic castle, a sort of Highland fortress, only gargantuan, and filled it with everything they could think of, to show off. Goods and chattels and art and inventions. All the world came. It was like the Paris Exhibition, only earlier. And less frivolous.' He blew a reflective bubble. 'It was made of papier mâché specially treated to withstand the weather. It was ever so ingenious, the castle.'

'What happened to it, then?'

'Someone dropped a match in 1914. It was apt enough. It went up in flames as the lights went out all over Europe. Victoria's final death pyre. You'd have thought it would occur to them to make it fire-proof, as well. But no. I painted the fire once as an allegory. The castle was a fat woman in nothing but a Highland plaid.' He blew another bubble. 'It was in the manner of a Rubens allegory.'

She saw in her mind's eye rude naked women and flames as upright and stiff as those on the covers of boxes of fireworks.

'It must have been an extraordinary picture,' she said.

'Jesus, it was that.' He looked at her sideways and she saw that he was laughing. She walked uncomfortably beside him. There was nothing to say. They said nothing. Soon they came to a stout fence of raw, new, wooden palisades with a door in it that said 'Private' above a grim-toothed lock. The fence stretched as far as she could see and, above it, waved the brown tops of trees.

'In here, Melanie.'

'But—'

'They are planning to bulldoze the park and build workers' flats. But I've read that in the local paper since I came here.'

He took a key from his pocket and opened the door. They stepped directly from the road into a dense hazel thicket and Finn closed the door behind them. The ground gave under their feet, a yielding mire of rain-sodden dead leaves. Leafless twigs rapped their faces like bony knuckles. Melanie smelt the cloying plastic of Finn's coat and impulsively took his hand, for company. He gripped her fingers against his calloused palm and led her forward. The silence was like wet cotton wool pressed into their ears.

The park lay in sodden neglect, sprawling over its rank acreage as if it had passed out. Trees had carelessly let go great branches or had toppled down entirely, throwing their roots up into the air. Bushes and shrubs, uncared for, burst bonds like fat women who have left off their corsets, and now many spilled out in mantraps of thorny undergrowth. It was a claggy, cold, moist, northern jungle. But Finn stepped firmly. He seemed familiar with every inch of this riot. They came out of the wood into a bare field where coarse grass lapped limply around their ankles. It was the sort of grass which cuts your hand if you pull it incautiously. In grey billows, it rolled into nothing, into the mist which was already descending. Nothing moved. There was nobody else.

'This is the graveyard of a pleasure ground,' said Finn. 'That is why there is such pervasive despair.'

They skirted the edge of the open space, keeping to the borders of woodland which had once been landscaped, and Melanie was grateful, for she would have felt too visible, too exposed out on the sea of grass – a sitting target for some marksman, for the arrow of any figure in Lincoln green who might be flitting among the mossy trunks. But here was cover. Finn helped her over a fallen-tree stump blooming with yellow fungus.

'There would have been stalls for coffee, gingerbread and souvenirs,' he said. 'And also theatrical performances in tents. And running patterers and ballad singers. That sort of thing. And little arbours to sit in with your girl, if it rained. And a genteel festive spirit, I suppose, though it is hard to credit.'

'It is weird,' she said. She found she was talking in as low a voice as Finn, feeling there was something which she did not wish to disturb.

'Look,' said Finn, drawing aside a fringe of branches. She saw a stone lioness at the mouth of a stone cave, guarding her cubs. A hundred years of weather had stained her haunches a blackish green and generations of birds had dropped whitely on her domed head. Her carved eyeballs stared back at them with the uncanny blindness of statues, who seem always to be perceiving another dimension, where everything is statues. The cubs clung stonily around her.

'She should wear a crown,' said Melanie, remembering the Noah's Ark lioness.

'I'll show you the queen in a minute,' said Finn. 'She's the Queen of the Waste Land.'

He was not grinning so much. He was in a curiously elegiac mood, moving soft on silken feet in deference to the sadness in the place, now and then touching a tree or a still-surviving piece of stone in a placating greeting, apparently apologising for his presence. Melanie wondered what the significance of this desolation was to him, for it seemed to mean a great deal. She had not expected his mind to contain this kind of land-scape. In showing this place to her and wanting to see her walking in it, he was making her a deep gesture of friendship; she was sorry that she did not care more.

'It smells of rotten mortality,' said Finn, looking into the invisible distance.

'What smell is that?'

'Mud.'

She did not care because a cold misery was seeping into her bones as surely as the damp seeped through her thin shoes. But she followed him or she would get lost.

'All these gardens were filled with statues,' he said. 'Dryads, slave girls, busts of great men, great men on horseback and on foot. A handsome yet sylvan prospect where you could promenade to the music of brass bands. They have managed to sell some of the statues though I can't think who'd want to buy them. But the rest of the statues stay because they can't bear to go away.'

'You do talk funnily,' she complained because her feet were wet. He shot her a backward glance over his black gleaming shoulder.

'You mean, I talk funny for an ex-bog-trotter slum-kid?'

She blushed.

'I read books from the library now and then. And living with your uncle is, God knows, an education.'

Suddenly the ground fell away before them and they came out on an open plateau with a floor of chequered marble, white on black, and a wide stone staircase with balustrades running down to the dried bed of an ornamental lake, which the mist turned to a bowl of milk. The staircase was ornamented at intervals with classical figures, chastely draped, and there was still a sweet primness in the graceful propriety of their attitudes though some were lacking a hand or an arm and others had had their noses rot away or even been entirely decapitated by exposure to the elements, and all were soot-stained and weather-beaten. The stairs were littered with broken masonry and rubble.

They walked out onto the marble floor, a dancing floor. A string orchestra should have started to play an old-fashioned waltz.

Melanie, a few paces behind Finn, trod carefully, carefully on the white squares only. If she did not tread on any of the black, perhaps when she got to the end of the floor she would shiver and rouse in her own long-lost bed, in her striped sheets, and say good morning to the apple tree and look at her own face in the mirror she had not broken. She had not seen her own reflection since. She was seized with panic, remembering that she had not seen her own face for so long.

'Do I still look the same? Oh, God, could I still recognise myself?'

Almost shyly, almost ashamed of her superstitious fear, she touched her cold cheeks and nose with her stiff, ungloved fingers. But the touch told her nothing.

Walk carefully, keep to the white squares. And this could never be real, this never could be happening to her, walking on the white squares behind Finn, who moved as if he did not set his feet to the ground, so gracefully, so uncannily. And what would happen, though, if she trod on the black – would all this simply go on, this bleak nightmare, for the rest of her life, sixty or even seventy years? And if she trod on the cracks, where the grass peered through, would they open up and engulf her and it would all be over, whatever it was?

She stepped off onto grass at last. She had religiously adhered to the white squares. Finn's shining carapace remained solidly before her. She did not know whether to believe in him or not.

'Here she is,' he said tenderly.

'Oh – your queen.'

At the end of the low, pillared barrier at the front of the dancing floor was a rococo stone plinth, tiered and orna-mented in the manner of a wedding-cake. On a smooth piece of icing, someone had inscribed, with lipstick, the motto: 'Gordon Cox (Cocks) has a fucking great penis.'

'I'm sorry about that,' said Finn. 'Vandals must have done it.'

From this plinth had, a long time ago, fallen sideways a tall figure which now lay face-down in a puddle, narcissistically gazing at itself. The figure had snapped in two at the waist, and was prone at right angles to itself. Slime and fungus streaked it but it remained recognisably, unmistakably, Queen Victoria in young middle-age.

'Albert stood at the other end, to balance her,' said Finn. 'But someone took him away. I often wonder where he went. He was probably glad to be away from her nagging.'

He pulled out a handkerchief and, kneeling, gently wiped away a little of the mud from the pale, marble face. Melanie nudged the detached torso with her foot but it was too heavy to shift.

'I don't like it,' she said involuntarily. 'And, poor thing, to be flat on its nose in the dirt.'

'That's the way of it,' said Finn philosophically. He splashed her with the grey-green ocean of his eyes.

It was growing dark, for the clocks had been turned back weeks ago and the nights were drawing in. Far away, through the mist, the blur of the city deepened like a sooty thumbprint and a few lights came out. Trees and bushes lost the precision of their leafless outlines. The white marble squares on the pavement glowed as if on a phantom chessboard. Melanie felt a drop or two of moisture on her face – rain, maybe, or the coagulated damp of the wet night air, or spray from Finn's regard. He took the bubble-gum (by now exhausted) from his mouth and stuck it deliberately on Queen Victoria's swelling stone backside. When she saw him do this, Melanie knew he was going to kiss her or to try and kiss her.

She could not move or speak. She waited in an agony of apprehension. If it was going to happen, it must happen and then she would know what it was like to be kissed, which she did not know, now. At least she would have that much more experience, even if it was only Finn who kissed her. His hair was marigolds or candle flames. She shuddered to see his discoloured teeth.

They were standing on opposite sides of the fallen queen. He lightly set his feet on the stone buttocks and sprang across, and, seized by some eccentric whim in mid air, raised his black p.v.c. arms and flapped them, cawing like a crow. Everything went black in the shocking folds of his embrace. She was very startled and near to sobbing.

'Caw, caw,' echoed his raincoat.

'Don't be frightened,' he said. 'It is only poor Finn, who will do you no harm.'

She recovered herself a little, though she was still trembling. She could see her own face reflected in little in the black pupils of his subaqueous eyes. She still looked the same. She saluted herself. He was only a little taller than she and their eyes were almost on a level. Remotely, she wished him three inches taller. Or four. She felt the warm breath from his wild beast's mouth softly, against her cheek. She did not move. Stiff, wooden and unresponsive, she stood in his arms and watched herself in his eyes. It was a comfort to see herself as she thought she looked.

'Oh, get it over with, get it over with,' she urged furiously under her breath.

He was grinning like Pan in a wood. He kissed her, closing his eyes so that she could not see herself any more. His lips were wet and rough, cracked. It might have been anybody, kissing her, and, besides, she did not know him well, if at all. She wondered why he was doing this, putting his mouth on her own undesiring one, softly moving his body against her. What was the need? She felt a long way away from him, and superior, also.

She thought vaguely that they must look very striking, like a shot from a new-wave British film, locked in an embrace beside the broken statue in this dead fun palace, with the November dusk swirling around them and Finn's hair so ginger, hers so black, spun together by the soft little hands of a tiny wind, yellow and black hairs tangled together. She wished someone was watching them, to appreciate them, or that she herself was watching them, Finn kissing this black-haired young girl, from a bush a hundred yards away. Then it would seem romantic.

Finn inserted his tongue between her lips, searching tent-atively for her own tongue inside her mouth. The moment consumed her. She choked and struggled, beating her fists against him, convulsed with horror at this sensual and intim-ate connection, this rude encroachment on her physical privacy, this humiliation. She swayed to and fro; she almost slipped down onto the ground beside the dead queen in the mud but Finn kept hold of her no matter how hard she struck at him, lightly clasping her shoulders so that she would not fall. When she grew calmer, he slowly released her and she walked away a few paces, staggering, digging her hands in her pockets and turning her back on him. He wiped his mouth with the back of his hand.

'Look on my works, ye mighty, and beware,' he said to the statue, prised off his bubble-gum, examined it for impurities and put it back in his mouth.

There would be potato scones for tea, split down the middle, butter melting in their golden hearts, and probably jam tarts, for Aunt Margaret was making pastry. The kitchen was fragrant with cooking. The light hurt Melanie's eyes and the heat made her nose and toes tingle. Victoria, on the floor, used the pastry trimmings for Plasticine.

'A bird,' she said to Melanie, holding up a grey lump.

'I suppose so,' said Melanie. She squatted by her sister and cuddled her because she was small and plump and happy. Victoria writhed.

'Don't do that,' she said. 'I'm busy. I'm playing.'

'It is a lovely bird,' said Melanie conciliatorily. 'I knew it for a bird at once.'

'You made me squash it,' snapped Victoria and pettishly threw it across the room, where it struck the sleeping dog sharply on the flank. The dog woke, sniffed it, ate it and belched. Melanie had never seen a dog belch before. It was a day of firsts. She continued to sit limply on the floor. Aunt Margaret wiped floury hands on floury apron.

'Did you have a nice walk?' she chalked. Her face was sharp, bright and inquisitive. Did she guess Finn had kissed her? Or had they all planned it beforehand, for a joke – but it was silly to think that.

'My feet are wet,' said Melanie. 'Perhaps I shall catch a

cold.' Which will turn into pneumonia and I shall die and nobody will care.

She thought Finn must have gone down to the workroom. He had come into the shop with her but had not followed her upstairs to the kitchen. She did not want to see him or speak to him. She wanted to be by herself, where there were no lights. She escaped to her own room and sat down on the bed, huddling in her damp raincoat and picking at the stitches of the band on her arm.

'Is there something wrong with me that I felt such a blankness? And after that it seemed so horrible, is there something even more wrong with me because I thought it was so horrible?'

Or was it because it was Finn who kissed her and not a man like the men in whose arms she had imagined herself when she used to imagine things like that, in the past? And now she would never be able to imagine them again because she would think of Finn's wet kisses. She found she had torn most of the mourning band away from her sleeve and there was nothing for it but to pull it off entirely.

The curtains moved at the windows. Against them, the geranium cast a fantastic shadow, umbrellas for leaves, cabbages for flower heads. The bars of Victoria's cot were black and menacing and the line of light under the door from the landing was a brilliant pencil which might at any moment rear up and scrawl 'She is not normal!' lambently on the wall. To soothe herself, she counted the roses on the wallpaper; she could just make out their heavy, dark faces. One rose, two roses, three roses . . . and, at the heart of the third rose, a gleam of light. A round gleam. She looked at it idly at first and then with increasing curiosity. A hole in the wall, through which light shone from the next room. A neat, round hole.

Finally, she got up and knelt by the hole, which was the size of a penny. Remembering the first night, when she watched the Jowles through the kitchen key-hole, she thought that she was always spying on them. Now she saw the terra incognita of the brothers' bedroom, lit by an unshaded central lamp.

Two small white beds, the sheets turned down over quilted satin eiderdowns. A black and brown rug on the floor, a very cheap one. A wooden chair painted with castles and roses, like a barge. That would be Finn's chair. A square of mirror propped against a pink-washed wall. Beside the mirror hung a painting. She squirmed around for a better view of it. It was a peculiar painting. She found it difficult to believe.

Aunt Margaret sat on a bank of primroses, naked but for a cloak of brilliant green loosely slung around her shoulders. Her famine leanness was softened by all the scarlet hair drifting around her. Her pubic hair was a mound of fire. Her breasts were on the point of turning into roses. Her flesh was a glaring white. Finn must have used white paint raw from the tube unmixed with any other colour. Down her white cheeks rolled two fat tears which glistened because they were round, faceted, crystal beads stuck onto the canvas. Over her head was a florid, curling garland of curious flowers, tulips, auriculas and daffodils, tied with a green bow at each end. Two cupids clutched the bows and kicked fat heels. They were executed in low relief in pink Plasticine. The whole painting had a secret, private quality about it, the quality of a whisper behind the hand. It, too must be an allegory, though not in the style of Rubens.

Finn's raincoat lay on the floor beside a fiddle-case shaped like the coffin of some dwarf. Then Finn himself crossed her field of vision. His hair brushed the splintery floorboards. He was walking on his hands. She could not be surprised any more. Walking on his hands, he made hardly any noise, only a carpet-slipper slapping of palms against the floor. She sat back and considered the evidence of the spy-hole.

The spy-hole was neat, round and entirely premeditated. Someone had made the spy-hole. Why? Presumably to watch her. So she was not only watching but being watched when she thought she was by herself, when she was taking her clothes off and putting them on and so on. All the time, someone was watching her. All the time she had been in the house. They had not even let her keep her own loneliness but had intruded on it.

She guessed it was Finn who watched her most, unless the brothers took turns. But somehow she could not imagine Francie putting his eye to the keyhole, even only once, just to see her without her knickers – his back was too stiff, his neck too rigid. Finn it was who was Peeping Tom and had put his tongue in her mouth. She flushed with anger.

'The dirty little beast,' she said to herself. 'Oh, what a little animal!'

And he was walking on his hands in the very next room this very minute. She was angry enough to go into his room and accuse him; but she thought better of it, for he was shifty and quick and, besides, she did not want to see him. After some thought, she pulled a chair in front of the hole and hung her coat over the back, so that the hole was blocked up. Perhaps this was enough. And she would not go walking with him again and she would not be alone with him if she could help it and she would freeze him with a look when he tried to talk to her. He was no friend of hers. A series of thumps from the next room indicated Finn was practising cartwheels or somersaults.

6

Aunt Margaret had one single piece of jewellery, besides her fat gold wedding ring. This was a curious necklace which she wore on Sunday afternoons after lunch, when she changed from her drab, black, weekday clothes into her best dress. The week's work was done and she waited for another hard week to start in this ugly, holiday dress. The dress itself was old-fashioned and made of cheap, unyielding woollen material in a deadly, flat shade of grey, a shade which was a negation of colour, an annihilation of any possibility of prettiness, an ulti-mately dejected and miserable grey. It had a high neck and narrow sleeves too short for her, from which her chapped, bony wrists and her hands on which every knotted sinew and vein was visible protruded limply, as if they were stitched separately to the cuffs and not part of her arms at all. It was her best dress because it was her only dress; otherwise her wardrobe consisted only of three or four shabby black skirts and four or five shapeless black sweaters all with snagged stitches slowly unravelling themselves, and the elbows worn thin and pale.

The dress fell straight from her shoulders to a hem midway down her shins in a long, vertical line. It fitted her badly, barely skimming her body and catching on her bony hips. It was difficult to imagine she had bought the dress on purpose, had one fine day long past gone into a shop and tried on dress after dress and, finally, taking this grey and unbecoming tube of cloth from a rack laden with many-coloured garments, slipped it over her head, examined herself fore and aft in the changing cubicle mirror, smiled with pleasure, clapped her hands in approval and said to herself: 'This is lovely, this is the very thing,' while a curled, perfumed salesgirl hovered, saying: 'But it's perfectly *you*, madam.' Rather, she must have inherited it or bought it at a jumble sale for the sake of something to cover herself as a rest from her everlasting black or perhaps (most likely) found it in a drawer of her newly married bedroom, chosen for her by Uncle Philip as suitable for his wife to wear on Sundays.

It was a very dowdy dress, and old, and it smelled of mothballs and, faintly, of years of perspiration soaked into the fabric, but it had been well and carefully preserved. Also, it was nevertheless her Sunday best and, as such, had a certain innate dignity in spite of its nastiness. Somehow, too, because it did not quite fit her and hung gauchely in parallels and was kept with such care, spots of dirt sponged out and the dress frequently brushed and pressed, it made her seem, touchingly, much younger.

It was a dress the good girl in Sunday school might wear. She looked naive and youthful in it. With it, she put on stockings with the holes and ladders neatly darned, saved for Sundays, and a pair of round-toed, low-heeled, strapped shoes, very old but nicely polished and also kept only for Sundays.

And when she was dressed and ready, she took her necklace out of some box or cupboard and clasped it round her throat, to complete her outfit.

The necklace was a collar of dull silver, two hinged silver pieces knobbed with moonstones which snapped into place around her lean neck and rose up almost to her chin so that she could hardly move her head. It was heavy, crippling and precious and looked as though it might be very ancient, pre-Christian or possibly even pre-Flood although, in fact, it was not. Topping off that scrawny, grey dress, the collar looked almost sinisterly exotic and bizarre. Wearing the collar, Aunt Margaret had to carry her head high and haughty as the Queen of Assyria, but above it her eyes were anxious and sad and not proud at all.

On Sundays, she did her hair with far more care than usual, arranging it in smooth red coils and loops, and, with her uncustomary neatness and her grand necklace and her look of youth, she acquired a startling, hare-like, fleeting beauty, pared to the bone; a weird beauty that lasted until bedtime, when she took the necklace off and put it away again. Because she possessed this eldritch beauty so briefly each week, it was almost shocking. With Victoria on her knee and her head held regally erect because of the pressure of the collar, she looked like an icon of Our Lady of Famine, pictured as a spare young girl.

When she wore the collar, she ate only with the utmost difficulty. Sunday teas never varied. Always shrimps, bread and butter, a bowl of mustard and cress and a rich, light, golden sponge-cake baked that morning in the oven with the Sunday joint so that it had a faint savour of burnt meat fat. The table was littered with shrimp whiskers, the sponge-cake gobbled up to the last crumb – but all she could do was to sip painfully at a meagre cup of tea and toy with a few shoots of mustard and cress, although she had prepared the extensive meal. Uncle Philip broke the armour off a pink battalion of shrimps and ate them steadily, chewed through a loaf of bread spread with half a pound of butter and helped himself to the lion's share of the cake while gazing at her with expressionless satisfaction, apparently deriving a certain pleasure from her discomfort, or even finding that the sight of it improved his appetite.

'He has no feelings,' thought Melanie. But it was the regal and hampering collar which made Aunt Margaret beautiful. *Il faut souffrir pour être belle.* Bristling with moonstones, the collar was primitive and barbaric; the mastiff of a prince of medieval Persia might have worn it for going out hawking in a miniature. It was not what one would expect Aunt Margaret to have chosen for herself. At a guess, she would have a taste for cultured pearls like Melanie's confirmation present, and maybe rhinestones, and flower brooches in fragile, glittery stones, and small, gold lockets with tinted photographs of babies and soft curls of new-fledged hair inside. But she was proud of her collar. It was real silver.

'It was his wedding present,' she chalked. 'He made it himself. To his own design.'

'Heavens, he is clever,' said Melanie.

'He can make anything, in wood or metal. Perhaps he'll make some jewellery for you, one day.'

'That might be nice,' said Melanie politely. To herself, she thought: 'God forbid.'

Talking about the collar, Finn said: 'You see, they make love on Sunday nights, he and Margaret.' His eyes were cold water and he spat, which distressed Melanie so much she did not take in what he said. The ball of spittle lay on the floor like a shed moonstone.

'You don't like Uncle Philip very much, do you?' she said.

'Why should I?' he said, fingering a great purple bruise under his right eye. It was a bad day, that day. The chisel had slipped and sliced his flesh to the bone; he could not work. Even in the shop, Melanie could hear Uncle Philip shouting: 'You done it on purpose, you Irish bastard!' and the dull thud of blows. Then Finn had come up, grim, silent and dripping blood, wordlessly shown her the dreadful cut and gone upstairs to his sister for a bandage.

He was sitting on the counter in the shop, now, playing with the fiddling and fluting monkeys with his good left hand. Suddenly he said: 'Rot him!' and flung the toy into a corner with great force. It shattered against panelling and crashed to the floor in jagged shards of tin. The music box mechanism died with a twang.

'Oh, Finn!'

'I should like to smash it all up,' said Finn, who had been beaten. He looked young, a little boy, as he said this and like a little boy who has been thrashed by playground bullies and cannot do anything in return but hate them. 'I should like to huff and to puff and to blow his house down and take Maggie away from him and she and me and Francie could go back to Ireland and live quietly together and play music and have a little step dancing from time to time.'

'What would happen to me and the young ones, then?'

'Ah, that I couldn't say. It's every man for himself.' He cradled his hurt hand. The bruise was a black mark underlining his squint. 'Didn't it have to be my right hand that's out of action? My painting hand?' Melanie went to clear up the broken toy.

She had not wanted to talk to Finn but she could not help it when he came and sat on the counter. Besides, if she did not talk to him at all, ever, then she talked to nobody, unless you counted her communication with Aunt Margaret; and her loneliness was unbearable. She was not brave enough to cut herself off from Finn entirely, in the end. And he seemed to be pretending that he had never touched her with his hot, wet mouth, anyway. So, after a time, she began to think – when he was so collectedly friendly – that she had imagined more than had really happened, or had imagined it all. Yet if she moved the chair, she saw the spyhole. So she did not move the chair.

'About Jonathon,' she said. 'What does Jonathon do when Uncle Philip hits you?' For she did not like to think of Jonathon sitting a silent audience to the scenes of cold violence in the work-room.

'He doesn't see. He rigs.'

'I shouldn't want my little brother to be upset.'

'He is thinking about something else, mostly. Your uncle is delighted with him. He will probably apprentice him, like he apprenticed me. The ships impress your uncle very much. He was talking about branching out into the ship-in-a-bottle business because Jonathon will make only ships. But he is good at making ships.'

'It is a kind of craze.'

'It seems more like an obsession.'

'I don't know.'

'He is only twelve years old, though, and that seems young to be obsessed or possessed.'

'Most of the time,' she said slowly, 'Jonathon hardly seems

to be there. As though the real Jonathon is somewhere else and has left a copy of himself behind so that no one notices he's gone. He has always been like that, even when he was quite small.'

'When he takes his glasses off, his eyes flinch from the impact of the open air,' said Finn.

'His school reports always used to say, "Jonathon could do better if he tried."'

'Isn't that just like schoolteachers? Don't fret about Jonathon, Melanie. He is content. He is of your uncle's flesh. A Flower.'

'A Flower,' she said, tasting the never-before perceived strangeness of the name.

'I thought at first, what was the mother like since there's so little of the Flowers in any of them, since they are so good and clean and wipe their noses always on their handkerchiefs and never on their sleeves? But the veneer is rubbing off already.'

'My mother,' said Melanie, invoking her with difficulty, 'wore hats and gloves and sometimes sat on committees.'

But Finn was no longer listening, brooding instead over his injured hand, his eyes veiled and murderous.

That evening, Melanie washed up by herself since her aunt was bathing Victoria. Once a week, Aunt Margaret defied the banging, popping, gangrenous, gas-flaring monster of the bathroom geyser all for Victoria's sake, to give her a bath in three inches of snot-green, brackish, warmish water, which took ten minutes to trickle from the geyser's brutish snout into the tub. Melanie thought Aunt Margaret was exceedingly brave to dare the rusty, maniacal geyser and to light it, against its wishes, and force it to spew out hot or fairly hot water. Melanie had tried to fill the bath from it only once and then it had exploded with such ferocity that the toothbrushes leapt and quivered in the rack and Uncle Philip's toothglass had taken a suicide jump from the shelf and bounced on the floor, fortunately without breaking.

After that, she never washed in any water but cold water except when she could borrow a steaming kettle from her aunt in order to wash herself piecemeal in the kitchen or the cramped wash-basin in the bathroom. The clean patches of flesh came up under her damp flannel with an apricot glow, first one leg, then the other. She remembered how she had submerged herself in scented water every day and sometimes twice in the sticky summertime and never would again, until she grew up and had a bathroom of her own. It was also difficult to wash her hair properly.

Finn and Francie never attempted to light the geyser. Melanie did not know how Finn washed, when he washed, if he ever washed; but Francie would sometimes fill an oval tin bath from kettles and saucepans boiled on the stove and sit impassively in it in the kitchen behind a locked door. And Aunt Margaret did the same, quite often, after she shooed Melanie off to bed early. But Uncle Philip bathed in the tub as often as once or twice a week; he seemed to exercise some occult authority over the geyser, for it never erupted when he lit it. He left the bathroom in a terrible mess, with water slopped all over the floor and the towel sopping. Melanie never found out to whom the plastic toy she discovered in the bath on her first morning belonged. The evidence pointed to Uncle Philip, but this seemed improbable.

However, Victoria's weekly bath was a ritual, a ceremonial, absorbing all Aunt Margaret's attention and taking up a great deal of time, and Melanie was by herself in the kitchen, which was warm and smug and complacent since its work was finished for the day. The pots on the dresser and the straight-backed, hard-backed chairs and the rag rug all seemed to be at peace with the world. It was pleasant to be in the kitchen and Melanie hummed to herself as she hung cups from their hooks and propped the plates. She opened the dresser drawer to put away the knives and spoons. In the dresser drawer was a freshly severed hand, all bloody at the roots.

It was a soft-looking, plump little hand with pretty, tapering fingers the nails of which were tinted with a faint, pearly lacquer. There was a thin silver ring of the type small girls wear on the fourth finger. It was the hand of a child who goes to dancing class and wears frilled petticoats with knickers to match. From the raggedness of the flesh at the wrist, it appeared that the hand had been hewn from its arm with a knife or axe that was very blunt. Melanie heard blood fall plop in the drawer.

'I am going out of my mind,' she said aloud. 'Bluebeard was here.'

She closed the drawer and leaned forward against the dresser. She was drenched in sweat and her mouth was dry. After a moment, her knees gave way and she slithered to the floor in a clattering hail of cutlery. All the furniture in the room danced up and down. The chairs jigged from one leg to the other. The table waltzed ungracefully. The cuckoo clock spun round and round. She lay on the heaving ground, frozen for fear of moving.

The next thing she knew was a cup held against her mouth. The cup contained water with the faint peat-coloured addition of a little whisky. Francie held her stiffly upright in his arms. In one hand, he held the cup, in the other, an open quarter bottle of Teacher's Highland Cream. Even though his hands were full, she felt quite safe. She could see the small, sandy hairs in his nostrils. Her teeth chattered against the cup.

'Drink it up, there's a good girl,' said Francie. Today he wore a tie-pin shaped like a St Bridget's cross, of badly tarnished grey metal. His tie was dark blue and red in diagonal strips. His cheeks were sandpapery with stubble. He looked like any Irishman. She was glad he had found her with his navy-blue suit on and his tie-pin.

'You are ordinary,' she said, blessing him. He smiled his rusty smile.

'So I am,' he said. 'Just an ordinary chap.'

She lolled her head against his shoulder.

'I fell down.'

'Fainted, maybe. I come in for me rosin and you're lying on the ground. The dog sniffing.' He talked as if he never thought in words and had to invent them to describe the shapeless, bulky concepts in his mind as he went along.

The dog, its eyes full of concern, pressed its nose into the palm of her hand, making reassuring, snuffling noises. With an effort, she patted its head. Suddenly she and the dog were friends. She sipped the sweet, weak whisky and water and began to feel better.

'I would have thought you would have drunk Irish whisky,' she said, curious.

'It all goes the same way,' he said. 'I like a drop of good stuff, though.'

Slowly, creakily, he talked, like a cart pulled by a wise old horse going along a rough road. She finished her drink, smiling at him over the rim of the cup. He took a drink from the bottle himself, leaning across her to do so. Then he asked her: 'What was the matter, pet?'

She shuddered and the nightmare came back.

'Something in the knife drawer. I saw it. It was bleeding.'

'Knife drawer? But she keeps knives there, only. Maggie would only keep knives there. After all, it is the knife drawer.'

'Go and see for me. Go and look. See if it's still there.'

'I'll put you nice and comfy in the chair, first, pet.' It did her heart good to hear him call her pet. He carried her easily to Uncle Philip's armed chair and settled her down, drawing the electric fire near to her on its cord. Then he opened the drawer. She bit on her fist in nervous fright.

'Nothing in there,' he said. 'Nothing but knives and forks. And spoons, too. Spoons. You must have been dreaming.'

'Are you perfectly sure? I mean, quite sure?'

Shaking his head, he opened and closed the drawer several times as if to demonstrate its innocence.

'What did you think you saw, girly?'

'A hand,' she said. 'Cut off.'

He turned his head to her in surprise. His eyes were grey-green, like Finn's, but had warm brown flecks in them and looked straight and candid ahead, as though they saw too directly to look from side to side.

'What a terrible thing!' He thought for a few moments. 'Perhaps you were thinking about Finn's hand and that made you think you saw a hand?'

'I don't know. I don't know.'

'I'll make you a nice cup of tea. That will soothe you.' He filled the kettle carefully and set it on the gas stove but in spite of his care he slopped water. His clumsy body made angles under the weight of his solicitude.

134

'How nice he is,' thought Melanie, astonished. 'And I never knew him till now.'

She was sure she had seen a hand in the drawer, a hand with little pink nails and a silver ring on one finger. The fourth finger from which a vein leads to the heart. However, Francie saw no hand and she trusted him. While she drank his hot, sweet tea, he continued to look in the drawer, picking over its contents and clicking his tongue.

'Nothing,' he said, 'you might think was a hand unless it is still your distress. The distress of your loss might make you see things. It is only natural.'

He was out of place among the pots and pans and plaster Alsatians and bread crocks; he was an Easter Island figure, ungainly and antique, put together on another, earlier pattern than that of most men, so that you would not guess, to look at him, that he had a loving heart. His sweetness was as unexpected and overwhelming as that of the spring in his own country where the fields grow rocks, only, and a little grass. She finished her tea. He emptied the dregs in the sink.

'Look,' he said, showing the pattern of tea leaves among the melted sugar at the bottom. 'A ship. That means a journey.'

'For me?' she said and could not keep the longing out of her voice.

'Or someone. Ah, you're not well, you should go to bed.'

'Well, yes,' she admitted. 'But you'll have to help me upstairs. My legs still feel funny.'

In her blue-lit room, Aunt Margaret was dressing sweet, clean Victoria in her night gown in an odorous fog of damp talcum powder. They both rolled on Melanie's bed. They were making a great game of it. Aunt Margaret, radiant, tickled the fat baby padding on Victoria's ribs and the soles of her soft feet, bouncing and wrestling her, shaking with soundless laughter while Victoria crowed her delight. It was a wonder to see Aunt Margaret happy. Her hair had fallen down and there were scattered hairpins everywhere.

'Melanie fainted,' said Francie.

The game stopped at once. Anxiety flooded over Aunt Margaret's face, washing away the joy. She scooped up Victoria, ignoring her protests but for a quick kiss, and dropped her into her cot, gesturing Melanie to lie down. She caressed Melanie's forehead with a cool, fresh touch like the wind with rain in it. She throbbed with the effort of containing words she could not speak.

Some sort of wordless communication passed between her and Francie, something too deep and personal for Melanie to comprehend. Then she smiled, stroking Melanie's face again, so tenderly that Melanie closed her eyes and imagined it was her own mother caressing her or any mother caressing any child. But the moment she closed her eyes, the severed hand flashed onto her eyelids like a still from a Hammer film and she moaned and twisted about.

'There, there,' said Francie. He and his sister stood on either side of the bed, bending over her as if to protect her from the perils of the night with their own flesh and bone. To Melanie's dazzled eyes, they seemed to mingle and become one single arch of living substance raised up over her, beneath which she could sleep in safety.

> *Matthew, Mark, Luke and John,*
> *Bless the bed that I lie on,*
> *Four angels round my head . . .*

Not four but three angels. Here was Finn, appearing at her bed foot. All the red people lighting a bonfire for her, to brighten away the wolves and tigers of this dreadful forest in which she lived.

'I'll stay with her until she goes to sleep,' said Finn. He was Francie's brother and the dumb woman was his sister There could be no harm in him. 'It is only poor Finn, who will do you no harm.' He had said that before but she had not believed him. Well, she believed him now.

Francie and Margaret gave her light, dry, affectionate kisses on each cheek. Then they vanished. A night light was burning and the main light switched off. She had not seen where the night light came from. It burned with a pure and nursery flame in a blue and white saucer filled with match-sticks. Finn sat on a chair by her bed. In the dimness, his tousled hair seemed to send out rays of its own brightness. Shadows carved the flesh from his features so that she could see the fine lines of his skull, the hard mystery of essential bone. His hands lay peacefully folded in his lap. His bandage was grubby, now.

'Does it hurt where you cut it, Finn?' she asked drowsily.

'It wasn't mortal. I'll live.'

In the next room, Francie tuned his fiddle and Aunt Margaret made a trial run on the flute.

'Shall I send them away or can you sleep through that?'

'I like to hear them.'

Victoria, ignored, slept already, murmuring in her sleep with a noise like the inside of a beehive. Finn lit a cigarette and the smoke curled and twirled around him. They were private and close together.

'Finn,' she asked because the approaches of sleep loosened

her inhibitions, 'why did you make the peephole in the wall and look at me?'

'Because you are so beautiful,' he said very softly, from a mouth redder than wine. He could have been her phantom bridegroom sleeping and, overwhelmed, she slept.

After this, she loved them, all reservations gone. She had not realised they could reach out from the charmed circle of themselves. Now she felt part of that circle. Francie, especially, she loved and would help her aunt gladly to mend his clothes. And she polished his shoes for him, whenever she got the chance. She threw in her lot with the Jowles. They adopted her. They smiled when she came into the room. Even doing the housework with Aunt Margaret satisfied her; she had a part to play in the running of the home. She was a help to Aunt Margaret. As they prepared a meal one day, Aunt Margaret chalked:

'I don't know how I coped before you came. It is lovely to have another woman in the house.'

Melanie played with the taps in the sink to hide her embarrassed pleasure. She was wrung with pity for her aunt, whose silence was so haunted when her brothers were not there.

'She must live for her brothers,' thought Melanie. 'She must have married Uncle Philip just to make a home for them when they were little. How can she ever have felt anything for him as a man?'

Uncle Philip never talked to his wife except to bark brusque commands. He gave her a necklace that choked her. He beat her younger brother. He chilled the air through which he moved. His towering, blank-eyed presence at the head of the table drew the savour from the good food she cooked. He suppressed the idea of laughter. Melanie chose her side the night she thought she saw the hand; she began to hate Uncle Philip.

And he had never yet directly addressed Melanie by her name or even acknowledged Victoria's presence. He glared across the breakfast table at them, quenching the morning cheerfulness in the kitchen, and fiercely examined them at tea-time as if to see what the day had done to them. Simply by sitting there, he rendered the dining-room as cold and cheerless as a room in a commercial traveller's guesthouse. He knew his nieces lived in the house. He saw them. But never spoke to them, having other things to do.

Melanie soon learnt what these things were.

One day, she prepared the brussels sprouts for dinner, cutting a cross on each base as her Aunt had taught her. Aunt Margaret was on edge that day. She had dropped stitches continually in her knitting (she was knitting a yellow angora sweater for Victoria) and started whenever the shop-bell jangled or the parakeet muttered a few words to itself. Now she agitatedly trimmed lamb chops, paring away the hard, white fat for Uncle Philip could not abide grease, glancing now and then at Melanie and opening and closing her mouth in a distressing, uncertain way. As if she could bear it no longer, she dropped her knife and seized the chalk.

'There is a performance tomorrow,' she wrote. There were ladders in both her stockings today and her hair spilled from its bun at all sides.

'What do you mean?'

'Puppets. A puppet show. We must all go and admire the puppets. It is special because you children haven't seen them before.'

'Well,' said Melanie. 'It will make a change.' She cut

another cross, wondering vaguely if it had a religious significance. They were Irish; were they Catholics? But they never
went to church, as far as she knew. She was not interested in
the puppets because Uncle Philip made them. Aunt Margaret
scrubbed at her board for more space.

'You don't understand. It is terribly important to him!'

'I see,' said Melanie, mystified. Such a fuss about a puppet
show!

Tomorrow was Sunday, a roast for dinner and no shop to
look after. Aunt Margaret told her to dress herself in her nicest
dress and Melanie put on a dress she had never worn in her
uncle's house, a best dress from the old days, dark green corduroy with lace at the neck. It had hung limply in the
cupboard for nearly three months. Now she felt strong enough
to shake the memories out of it. She smoothed the skirt and
wished, once again, for a mirror to see herself, to see how
much she had grown since she last wore this dress one blus-
tering, pink and white Easter holiday. Or if she was looking
older, if she had changed at all. She combed out her hair, to
please Finn. She could see that her hair had grown by perhaps
half an inch. Her hair felt rough and unpleasant to the touch
because she was no longer washing it properly but improvising
with a kettle of hot water in the kitchen sink. And it was a
particular nuisance since it was so long. It would be sensible to
cut off most of her hair, but so much of it had grown when her
parents were alive that it seemed somehow unfaithful to their
memory to scissor it all away. Her hair was never quite clean;
but she was getting used to being never quite clean all over.

After dinner, her uncle and Finn went again to the work-
room and her aunt put on her grey dress and silver collar and
did up her coiffure. Victoria's mucky bib came off her flower-

sprigged Viyella dress and the chocolate pudding was sponged from her face. Jonathon's neck and ears were examined and polished once again for luck with a damp face-cloth and he was instructed to change his shirt. Francie appeared, wearing his harp tie-pin and carrying his fiddle-case.

'I like your harp,' said Melanie because she loved him.

'They gave it me St Patrick's night,' he said. 'At the Dagenham Irish Club.'

They were all ready, spruce and clean as for going to church, Sunday trim. They filed downstairs, the dog following them with the air of a dog doing his duty. The workroom was extremely tidy and four chairs were set in a row in front of the puppet theatre. They were the upright chairs from the parlour behind the shop. Melanie had not been down to the workroom since her very first morning; she tried not to look at the partially assembled puppets, hanged and dismembered, on the walls. The red plush curtains bulged and bumpings and thumpings came from behind them. They took their seats with some ceremony, arranging their good clothes around them. There was a notice in red paint pinned to the curtains: NO SMOKING: On the wall was a poster in crude colours announcing: 'GRAND PERFORMANCE – FLOWER'S PUPPET MICROCOSM', with a great figure recognisably Uncle Philip by virtue of the moustache and wing collar, holding the ball of the world in his hand. Finn must have painted it.

Finn came from between the curtains, tense and preoccupied. He turned off the lights and scurried back to the theatre. They sat in expectant darkness. From above the curtains came a muffled roar: 'Play your blasted fiddle, Francie Jowle! What else do I keep you for?'

Francie tuned up and began to play an unexpected, tearoom

kind of music. Melanie glanced at him in surprise but his face was expressionless, living stone. The curtains swung open, revealing the peacock-coloured grotto she had seen there before. Now it was lit luridly in green and the puppet in the white ballet dress was standing upright facing them. Her hair was screwed into a ballerina chignon and her wooden lips set in a smile of excessive sweetness. A network of wires supported her. Jerkily she rose *en pointe* on one wooden leg and twisted round in a pirouette.

Over Francie's playing, Uncle Philip recited: 'Morte d'une Sylphe, or, Death of a Wood Nymph.' Audibly he commented to himself, 'Poor little girly.' So he was a sentimental man, at times.

The puppet spread its arms and effected a backward kick. Aunt Margaret began energetically to applaud, nudging Melanie to join in with her. They clapped in chorus. Their hands made a seaweed swish in the submarine gloom. When Aunt Margaret stopped applauding, Melanie stopped, too.

Now the puppet raised its hands above its head and swayed from side to side. Its wooden feet (in pink satin slippers) made tick-tocking noises on the boards. The light deepened till she looked like a ballerina in a green glass bottle. She clasped her wooden hands to her heart and tilted her head backwards, upwards. Leaves of various shapes, sizes and colours, cut out of paper, came fluttering down.

'Funny lady,' said Victoria audibly. Aunt Margaret hastily unwrapped a toffee and stopped Victoria's mouth with it.

'With the approach of autumn,' intoned Uncle Philip, 'the wood nymph feels its end drawing nigh.'

Aunt Margaret applauded. Melanie applauded. Then stopped. The fiddle sobbed and wailed. The nymph attempted a final arabesque but the effort proved too much for her weak heart. She gracefully collapsed in a waterfall of white tulle while the leaves thickly and fast filled the grotto. The lights went out. The curtains closed. Francie made a final plangent chord and took the fiddle from under his chin.

Melanie and Aunt Margaret applauded until their hands hurt. The curtains opened and there was the nymph, alive again, smiling and curtseying stiffly. The curtains closed. Melanie and Aunt Margaret continued to applaud. The curtains opened again and Uncle Philip stood next to his doll, beaming proudly. Yes, beaming, grinning like a shark; Melanie was reminded of the barren, professional, show-biz smiles on the faces of the toy acrobats. He bowed from the waist. He was got up in rusty finery, striped trousers and a dinner jacket with a white carnation in the button-hole and a clip-on bow tie. It was an imitation carnation. All the clothes were unused looking and old, as if kept for years in jars of formaldehyde. This was his puppet master's outfit.

The nymph swayed dangerously now Finn was controlling her from above. She swayed and bumped against Uncle Philip and he dropped his joviality like a brick and shook his fist balefully at Finn over his head. Finn was an inexperienced and inexpert puppeteer.

'Watch it, young Finn!'

Aunt Margaret hastily took a bunch of paper roses from a bag she carried and threw them at the stage. They glanced off the puppet's head and fell to the floor. Uncle Philip picked them up and stuck them briskly in the gap between the puppet's wooden breast and its white satin bodice. They took two more curtains and then he bawled: 'Houselights!' Francie turned them on. The whole performance had taken perhaps seven minutes.

'Is that all?' whispered Melanie.

Her aunt shook her head emphatically and pushed a toffee into her hand, with a soft pressure of her fingers. Inside the toffee paper was a scribbled message: 'Look as though you're enjoying it, for my sake and Finn's.' Melanie, to please her, put on a false, bright smile.

Francie accepted a toffee.

'I think you are a marvellous fiddler,' said Melanie. He chewed, putting his finger reflectively along his nose. 'Not on this rubbish,' he said. 'But I do my best. I'm fair on jigs and reels.'

Finn dashed through the work-room and out of the door, returning carrying an elaborate gilded throne made of cardboard. His face was streaked with sweat and dirt. The curtains heaved and billowed.

'Like a sail,' said Jonathon. Aunt Margaret gave him a toffee. He did not eat it but put it in his pocket, where it would lie forgotten for months.

'Can I go now?' he asked. Melanie was shocked to see the horror on her aunt's face.

'Not yet, Jonathon.'

'Turn the lights out, Francis Jowle, and tune up your fiddle!'

The curtains parted again as Francie played 'Greensleeves'. Golden artificial sunlight filled a wainscotted room with a frieze of unicorns butting one another with their horns. On the top of three steps in the centre of the stage was the cardboard throne.

'Holyrood Palace,' said Uncle Philip. His wife and niece applauded with dutiful enthusiasm.

'A historical sequence,' he announced. 'Mary, Queen of Scots, and Bothwell enjoy a secret rendezvous.'

Francie began to play the love theme from the 'Romeo and Juliet Fantasy Overture' with excessive, perhaps derisive, use of tremolo. A female puppet with a fine, domed forehead entered, swishing black velvet. They applauded. She curt-seyed. She walked up the stairs, one, two, three – a tense moment on three as the wooden foot hovered over the step for a long moment before descending. The Queen turned slowly round and sat down. She wore a collar like Aunt Margaret's but it could not chafe her neck because she was made of wood. Aunt Margaret surreptitiously ran her finger round her own silver choker as if the sight of the Queen's collar had reminded her how much her own one hurt. There was a lengthy pause while the Queen's cunningly articulated fingers played with a pomander.

Then Bothwell came in. He was a fine figure of a puppet, in a red cloak and a hat with a feather. He had a winging moustache and a goatee beard but he moved tentatively, uncertainly, and Melanie guessed it was Finn who worked him. Bothwell walked with Francie's toppling fall. It seemed forever before he got to the centre of the stage. A seismic rumbling and a muffled yelp from the flies indicated that Uncle Philip was not pleased with Finn. Melanie felt Aunt Margaret flinch beside her. Mary, Queen of Scots, descended her rostrum extending her hands in greeting. Bothwell raised his arms.

'Lovers' meeting,' commented Uncle Philip.

The puppets embraced, their two faces clicking together a morse code of passion, arms folded closely about one another in a flurry of black and red velvet. Aunt Margaret and Melanie clapped and clapped and clapped. The embrace lasted a long time. Francie finished the love theme from the

'Romeo and Juliet Fantasy Overture' and began to play the *Liebestod* from 'Tristan and Isolde' in the manner of a slow air. Melanie's hands tingled but they went on clapping.

The puppets clung together as if they would never part. Tension began to mount. They were like a needle stuck in a gramophone record, inexorably repeating embrace after embrace. Uncle Philip began to rumble again. Still entwined, the puppets threshed violently against each other as if overcome with concupiscence. Melanie saw, with a sinking of the heart, that this was not written into the script. The clapping petered out. She saw how Bothwell's strings had become hopelessly entangled with those of his royal mistress; bound in a true lover's knot, the puppets wrestled. The *Liebestod* went on and on.

Aunt Margaret cowered in her chair, covering her eyes, awaiting the end. Jonathon stared vacantly before him, seeing a tall mast and a red plush sail. Seagulls circled, mewing, over his head. Victoria, bored, pulled up her smock and tucked down her white lock-knit knickers to make sure her navel was still there. It was.

'Can I have another toffee?' she asked and was ignored.

There was a dreadful noise of rending wire. Finn had at last wrenched Bothwell free but at the cost of tearing apart his controls; in a spiky halo of torn wire, Bothwell crumpled to the floor. His head knocked on the steps of the rostrum as if asking to be let in. Mary tottered backwards. Francie stopped playing in mid cadence. There was a deadly silence.

Broken by a clear and penetrating, irrepressible gush of Finn's laughter.

Which modulated into a high-pitched scream. Then Finn came falling from the flies, as the leaves had fallen; only the leaves fell soft. His hair blew free like the tail of a comet. He plunged down for an interminable second, arms and legs splayed out in abandon, forgotten, tumbling anyhow, and crashed onto the stage on his back, lying across Bothwell, whose cloak was the colour of blood.

Mary, Queen of Scots, turned on her majestic heel and stalked off stage, her head held high. Her footsteps and the faint noise of her limbs striking one another as she walked sounded like the mechanism of a time bomb. Victoria began to wail. Jonathon pushed back his chair and got up.

'I think it is all over,' he said. 'I shall be going.' He went.

Slow tears ran down Aunt Margaret's face and splashed onto Victoria's cheeks and she comforted her, hampered by her hateful collar. Francie knelt beside them, sheltering them with the dry-stone wall of his body.

'How can she cry without making any sound at all?' thought Melanie.

Finn did not move.

'And is he dead, because she is crying so much?' thought Melanie. 'What if he is dead? Oh, God, make him not dead!'

And still he never moved. His eyes were open and staring. He looked broken like the toy he threw against the wall. All his lovely movement was shattered. Melanie tried to grasp how dreadful it would be if Finn were dead but she could not think coherently because of the terrible sound of Aunt Margaret's silence. Uncle Philip, huge and sombre, came onto the stage, straightening his bow tie, which was askew. He brusquely kicked Finn's stomach but Finn did not move.

'He's not going to work my lovely puppets again,' he said. His voice was thick and coarse like a peasant salami. 'I'll never let him put another hand on their strings.'

He shoved Finn's body off Bothwell with the casual brutality of Nazi soldiers moving corpses in films of concentration camps. He gathered up the puppet in his arms. At last, slowly, Finn moved, struggling onto his side, then onto all fours. He crouched doggily, panting. His face was whiter than he had painted his sister's.

'I wish you'd killed me,' he said hoarsely to Uncle Philip. 'If you'd killed me you'd be damned.'

Uncle Philip took no notice of him; he was tenderly smoothing Bothwell's cloak.

'Can't use Finn for me puppets again,' he grumbled. 'Useless bastard. Useless.'

Finn tried to get to his knees, but groaned and collapsed.

'Humans can act with my puppets,' said Uncle Philip. 'That's it. That'll be a novelty. Puppets and people. I'll use the girl.' He swung round and jabbed his forefinger at Melanie. 'I'll use you, miss!'

'Ah, no!' exclaimed Francie.

'No!' mouthed Aunt Margaret.

'God rot you to hell,' said Finn and vomited. His vomit was streaked with blood. He looked down at it with a horrified surprise.

'Why shouldn't the girl do something for her keep? God knows she eats enough. She can act with my puppets up on my stage. She's not too big, she won't be out of scale.' He rubbed his hands with satisfaction. 'What's your name, girly? Speak up.'

'Melanie,' she said, though her mouth was dead, as at the dentist's after the injection. But surely he knew her name?

'Daft kind of name,' he said. 'But that's settled. Now clear out, all of you.'

'But Finn—' said Francie.

'Take him and good riddance. Buggering me Bothwell. And you can mop up this filthy mess he's made, Maggie; he's your brother.'

Uncle Philip took up Bothwell and walked from the stage to his workbench. He laid the puppet out, a corpse on a slab, wailing: 'Poor old Bothwell! All his wires gone!'

Francie helped Finn to his feet. Still clutching Victoria, Aunt Margaret ran to his other side, her face that of the Virgin in a pietà. Melanie and the dog, who had been quietly sitting beneath her chair observing all this, went to join them. Melanie stumbled with joy because Finn was alive and could walk.

'I'm not hurt,' he said. 'Well, I don't think so. But I feel rocky. Rocky. And I can taste blood. Why can I taste blood, Maggie?' He asked her again, with bewildered innocence: 'Why?' His eyes seemed unable to focus.

Aunt Margaret, moaning, covered his face with kisses.

'Piss off, the lot of you!' cried Uncle Philip in a sudden, towering rage. 'Piss off!'

7

After this, Finn stopped grinning.

After he fell, he changed. His mouth turned sullenly down at the corners, like the mouth of a joke mug Melanie had once seen in an antique shop. On the mug was a face and, right side up, lettering over it said: 'FULL' and the face was beery, jolly and merry; but, bottoms up, it read: 'EMPTY' and the peaked eyebrows were turned into a drooping and despondent mouth. Finn read: 'EMPTY' all the time. He rarely spoke. His stream of talk was dried up at the source. His head hung down. He grew dirtier than ever and often would not shave for three or four days together, till his jaw looked coated or grown over with yellow fungus or sprayed like a car with glistening tangerine.

Worst of all, his grace was gone. Miraculously, the fall left him whole, with no injury internal or external, but it had shaken the beauty out of his movements. He stumped like an old man. It hurt Melanie to look at him. He was transformed into this sour lump of unbaked dough and, if the old, soft-voiced, slippery-tongued Finn had disturbed her, this new one cut her heart. He ignored her; not, it seemed, on purpose, but because only Uncle Philip was real to him any more. Mealtimes were desperate. He hardly ate, watching Uncle Philip all the time with fierce, twisted eyes.

Finn had moved into a glass box and never noticed if she or Francie or Aunt Margaret scratched on the glass to attract his attention. Aunt Margaret grew even thinner and more spectral. Her hair, red snakes struggling to free themselves from the hairpins, was the only vital thing about her. Under her red eyebrows were eyes often red with private weeping. Finn still treated her gently, if absently, kissing her goodnight; but as if he had already said good-bye to her, somewhere else. Her face was a tragic mask, that of a woman who has sent all her sons to a war and waits hourly for the death telegram.

The circle of the red people was broken. Melanie clung, above all, to Francie, who was always the same. Sometimes she sat in his room with him in the evenings when he practised, curled up on one or other of the narrow beds, with her sewing. She had started to help her aunt with the never-ending sewing. Melanie realised, now, that she had never needed an invitation to listen to his dancing music; all she had to do was to open the door and walk in. Aunt Margaret never left the kitchen to play her flute with Francie, after the fall.

'Philip might come up for something,' she chalked.

But that was pretending. She waited alone in the kitchen for her husband to kill Finn. Melanie knew what she was waiting for although she had not told her. Melanie expected it herself. Her uncle, in a fury, would lunge at Finn with a knife or a block of wood. Finn, sullen, vindictive, was forcing the killing blow to come to him.

The violence in the house was palpable. It trembled on the

cold stairs and rose up in invisible clouds from the thread-bare carpets. Melanie was afraid at nights, when her blue lantern was out and Victoria's cot loomed like a rat-trap. She shivered in her lavendered sheets, imploring herself to rest, trying not to think of the dreadful thing Finn had said. That he wanted her uncle to kill him so that her uncle would be damned. One night, she got up and turned on the light and looked at the sweet, bland face of Jesus, the Light of the World, in the picture over the mantelpiece. He smiled beneath his crown of thorns.

'Sweet Jesus,' she said. 'Help me. Help us all.'

But no help came. Her youth was a rock round her neck, her albatross. She was too young, too soft and new, to come to terms with these wild beings whose minds veered at crazy angles from the short, straight, smooth lines of her own experience. She got in the way of their passionate preoccupations. And Finn forgot her; she was a child. He could easily forget her, although he had pulled her hair and teased her and kissed her (had he kissed her?) and played Battleships with her. But never any more.

He was painting another picture, late at night, after Francie had gone to sleep, when the day's work was over. For his days still went on the toys and his evenings on the puppets, in dangerous and uneasy silence, down there. Then he painted his picture. Melanie knew because she watched him. She acknowledged the spyhole and peered through it, sometimes, when the sleeplessness got very bad. In the spot-light of an Anglepoise lamp which crouched on a chair like a big, black praying mantis, Finn worked quietly so as not to disturb Francie. He painted a triptych. Francie, Aunt Margaret and Finn himself, each on a separate panel, each wrapped in a bloody loin-cloth, each tied to a stake, each a St Sebastian full of arrows.

Meanwhile, Christmas was coming and the shop was busy. The first of Jonathon's wooden ships were up for sale at ten guineas each; Jonathon was earning his keep and so was Melanie, in the shop on her feet all day. Her legs began to hurt and she considered from time to time the possibility of varicose veins. Mrs Rundle had once had varicose veins but they had been cut out.

There were special lines for Christmas – wooden Christmas trees that opened out green painted branches on the principle of an opening umbrella; Santa Claus masks, red and white as raw beef; little tin candleholders shaped like gnomes and sprites for the tops of Christmas cakes. Also a special Christmas wrapping paper all over flowers, because of the name of the firm. Pretty pink and blue daisies. Finn had designed it, when he had had the heart to be pastoral. Every day, she and Aunt Margaret wrapped sheet after sheet of pink and blue daisies round toy after toy and the drawer where the money was kept sometimes would not shut because of all the pound notes inside.

'Well, I'm a sales girl, now,' Melanie thought the day she sold the Noah's Ark. A plump woman in a white wool suit and dark glasses bought it and tried to pay for it by cheque. Melanie took the cheque to her aunt to find out how she should deal with it; her aunt's hands fluttered in dismay. 'Philip won't take cheques. He says they're unnatural.'

Melanie said to the woman: 'I'm afraid we don't take cheques. I'm sorry.'

'Gee,' said the woman, who was American or, at least, had a transatlantic accent, 'don't be sorry. I think it's charming. It suits your old-fashioned kind of shop. Kind of Dickensian.'

And she returned shortly afterwards with a thick roll of notes fastened with a rubber band and Melanie counted out seventy-eight pounds and a ten shilling note and the woman gave her five shillings from her alligator purse. Then Melanie realised how profitably the shop purveyed old-fashioned charm. She began to respect her Uncle Philip's commercial acumen; although he was a swine, he was a clever swine. She was pleased with herself for selling the Noah's Ark but sorry to see it go, with the little Finn in jeans and tee-shirt inside it.

She put plastic holly in the windows, to keep up appearances. All the shops in the square, even the secondhand shop, were decorated with greenery and paper-chains. The greengrocer's was a bower of fir-boughs. Melanie and Victoria each had a fat, foil-wrapped tangerine from an aromatic, tissue-padded cardboard box, which was being unpacked when they went in together for potatoes and cooking apples; and the greengrocer lady, nodding her gold earrings, promised Victoria a solid triangle of muscatel raisins if she was a good girl and if the muscatel raisins did not sell. There were mauve-fleshed turkeys hanging by their feet in the butchers and rows of little chickens on their backs kicking their legs in the air.

'We don't celebrate Christmas,' wrote Aunt Margaret. 'Philip thinks it is a waste of money and over-commercialised.'

'He would,' thought Melanie bitterly.

'But there is a special show downstairs on Boxing Day,' wrote Aunt Margaret. 'It is his big show.'

Then she broke down and cried onto the flowery wrapping-paper. Melanie put her arms round the poor, thin body. What is Aunt Margaret made of? Bird bones and tissue paper, spun glass and straw. Cradling the worn, sad woman, Melanie felt herself to be very strong, young and vital and tough. She knew and trusted her firm, quick, resilient body, fed on wholesome food all its life, washed and tended so carefully. Aunt Margaret was as fragile as the first white shoots put trembling out by a bulb kept in a pot in a dark airing-cupboard. And Melanie knew that she, too, had been put away in the same close airing-cupboard, this grey, tall house. Would her strength wither away?

'Don't cry,' said Melanie, who was too strong to be withered. She was certain of it.

'He wants you to be in his next show.'

'Oh. Oh, dear.'

'He won't harm you. You are his sister's child.'

Then why was she crying? Was she remembering the last puppet show? Melanie hugged her aunt more tightly. Besides, Christmas was coming and Christmas must be especially hard for her, because she loved children and had none and all day and every day she sold toys for other people's beloved children.

It was not going to be a merry Christmas at Philip Flower's. Well, Melanie had had fifteen merry Christmases, when they tied wreaths of holly to the doorknockers and fed visiting choirboys on mincepies, and perhaps that was a sufficiency of merry Christmases. Besides, she was too old for Santa Claus. All the same, she put a little more plastic holly in the shop-window. She hoped Uncle Philip would not notice it.

A card came from Mrs Rundle, a tall, pious card, Jesus in the manger with ox and ass and kneeling shepherds; her love was on it, inscribed in her monumental handwriting. Melanie set it on her mantelpiece under 'The Light of the World'. The card had the price 1s 3d still lightly pencilled on the back and this seemed reassuringly normal and cosy. It had been bought with real money in a bright, well-lighted shop where they sold newspapers full of facts and human events, births, deaths and marriages, and chocolate and cigarettes for ordinary people to enjoy. Mrs Rundle also sent a squashy parcel addressed to all the three children. The parcel was stuck all over with 'Not to be opened until December 25' labels. Melanie put it away in a drawer. It was the only present any of them was likely to receive and she was deeply touched. They were all, three of them, remembered.

She was also embarrassed. She must send Mrs Rundle a card and perhaps a present but she had no money. Uncle Philip locked away all the takings every night. There was, Aunt Margaret said, a safe in their bedroom where he kept the money until he took it in to the bank at the end of the week in the massive, gleaming, opulent-looking calf-skin briefcase with a very large lock. Melanie pictured the safe, made of very black metal, set squarely at the end of the bed where he could see it all the time, in the strange bedroom where he slept with Aunt Margaret in a bed that must sag deeply on his side, since he was so heavy and she was no weight at all. Melanie had never been given so much as a sixpence for herself all the time she had been at the shop. She asked her aunt for a little money, for the first time, shuffling her feet and keeping her eyes shyly down.

'Just five shillings for – oh, some scented soap. That would be nice, scented soap. She was so kind to us, you see, and she is still fond of us and thinks of us.' There was an odd lump in her throat, thinking of Mrs Rundle thinking of her and Jonathon and Victoria as she stirred a Christmas pudding or chopped fruit for mincemeat in her new home. She would be pleased that the orphans were having a Christmas in the bosom of a family, since Christmas is a time for families. It would be a comfort to her and she would never know it was not true.

Her aunt twisted her eloquent hands.

'But he doesn't let me have any money, myself. Or you could have whatever I had.'

'Well,' said Melanie.

'I am so sorry!' The tail of the 'y' drooped with her sorrow. 'It is his way. He doesn't trust me with money.'

In case she ran away?

'Then it doesn't matter,' said Melanie.

'There is credit at the shops. I don't really need ready money, you see. And it is his way.' She tried to gloss over the humiliation of it.

'I understand,' said Melanie. An ancient, female look passed between them; they were poor women pensioners, planets round a male sun. In the end, Francie gave Melanie a pound note from his fiddling money. He slipped it into the pocket of her skirt and she hardly knew how to thank him.

She bought a box of rosy smelling soap and packed it off to Mrs Rundle. Because she felt no Christmas was hard on the young ones, she also bought a tin of boiled sweets for Victoria (the tin had a cheerful scene of rabbits in top hats on it) and three handkerchiefs marked 'J' for Jonathon, because he was careless with handkerchiefs. There was still a little money left so she bought a tiny bottle of scent for Aunt Margaret. It was not very good scent but it was something. She felt defiant, buying presents in the teeth of Uncle Philip's disapproval, though he could not have known she was keeping the Christmas economy going.

'I'll clean Francie's shoes every day for a year for a present,' she thought. But she did not think about giving anything to Finn; he lived, now, in a country where presents and affection and loving and giving meant nothing. She tried not to think about Finn because then she felt weak and hopeless. She could still see him, dancing. But never again.

One night, her aunt drew a length of white chiffon out of a paper bag. The painted dog's eyes shone with white lights, reflecting it. She gestured Melanie over to her and draped the material around her shoulders. All at once, Melanie was back home and swathing herself in diaphanous veiling before a mirror. But the cuckoo clock poked out its head and called nine o'clock and there she was, in Uncle Philip's house.

'Your costume,' wrote Aunt Margaret on a pad, to save herself getting up. 'For the show.'

'What am I?' asked Melanie.

'Leda. He is making a swan. He is having trouble with it. He says Finn is trying to spoil it.'

This seemed very likely to Melanie.

'How big is the swan?'

Her aunt sketched a vague shape in the air.

'I don't think,' said Melanie, 'that I want to be Leda.'

'That is how he sees you. White chiffon and flowers in your hair. A very young girl.'

'What kind of flowers?'

Aunt Margaret drew out a handful of artificial daisies, yellow and white like fried eggs. Melanie would be a nymph crowned with daisies once again; he saw her as once she had seen herself. In spite of everything, she was flattered.

'Needs must,' she said. 'I suppose.' Her aunt's scissors flashed in the light like exclamation marks as she snipped into the flimsy stuff.

When the dress was roughly tacked together, Melanie had to put it on and go down and show it to Uncle Philip. She had to take all her clothes off and wear just the chiffon tunic with the white satin ribbons criss-crossed between her breasts (which, she observed with interest, seemed to have grown and the nipples to have got rather darker.) Aunt Margaret brushed her hair with the silver-backed brush which, like Winnie the Pooh, had survived the crash; she brushed and brushed until Melanie's black hair swirled like the Thames in flood, and then she floated all the daisies on it. She took a cigar box from a cupboard, opened it and displayed a number of sticks of greasepaint. Melanie's eyelids were painted blue and her lips coral. She felt greasy, basted with lard.

'Have you any nice jewellery?'

'Only my confirmation pearls.' They, too, had survived. Aunt Margaret stroked them and adored them and fastened them round Melanie's neck. A few pins left in the chiffon tunic scratched Melanie's flesh. She wriggled.

'The pearls are the finishing touch. You look so pretty!'

'Well, I wish I could see myself. It is a long time since I dressed up.' Recollecting, she bit her lip.

'Go down, now.'

'By myself?'

Aunt Margaret nodded. Melanie slung her coat round her shoulders for the thin silky stuff hardly kept out the draughts and the house was freezing cold. Tea was long over and, downstairs, the evening's work was well under way. The curtains were open and Finn stood on the stage surrounded by cans of paint, open eyes of pure colour, working on a backcloth showing a sea with a blood-orange sunset, something like the background to the picture of the dog in the kitchen. Under the crude strip lighting, Uncle Philip squatted on the floor with a mound of feathers on a spread sheet before him. He was sorting the feathers into smaller piles. His moustache was lightly furred with down.

'Here I am,' said Melanie.

He stayed on his heels, resting his bulky hands on his dirty white overall knees. Tonight, his eyes were the no-colour of old newspapers.

'Why, his head is quite square!' thought Melanie. She had never noticed before. This evening, some disarrangement of the pale hair emphasised the corners. His head was a jack-in-a-box. A pin stuck in her armpit painfully.

'Take off that wrap,' he said.

She obeyed, shivering, for the basement was heated only by a miserly, inefficient little oil stove. Finn painted on. She heard the slap-slap of his brush as he filled in a large area of sky.

'You're well built, for fifteen.' His voice was flat and dead.

'Nearly sixteen.'

'It's all that free milk and orange juice that does it. Do you have your periods?'

'Yes,' she said, too shocked to do more than whisper.

He grunted, displeased.

'I wanted my Leda to be a little girl. Your tits are too big.'

Finn flung down his paintbrush.

'Don't talk to her like that!'

'Keep your mouth shut and mind your own business, Finn

Jowle. I'll talk to her anyway I please. Who is it pays for her board?'

'I can talk how I like, as well as you!'

Uncle Philip stroked his moustache thoughtfully, not looking at Finn at all.

'Oh, no,' he said calmly. 'Oh, no, you can't. Get on painting. You haven't got all day.'

The discord jangled between them. Melanie's head ached.

'Finn,' she said. 'Please. I don't mind.'

'You see?' said Uncle Philip with a queer inflection of triumph. Finn shrugged and picked up his brush.

'And wipe out that paint mark you just made!'

Scowling, Finn scrubbed at the brush-mark on the floor with the elbow of his paint-stiffened overall.

'You'll do, then,' Uncle Philip said to her. 'I suppose you'll have to do. And you've got quite nice hair. And pretty legs.' But he was resenting her because she was not a puppet.

'Turn round.'

She turned round.

'Smile.'

She smiled.

'Not like that, you silly bitch. Show your teeth.'

She smiled, showing her teeth.

'You've got a bit of a look of your ma. Not much but a bit. None of your father, thank God. I never could abide your father. He thought 'isself too good for the Flowers by a long chalk, he did. A writer, he called 'isself. Soft bastard, he never got his hands dirty.'

'But he was awfully clever!' protested Melanie, stung with defiance at last.

'Not so clever he thought to put a bit by to take care of you

161

lot when he'd gone,' Uncle Philip pointed out reasonably. 'And so I've got his precious kids all for my very own, haven't I? To make into little Flowers.'

He began to sort the feathers again. Jesus wants me for a sunbeam, Uncle Philip wants me for a little flower. The feathers moved about in the current of air that blew in under the door. Uncle Philip sighed heavily, the sigh of a man being thankful for exceedingly small mercies.

'You'll do,' he said. 'I suppose. Now piss off.'

Finn looked up angrily and Melanie ran upstairs before the sharp words and blows began. Why was Finn standing up for her, quixotically acting her champion like this? Because it was such an easy way of rousing her uncle? But did Finn care how much it upset her to see them so fierce with each other? He probably did not even notice. She took the flowers from her hair and carefully stepped out of the tunic. She did not think she would like herself in it if she could see herself and she did not think she would like to see her face bright and thick with greasepaint.

'I wish the show was all over,' she said.

Her aunt nodded and her eyes strangely spilled over with quick tears. She thrust her fists into her eyes and her shoulders shook. She cried often, these days. The bull-terrier at once left off lapping water from its baking dish and went and put its head on her knee. Melanie was again surprised at the quick, alert sympathy of the dog, how he combined the roles of guard dog and four-legged comforter. She wished she could act just as quietly, just as simply. She put her hand on the older woman's shoulder and Aunt Margaret blindly grasped it with her own bird-claw. They stayed together like this for a long time. Each time Aunt Margaret cried, she and her niece became closer.

Finn said: 'You must rehearse with me.' He did not raise his eyes to Melanie but stared at the backs of his hands. The chisel cut had left a broad, purple, crescent-shaped scar.

'What, on the stage?'

'Do you think he'd allow us onto his lovely stage? Never. We'll have to do it in my room.'

'Why with you and not the swan?'

'You're not to see the swan until the performance so that you will react to it spontaneously. But you've got to practise with me to get the movements right so I'm to stand in for the swan.'

His voice was softer than a goose's neck, almost inaudible, and he kept his eyes turned away.

'Are we to rehearse in costume?' she asked half apprehensively, thinking of the white chiffon and her own white flesh showing through like milk in white glass.

'What, you think I should feather myself?'

He looked like the petrol-soaked wreck of a swan come to grief in a polluted river. His trousers and shirt (an old-fashioned shirt of striped flannel which should have had a collar but did not) were motleyed with all sorts of paint and a welter of dirt and sweat. His bare feet were warty with dirt. There was a dark brown tidemark round his throat and heavy thumbprints of dirt under his ears. The fungus was on his chin again. He smelt sickening and stale, a sour-sweet stench as if he was going bad.

'You should take more care of yourself,' she said. 'Oh, Finn, wash yourself. And cut your hair, perhaps.' For orange tendrils of uncombed hair curled round the shoulders of his grimy shirt.

'Why should I?'

She could not answer that.

It was the becalmed middle of a Sunday afternoon. In the kitchen, Aunt Margaret sat in her grey dress and vicious collar, sewing at the greek tunic with the finest of stitches. Tea was already laid in the dining-room, the calm white cloth laid with green-banded Sunday china, milk and sugar standing on tiptoe to be used in jug and bowl. Victoria napped in her cage beside the blossoming geranium. Jonathon made ships downstairs while Uncle Philip constructed his swan and planned how it should be strung. Francie had taken his fiddle and gone off about his own business in his Easter Rising trilby and mackintosh. The house rested.

'Come on, then,' said Finn.

They climbed the stairs together past all the closed doors of Bluebeard's castle. Finn's hoarse, snoring breathing echoed noisily. They went into his room and he kicked the door to behind him. His face was a picture of sulky boredom.

'Let's get this stupid game over with, then.'

She looked around her, disconcerted. The room was as bare as if all the brothers' possessions were packed up in trunks and cases and put away in preparation for imminent departure. On the wall which she had never seen because it was the one with the peephole in it was a shelf with the only small and personal thing in the room standing on it, a single, faded photograph in a black, badly fitting frame. The photograph was of a woman with a broad face who looked the camera squarely in the eye without a smile. She wore a Galway shawl and there was a baby in the fold of it.

'Our mother,' said Finn, 'with Maggie in arms.'

Behind her head was a desolation of rocks.

'Back home,' said Finn and said no more.

Next to the photograph was the Anglepoise lamp coiled up ready to spring. But for the strip of mirror and the portrait of her aunt, the walls were empty. There was no sign of the St Sebastian triptych. He must have hidden it. By the shelf was a built-in cupboard but everything else she saw was familiar. She sat down on the roses-and-castles chair with a ludicrous sense of formality, as if paying a polite call in a tailored suit and a small, veiled hat.

'This is how it goes,' said Finn. He seemed to grudge every word he spoke. 'Leda walks by the shore, gathering shells.'

From his pocket, he took a convoluted shell, all milky mother-of-pearl. He set it down on the bit of rug.

'Night is coming on. She hears a beating of wings and sees the approach of the swan. She runs away but it bears down and casts her to the ground. Curtain.'

'Is that all?'

'It is only a vehicle for his handsome swan, after all.'

She rose and stooped for the shell. She moved badly because he was watching her.

'Make it more fluid,' he said wearily. 'Move from the hips.'

She stooped again, waggling her backside, which was the only way she could think of moving from her hips.

'For Chrissake, Melanie. Did they teach you hockey when you went to school?'

'Well, yes. They did.'

He sneered.

'Move – ah, like this.' He scooped up the shell. But he no longer moved like a wave of the sea. He creaked, indeed, like a puppet. He had forgotten his grace was all gone. He stopped short, fingering the shell.

'Anyway,' he said. 'Try again.'

She tried.

'Better, maybe. Now, do it again. I'm the swan.'

She walked by the shore, gathering shells. Finn stood on his toes. His hair was all over his face; she could hardly see him. He made swishing noises indicating the beating of wings.

'When you hear that, you worry. You run a few steps.'

She ran a few steps.

'Right.'

He ran after her. It was charades. She giggled.

'No, don't be silly! You're supposed to be a poor frightened girl.'

'I can't take it seriously.'

'But, Melanie, he'll turn you out if you can't work for him. And what would you do then?'

'He wouldn't,' she said wondering. 'He couldn't.'

'Yes, he could and would.' He was reasonable and serious. 'We could do nothing for you. You would starve.'

'I hate him,' she said. She had not meant to say this. Their eyes met and looked away again.

'Start from the beginning. Pretend. Act.'

This time, things went better. She screwed her eyes up and pretended she saw evening coming on. And pretended she could hear gulls mewing and the squeak of sand under the balls of her feet and the rhythm of wings. So it was easy to look frightened and to run a little way.

'You run and stumble and I bear you to the ground.' He concealed a yawn. 'Put the shell down and we'll go through it all.'

She obeyed him. The gulls mewed and the sand shifted and the swan hurtled down and it was easy. She sprang away from Finn and it was no longer a pretence – she stumbled over the knotted fringe of the rug. Overbalancing, she clutched at Finn to save herself but pulled him over with her. Clinging to each other, Melanie laughing, they toppled in slow motion to the floor.

But Finn did not laugh. And Melanie's laughter trickled to nothing when she saw his pale, bony face half-hidden by hair and could see nothing there, no hint of a smile or inflection of tenderness which might mean she would be spared. He lay as close as a sheet to a blanket; and he smelt of decay, but that no longer mattered. Shuddering, she realised that this no longer mattered. She waited tensely for it to happen.

She was seized with a nervous, unlocalised excitement. They lay together on the bare, splintered boards. There was no time any more. And no Melanie, either. She was utterly subdued. She was changing, growing. All that was substantial to her was the boy whom she touched all down the length of her but did not touch. The moment was eternity, trembling like a dewdrop on a rose, endlessly about to fall. Grudgingly, slowly, reluctantly, he put his hand on her right breast. Time began with a jolt, their time. She let her breath out in a hissing rush. He closed his Atlantic eyes. He looked like a death-mask of himself. It was killing him to leave his isolation, but leave it he must.

'This is the start,' she said to herself, clearly. She heard her own voice, certain and distinct, inside her head. No more false starts, as in the pleasure gardens, but the real beginning of a deep mystery between them. What would he do to her, would he be kind? She looked down with a fear that was also a pleasure at his stained, scarred hand. His workman's hand, which was strong and cunning. The light seemed to die about her, leaving her to see by her senses only.

'No,' said Finn aloud. 'No!'

He leapt to his feet and sprinted across the room. He jumped into the cupboard and shut the door. From the cupboard came a muffled cry. 'No!' again.

The tension between them was destroyed with such wanton savagery that Melanie fell limply back and struggled with tears. She still felt his five fingertips, five red cinders, burning on her breast. But he was gone. She felt cold and ill.

'No!' more faintly.

'What have I done wrong?' she asked the door of the cupboard. No answer. 'Finn?'

Still no answer. She felt a fool, lying on the floor with her skirt rumpled over her knees. She could see under the beds, a pair of shoes standing harmlessly under each one in no dust. The room was very clean although Finn was not. Francie's shoes were brilliant with polish but Finn's were caked with mud – though where could he have been, had he been walking in the pleasure garden by himself, talking to the broken queen and patting the stone lioness on the head? His shoes were lop-sided with walking.

'Maybe,' she thought, 'he wouldn't because I never polished his shoes.' Anything was possible, when he went to earth in a cupboard to get away from her.

From the keyhole of the cupboard issued a blue trail of smoke. She was horrified until she guessed he had lit a cigarette. Probably, in the close confinement, he would suffocate in his own smoke. Or set himself on fire like a Buddhist monk, but accidentally.

'Isn't he *silly*,' she thought. She felt very old, but not mature.

'Don't smoke in the cupboard,' she said.

A fresh puff of smoke answered her. Grumbling beneath her breath, she dragged herself upright and went and opened the door. The cupboard was just deep enough to hold him sitting cross-legged, his head concealed in the pinstriped folds of Francie's second-best suit, which hung on a hanger. There were also some ghostly white shirts there. On a shelf at the top of the cupboard were piled paintings of all shapes and sizes. Finn's hand, with a cigarette in it, poked out of the folds of clothing and tapped ash onto the floor. He said nothing. She examined the crossed soles of his feet.

'Finn,' she said, 'there's a splinter in your left foot.'

'Go away,' he said.

'If you don't take the splinter out, it will fester. They will probably have to amputate your leg, in the end.'

'Please. Go away.'

'Why are you hiding in the cupboard, Finn?' she asked like a mother to an inexplicable child at the end of a hard day.

'Because there's room for me,' he said. The Lewis Carroll logic of this was too much for her; she ran up a white flag, acknowledging defeat.

'Oh, Finn, why did you run away from me?' And the words issued out on the wings of a wail.

'You are too young,' he said, 'to say things like that. You must have read it in a woman's magazine.' His voice was muffled in serge, dressed up for the Arctic in cap and muffler.

She pushed aside the clothing and revealed him, all small and disconsolate and shrivelled looking, knees drawn up under chin in a foetal position. He scowled with squinting ferocity, like a balked Siamese cat.

'You see,' he said, 'he wanted me to fuck you.'

She had only read the word before, in cold and aseptic

print, never heard it spoken except in heat by rough farm-workers who did not realise she was walking by. She was deeply agitated. She had never connected the word with herself; her phantom bridegroom would never have fucked her. They would have made love. But Finn, she acknowledged with a sinking of her spirit, would have. She could tell by the way he ground out his cigarette on the floor.

'It was his fault,' he said. 'Suddenly I saw it all, when we were lying there. He's pulled our strings as if we were his puppets, and there I was, all ready to touch you up just as he wanted. He told me to rehearse Leda and the swan with you. Somewhere private. Like in your room, he said. Go up and rehearse a rape with Melanie in your bedroom. Christ. He wanted me to do you and he set the scene. Ah, he's evil!'

Melanie kicked at a knot in the floorboards with the toe of her shoe. She noticed that the toe was scuffed and the shoes would need mending. Did the household have credit at a cobbler's shop? She tried to concentrate on this so as not to have to think about what Finn was saying.

'Well,' said Finn, parting the clothes in order to light a fresh cigarette, 'I'm not having any, see? I'm not going to do what he wants even if I do fancy you. So there.'

Melanie abandoned trying to think about cobbling.

'Oh, but Finn, why ever does he want you to—'

'To pull you down, Melanie. He couldn't stand your father and he can't stand you and the other kids being your father's children, though he doesn't mind you being your mother's. You represent the enemy to him, who use toilet paper and fish knives.'

'We never had fish knives,' said Melanie.

He disregarded this. He became distraught and incoherent.

'And you're so fresh and innocent, all of you, and so you're something to change and destroy. Well, Victoria is Maggie's baby, now, and he has Jonathon working all day and all night under his eye and there is only you left not accounted for. So he thinks I should do you because he despises me, too, and he thinks I'm God's scum. He does, really. A dirty beatnik and he'd turn me out if it wasn't for Maggie and if it wasn't for the painting, and I'd go, anyway, if it wasn't for Maggie. And so I should do you because you shave under your armpits and maybe you would have a baby and that would spite your father.'

'My father is dead.'

'He knows. All the same, it's all the same to him.'

'I don't shave under my armpits.'

'It's a manner of speaking.' His face twisted in a grimace of pain or pure disgust and he threw away his cigarette and buried his head in his arms. She shifted her weight from foot to foot, uncertain and bewildered. She hardly took in what he said. Without understanding, she said: 'And you don't want me, then?'

'That's got nothing to do with it,' he snapped. 'Besides, you're too young. I found that out in the pleasure garden. Later on, perhaps. But you're too young.'

'I know,' she said. 'It is my curse.'

'Isn't it terrible?' Finn said. 'This is a madhouse. He is making me mad.'

He hid himself with the clothes again, jerking them about on their hangers. Disturbed, the pile of paintings on the shelf slithered to the floor. Melanie picked them up wearily. She was exhausted with surprises. First the St Sebastian triptych, all finished, down to the last arrowhead and gobbet of blood.

She made a face at it and thrust it away. Then she saw herself, and was touched.

She was taking off her chocolate sweater and was all twisted up, a rather thin but nicely made young girl with a delicate, withdrawn face, against a wall of dark red roses. Her wallpaper. She looked very scrubbed. She looked like a virgin who cleaned her teeth after every meal and delighted to take great bites from rosy apples. Her black hair exploded about her head in great Art Nouveau ripples. It looked as though Finn was trying his hand at curves. The picture was as flat and uncommunicative as all his pictures and seemed to be an asexual kind of pin-up. Round the bare upper part of her right arm was a black band. He did not see her precisely as she saw herself but it could have been very much worse.

'But why has he put in the mourning band?' she thought

Nevertheless, she was pleased.

'Did you make sketches of me through the spy-hole when I was undressing?' she asked.

'Don't look at my pictures.'

'I'm only putting them away.'

Then she saw the horrible picture. It was a hell of leaping flames through which darted black figures. Uncle Philip was laid out on a charcoal grill like a barbecued pork chop. He was naked, gross and abhorrent. His flesh was beginning to crack and blister as his fat bubbled inside it. His white hair was budding in tiny flames. Beside him stood a devil in red tights with horns and a forked tail. He held a pair of red hot tongs in his hands with which he was tweaking Uncle Philip's testicles. Uncle Philip's face was branded with a fiery hoofprint. His mouth was a black, screaming hole from which issued a banner with the words: 'Forgive me!' The devil had Finn's former, grinning face.

'So that is where his grin went,' thought Melanie. 'He wiped it off his face and slapped it onto the cardboard.' Finn would never grin again.

From Finn's painted lips, which were made of fire, came the one word: 'Never!' Over the top of the picture, in a white shield, was a title, also in Gothic script: 'In Hell, all wrongs are righted'. The inspiration of the whole was Hieronymus Bosch. Melanie dropped the picture with a sob.

'I told you not to look.'

'You are right. It is a mad house.' She began to cry. Finn crawled out of the cupboard on all fours and clasped her knees, burying his head between her thighs. She dug her fingers in his hair convulsively and said the words which floated on top of her mind, thoughtlessly; if she had thought about them, she would never have said them.

'I think I want to be in love with you but I don't know how.'

'There you go again, talking like a woman's magazine,' said Finn. 'What you feel is because of proximity, because I am here. Anyway, you are too young, we have been into that. And it would be a waste of your time, for I'm going to make him murder me, aren't I?'

Then the gong sounded for tea, which somehow had to be endured, the shrimps shelled, the bread buttered, the milk and tea poured into the cups, Victoria's cake to be cut into fingers so that she could eat it all up. In the witch-ball, they all sat, monstrously swollen, eating at a warped white table that stretched forever. Melanie kept her eyes on the witch-ball so as not to have to look at Uncle Philip.

The next day was Christmas Eve but it was no different to any other day except that the shop was very, very busy. It was crowded all through the day and Melanie and Aunt Margaret tottered on burning feet by the time they turned the sign on the door round to read 'closed'. The shelves were almost bare, the stock almost gone. Even the hobby horse and the toy puppets had gone from the windows, leaving only the plastic holly behind. Notes spilled out of the money drawer. They were down to the last roll of flowered wrapping paper. The shop had the look of a battlefield the morning after. On its perch, the parakeet drooped as if it, too, had been worked off its feet.

'Well,' wrote Aunt Margaret, 'at least we shall have a day of rest tomorrow.'

Although nothing more. Melanie wrestled with self-pity and memory as she sat in the kitchen with her book while her aunt sewed the last seams of the Greek tunic. No holly in the kitchen, no mistletoe over the lampshade. No Christmas tree with small coloured lights. Uncle Philip received Christmas cards and calendars from traders and wholesalers with whom he dealt but he destroyed them as soon as they arrived so there were no cards on the mantelpiece. Nothing. And the house was peculiarly cold. Perhaps it was freezing itself out of spite.

Melanie wondered if they would go to church, to Midnight Mass, because she, in a muddled way, thought they must be religious if they believed so firmly in Hell. But bedtime was at the usual time and, though Francie returned very late, he was slightly drunk so he could not have been to church. She heard his uncertain footsteps on the stairs and he was humming a hornpipe under his breath.

Finn must have been lying awake in the darkness, as she was, the wall separating them like Tristan's sword, for she

174

could hear the soft murmur of him and Francie talking together for a little while, but she could not make out one word. Then a little light came through the uncovered spyhole, a flickering, surreptitious light. And her nostrils caught the smell of charring wood. They were burning something. Guiltily, she got out of bed to look. Out of bed, it was colder than she would have thought possible, the temperature of Russia when nights are coldest there. The floorboards struck ice up through the unprotected soles of her feet. She felt gooseflesh rising up all over her.

The brothers' room was dim and shadowed; she made out their two shapes with difficulty. They were hunched together in the middle of the room. The strip of mirror suddenly flashed at a struck match. Francie's raincoat glimmered; he still wore his coat and hat. He knelt on the floor, steadying himself with one hand. In the other, he held upright a small, carved doll with a shock of yellowish white hair made from unravelled string. It had a small, dandyish white shirt with a bootlace tie. Aunt Margaret must have made the shirt, it was so small and fine. It must have been difficult to make it so small.

Finn was carefully applying matches to various parts of the doll. As soon as the clothing began to smoulder and glow, igniting the wood beneath, he pinched out the charred, burnt part and began again on another place. Both were quite silent and busy, absorbed. She saw the dog was also present, sitting watching them without blinking. When the matches shone out, its eyes were fluorescent raspberries. Its white fur looked unnatural, bleached on purpose, for a disguise. Finn put a match to the doll's trousered groin and he and Francie laughed very quietly. The Jowles were keeping Christmas in their own way.

Melanie went back to bed and pulled the covers over her head. But there was no warmth in the blankets and the stone hot-water-bottle had cooled in her absence. It was so cold she thought the mucus would freeze inside her nose and her brain congeal to a ridged knob of ice. She kept her head under the blankets so that she would not see the magic light.

8

When Melanie shyly gave the scent to her aunt in the kitchen on Christmas morning, her aunt hugged her and kissed her and showed such pleasure at the gift that Melanie was ashamed because it was such a small one.

'Why ever didn't I think?' she said to herself. 'I could have given her my confirmation pearls. I don't need them and I'll never want to wear them again, after tomorrow. And, oh, wouldn't she just love them!'

She visualised her aunt touching the pearls with scarcely believing, transfigured fingers, clasping the string of moony seeds round her poor neck. The pretty pearls, so much more fitting for her aunt's tender flesh than that tormenting silver-ware. And her precious pearls were the only gift she could give which would express what she felt for her aunt. Melanie would give them to her next Christmas, or for her birthday, if she could find out when it was.

'I wanted to buy presents for you all,' chalked Aunt Margaret. 'But I have no money, you see, and Philip—' The chalk sagged from her fingers.

'That's all right,' said Melanie with a rush of love. 'Oh, don't fret.'

In her own room, she opened her only parcel. Mrs Rundle had knitted them each a sweater – of a serviceable grey for Jonathon, of an edible, fruity pink for Victoria, and of a becoming sky blue for Melanie – and hollied them all up in pretty paper. Melanie tugged the new sweater over Victoria's head; dressing her in it was like putting a pillowcase over an unwilling pillow. There was no bulging stocking (no orange in the toe, nuts in the heel, cracker sticking out of the top), no nothing for Victoria this Christmas except the sweater and the sweets. But she did not remember last Christmas and she had not been told to expect a Christmas this year so she did not feel the lack of it, although Melanie felt it for her. It seemed hard to deprive the baby. But the sweater was just another draggy old item of clothing to Victoria, and she accepted the sweets incuriously, possibly thinking they were some kind of bribe. She began to eat them at once, after Melanie had opened the tin for her. It was wrong for her to eat sweets so early in the day but Melanie did not have the heart to stop her.

The Japanese paper lantern looked like a Christmas decoration this morning, it was so round, blue and gay. Had it originally been a Christmas decoration, in some distant past when the Flowers had been just an ordinary family? They must have been ordinary when her mother lived with them. Her mother could never have been eccentric. And the never-mentioned grandparents, what had they been like? They must have celebrated Christmas when Mother and Uncle Philip were small. If Uncle Philip had ever been a little boy. It was difficult to see him small, in schoolcap and short trousers, playing conkers and reading comics and collecting match-boxes.

But, thought Melanie in sudden dismay, what if Uncle Philip of the iron fists is not my mother's brother at all? Perhaps the fat man had, somewhere over the years, substituted himself for the thin man of the wedding picture. A strange fat man, an impostor, wearing Philip Flower's face and clothes but not really him at all.

Melanie wished they could have gone to live with her father's family, instead. All the nice people in the wedding photograph, no doubt each one at this very moment preparing huge turkeys and trimming Christmas trees in preparation for a huge feast. But if she had gone to Aunt Rose or Aunt Gertrude, she would never have known Francie and Aunt Margaret and Finn. And Finn.

Melanie put on her own sweater. The new wool tickled her but it was blessedly snug, with a deep collar that rolled around her throat. It seemed to warm her with more than wool, as if Mrs Rundle had purled and plained some of her love into it with every stitch. She was grateful for it, for the house was sunk deep in midwinter. The few electric fires seemed to intensify the cold rather than dispel it. These December days, Aunt Margaret's pointed nose was always a little red at the tip. But Melanie did not even need a cardigan over her June sky coloured sweater. She would write to Mrs Rundle and say thank you. She thought of Mrs Rundle's hairy moles; they were a significant and beautiful memory.

To her surprise, there was a special dinner, a roast goose, materialising unexpectedly on the table attended by a bowl of apple sauce like a ghost of Christmas past. Aunt Margaret must have ordered it secretly by herself, as a surprise. Old

Scrooge Uncle Philip frowned when he saw it and plunged the carving knife into its belly so fiercely that the stuffing spurted on the best damask tablecloth and Aunt Margaret had to scoop it back up with a spoon. He attacked the defenceless goose so savagely he seemed to want to kill it all over again, perhaps feeling the butcher had been incompetent in the first place and Aunt Margaret had not cooked it in a hot enough oven to finish it off. The reeking knife in his hand, he gazed reflectively at Finn. For a moment, Melanie feared he had merely been trying out the fatal blow on the goose and now, action perfect, would use it on Finn. But in the end all he did was to serve Finn a mean portion of skin and bone which Finn pushed moodily around his plate with his fork, not eating. Uncle Philip made a hearty meal and gnawed on the bones like Henry VIII. It was a gloomy table and they did not linger over it.

And all over London, men and women in hats of coloured paper were watching the Queen's speech on television, cracking walnuts and toasting one another in tawny port. It was hardly to be believed when, in this house, Uncle Philip and Finn and Jonathon went back to the workroom as soon as the mincepies and brandy butter were eaten, without zest. Aunt Margaret took out the chiffon tunic once the dishes were washed to put the finishing touches to the criss-crossing ribbons. Victoria was playing with a saucepan, banging it with a wooden spoon. There was brandy butter, already, on her pink woolly cuffs. She beat a tattoo and yelled. Melanie's head began to ache.

'The house is full of toys and Uncle Philip won't even give Victoria something she can play with quietly,' she thought resentfully. She tried not to look at the tunic because it made her think of the unknown and unknowing swan which was to ravish her the next day. She was scared of the very idea of the swan. The afternoon stifled her. Victoria hit her saucepan and chanted snatches of song and Aunt Margaret stroked her little head lovingly. They were so happy together. Melanie's headache grew worse. She slipped up to her room but Francie was playing slow airs, and phrases of music padded about her on small, soft, melancholy feet and she thought her heart was breaking. She did not know what to do with herself. She picked the dead yellow leaves of the geranium and crumbled them to fragrant dust between her fingers. She stared at her hand. Four fingers and a thumb. Five nails.

'This is my hand. Mine. But what is it for?' she thought. 'What does it mean?'

Her hand seemed wonderful and surprising, an object which did not belong to her and of which she did not know the use. The fingers were people, the members of a family. The thumb the father, short and thick-set, probably a Northcountryman, with flat, assertive vowels in his speech, and the forefinger the mother, a tall, willowy lady, of middle-class origins, who said: 'dahling' frequently and ate dessert oranges with a knife and fork. Had he married above his station, in the flush of self-made money? He had the bluff, upright stance of a man who has made his own way in the world. And three fine children, two full grown, a big boy and girl, and one just coming into its teens. She flexed her hand, and, obligingly, the family performed a brief dance for her. Then she was horrified.

'I must be going crazy!' In this crazy house, as Finn said he would, she, too, was going mad. She wrapped up her head in the curtains so as not to hear Francie playing and not see the room darken as it approached tomorrow. She felt the round world spinning towards the new day and carrying her, infinitely small, furious, reluctant, with it. She saw herself, minute, standing on the schoolroom globe of the world and it turning in vast, silent space and once again felt she was teetering on the edge of sanity. But did people have nervous breakdowns at fifteen going on sixteen? Well, she must be the first, unique. There was a swan over her head, dangling there like the sword of Damocles, following her wherever, insignificant as dust, she was blown by cross currents of fearful winds.

'Oh, I must not be afraid of the swan. It is all charades.'

But it was not precisely the swan of which she was afraid but of giving herself to the swan.

When her hair was done next day and she was dressed in the tunic, Victoria filled her sticky hands with chiffon and exclaimed: 'Pretty lady! Pretty lady!'

'Do you really think so?' said Melanie wistfully, as if Victoria's opinion counted or as if being pretty was a kind of protection.

'Yes,' said Victoria emphatically, round as a fruit in her fruit-coloured sweater. Aunt Margaret, pinning the flowers in Melanie's hair, nodded as hard as her collar would let her. She was wearing her straight grey dress and looked like a Doric column. But her hair was not skewered up quite so firmly as it usually was when she wore her best clothes and a stray lock fell down beside her ear, giving her an incongruous, faintly raffish air. She must have been too preoccupied to fasten her hair properly. She and the rest of them were so clean and Sunday-dressed, so nice and clothed that Melanie felt improper, like a chorus-girl taking Holy Communion in fishnet tights. So she was in show-business, now.

'I'm under-rehearsed,' she said, quaking.

'You'll do fine,' said Francie. 'Don't shilly shally, girly, it's nearly curtain-up time.'

'Oh, Francie,' she said and gulped. He patted her chiffon rump encouragingly.

'His bark is worse than his bite.'

She had heard this of her Uncle Philip before but she did not believe it. She thought, wincing, of what he might do to her if she performed badly, thought of her fresh blood staining the little stage. But when he saw her, he seemed sufficiently satisfied with her appearance, at least; he looked her up and down and said: 'All right. Get behind the curtains.' He looked huge in his dinner jacket and striped trousers, a bull. Perhaps he was a bull. Fire spurting from his nostrils, he was going to turn into Jove as a bull and, myths all awry, carry her off as Europa across this painted sea where dolphins sported. She was on edge and imagining all sorts of things.

There were only three chairs set, this time, since Melanie was no longer in the audience. The 'NO SMOKING' sign was on the curtains but a re-designed poster proclaimed: 'GRAND XMAS NOVELTY SHOW – art and nature combine with Philip Flower to bring you a Unique Phenomenon.' And Uncle Philip, surrounded by a dwarfish ring of skipping young girls, held aloft a pretty swan on strings.

The stage was a neat box with one red side and one sea side and a frame over the top with lights, where Finn sat grimly on his haunches like a toad. His face was black, blank and ill-tempered. She could not see the swan anywhere. It must be somewhere in the wings. The stage was strewn with innumerable shells of all shapes and sizes, clam shells, big, round, pearly shells, little, viciously pronged shells. On the other side of the curtain, in another dimension, Aunt Margaret and the children were taking their seats for the spectacle. Melanie stood in the middle of the shells. She felt a fool.

'Take your clodhopping shoes off, you silly bitch!' Uncle Philip was climbing a short ladder up to Finn. Melanie was still wearing the heavy, lace-up shoes which she had put on to walk downstairs. They must look absurd, with the tunic. She kicked off her shoes and threw them into the wings. She felt far more undressed without her shoes on.

The light went through a kaleidoscopic series of colour changes, as if Finn were trying out the whole battery of his effects. She tried to calm her nerves by thinking of something else, something nice, fluffy kittens, potato-scones for tea; but, oddly, the thought of such things made her want to cry. She began to recite the multiplication tables to herself, in order to make time pass. Over her head, Finn and Uncle Philip rustled and murmured.

'Music!'

Outside the red wall, Francie began to play selections from 'Swan Lake' in the style of 'Grand Hotel' on Sunday night radio. 'What else,' she thought, repressing a sudden desire to giggle, 'what else.' It was comforting to feel superior to Uncle Philip's mediocrity. He must have a taste for Tchaikovsky, for he nodded his heavy head in time. He rustled a script in his hand and read out:

'Leda gathers shells by the shore in the approaching dusk; little does she know that Almighty Jove has picked her out to be his mate.'

Finn threw a switch and the stage was filled with a brown-ish gloaming. A spotlight transfixed her. Uncle Philip hissed: 'Get started, what's yer name!'

She spread out her skirt and put shells into it, bending and rising, bending and rising, accompanied by the spotlight, while the curtains opened. There was Francie with his fiddle under his chin. There was her aunt and her brother and sister all applauding. It was like the school play. She had been an angel in the nativity play at school, this time last year, also in white draperies, but with a cardboard halo on her head. She picked up her shells.

'But what shall I do with them all?' she thought. She found out when Uncle Philip beat unexpectedly on a metal sheet with a padded stick, simulating thunder; startled, she dropped the lot. And the swan came on, then.

It was almost as tall as she, an egg-shaped sphere of plywood painted white and coated with glued-on feathers. She guessed its long neck was made of rubber, since it bent and swayed with an unnerving life of its own. Its head and beak, however, were carved of wood, with black glass eyes inset. The beak was painted with gold paint. The wings were constructed on the principle of the wings of model aeroplanes, but curved; arched struts of thin wood with an overall covering of feathered white paper. Its black legs were tucked up beneath it. It was a grotesque parody of a swan; Edward Lear might have designed it. It was nothing like the wild, phallic bird of her imaginings. It was dumpy and homely and eccentric. She nearly laughed again to see its lumbering progress. But she ran away from it as she was supposed to do, treading on shells, which cut her bare feet.

Its wings waved because Uncle Philip was pulling the strings. It followed her, jerking its mindless beak this way and that. The little audience was applauding again. The swan low-ered its legs, a model aeroplane coming in to land. 'That is clever,' thought Melanie. It landed with a light thump on its two webbed feet, which were made of p.v.c. She halted, at a loss what to do next. It waddled purposefully towards her. She prayed for a cue. Uncle Philip read out:

'Leda attempts to flee her heavenly visitant but his beauty and majesty bear her to the ground.'

'Well, I must lie down,' she thought and, kicking aside shells, went down on her knees. Like fate or the clock, on came the swan, its feet going splat, splat, splat. She thought of the horse of Troy, also made of hollow wood; if she did not act her part well, a trapdoor in the swan's side might open and an armed host of pigmy Uncle Philips, all clockwork, might rush out and savage her. This possibility seemed real and awful. All her laughter was snuffed out. She was hallucinated; she felt herself not herself, wrenched from her own personality, watching this whole fantasy from another place; and, in this staged fantasy, anything was possible. Even that the swan, the mocked up swan, might assume reality itself and rape this girl in a blizzard of white feathers. The swan towered over the black-haired girl who was Melanie and who was not. Its empty body was white and light as meringue, its head bobbed this way and that way on its prehensile neck. The music throbbed to an excruciating climax.

She had last heard the 'Swan Lake' music a couple of years before, also at Christmas, sitting in a red plush fauteuil at Covent Garden Opera House, when her father took her to the ballet for an end-of-term treat. The white figures turned and twirled around her. She had been fond of ballet for a time. Now she herself was on stage with an imitation swan. The swan settled its belly on her feet. She felt it. Looking up, she could see Uncle Philip directing its movements. His mouth

186

gaped open with concentration. She noticed that his black bow tie had glossy spots in the fabric which caught the light and shone. She shifted under the rustling swan, whose wings now beat strongly, stirring her hair. A daisy blew away. She could see nothing, after this, except the floury glare of the spotlight.

'Almighty Jove in the form of a swan wreaks his will.' Uncle Philip's voice, deep and solemn as the notes of an organ, moved dark and sonorous against the moaning of the fiddle. The swan made a lumpish jump forward and settled on her loins. She thrust with all her force to get rid of it but the wings came down all around her like a tent and its head fell forward and nestled in her neck. The gilded beak dug deeply into the soft flesh. She screamed, hardly realising she was screaming. She was covered completely by the swan but for her kicking feet and her screaming face. The obscene swan had mounted her. She screamed again. There were feathers in her mouth. She heard the curtains swish to amid a patter of applause and thought it was the sound of the sea.

After a gap of consciousness, she found that Finn was kneeling beside her, pulling her skirt decently down for her. The passionate swan had dragged her dress half off. Finn's face was set. She looked at him as if he were a stranger in tartan wool shirt-sleeves and worn-out corduroy trousers and unshaven stubble. 'He has nice ears,' she thought, noticing them for the first time. They were small and elegantly shaped ears. She tried to recall where she had seen him before; his face was familiar. But it was too hard and she gave up. She looked round for her swan. It had been hauled away. It hung on its strings, pathetic now its motive power was gone, waving about a little from side to side.

'Everything is all right,' said Finn. 'The play is over.'

Then she recognised Finn. Of course, he painted things and was her friend, whatever that was. She put Melanie back on like a coat, slowly. Uncle Philip came puffing and blowing down the ladder and brusquely ordered Finn back to the lights.

'You overacted,' he said to Melanie and cuffed her with the back of his hand. 'You were melodramatic. Puppets don't over-act. You spoiled the poetry.'

Her face stinging, she said: 'The swan upset me.' But he did not hear. He was arranging his bow tie. The stage flooded with brightness. She, Uncle Philip, and the swan received a tumul-tuous ovation. They seemed to go on for hours, bowing and curtseying and fielding paper roses thrown by her aunt, until her uncle shouted: 'Houselights!' and the curtains closed for the last time. He switched off his beaming smile at once. He put his arms round the neck of the limp swan.

'Well done, old fellow,' he said to it. The wooden head lolled.

'Is there anything more?' asked Melanie. She was trembling and sick with anti-climax.

'No. Clear off.'

She retrieved her shoes and went. Aunt Margaret and Francie kissed her and Francie said: 'You did fine, just fine.' It was all over. She had made her debut. She was alive again. There were feathers in her hair and she was dusty. She brushed her hair, removed the daisies and the feathers and put on her everyday skirt and her new sweater, which put friendly arms around her. Yet she still felt detached, apart.

For tea, they had a chocolate Yule log with a tiny sugar robin on top, which Victoria took and ate. The cake seemed extremely exotic and unlikely, a figment of the imagination. She ate her slice but tasted nothing. The company round the tea-table was as distorted and alien as its miniature in the witch-ball. She watched Uncle Philip empty four green-banded cups of tea and thought of the liquid turning slowly to urine through his kidneys; it seemed like alchemy, he could transmute liquids from one thing to another. He could also turn wood into swans. There was chocolate icing on his moustache; what would he turn it into? She waited, rapt. His silence had bulk, a height and a weight. It reached from here to the sky. It filled the room. He was heavy as Saturn. She ate at the same table as this elemental silence which could crush you to nothing.

Yet her eyes returned again and again to the plausible distortion of the witch-ball. She found herself wondering which was the real tea-table and which was the reflection. The chocolate icing on her knife was no empirical evidence, the lacquered paper holly sprig on the cake was itself artificial. Everything was flattened to paper cut-outs by the personified gravity of Uncle Philip as he ate his tea. She felt she cast no shadow.

She could not remember how the evening passed, but it must have passed somehow for then she was in bed, inhabiting a grey no-man's-land between sleeping and waking. Victoria, happy Victoria who still lived in the land of Beulah where milk and honey flow, an Eden where the snake still slumbers in futurity, mindless Victoria slept like a top, but Melanie heard a scratching at the door. She did not believe it and pretended she was asleep in her striped sheets at home and the apple tree blooming with frost outside. Nevertheless, the scratching went on. She opened her eyes.

A finger of moonlight poked through the curtains and rested on the end of the bed, illuminating a mound which, after a moment, she was relieved to perceive to be her feet. Scrabble, scrabble, scrabble on the door; then a whisper: 'It's Finn here. I want to talk to you.'

She lay in lavender and Finn wanted to talk to her. She tried to see the logic of this but failed.

'Come in, if you want,' she said letting herself drift on the tide.

But was it Finn or not? It was too dark to see and the whisper was anonymous, a metallic rasp. She had an uneasy time as the shadowy figure made its way around the room to her bed, treading the noiseless dark like a swimmer. But the breathing was Finn's. It must be. It sounded like a musical saw. No two people could breathe that way. He crouched by the bed. He smelt like Finn. No two people could smell that way. But there was a wild overtone of night on him and strong liquor on his breath, although he did not seem drunk. His teeth were chattering so loudly he might have been playing spoons. She was reassured that it was Finn and worried because he was in such a state.

'What is the matter, Finn?'

'Oh, Melanie, oh—' his teeth were chattering too much for him to speak coherently. His whole body was shaking. She touched his forehead, which burned with fever He jerked away as if the touch hurt him.

'You're ill!'

'I don't know. No,' he said, biting on his teeth to keep them quiet.

Sick and sorry, he came creeping to her bed. She could not be bothered with the how or why of it. Here he was. What now? A withered flower fell from the geranium at that moment, with a soft, tissue-paper noise. One flower less.

'Melanie,' he said, 'listen, can I come in with you for a little while? I feel terrible.'

When she was Victoria's age and saw ghosts at night, she would go to her mother's room in a flurry of nightgown and snuggle down in the cosy cleft between her parents and sleep securely, locked in by their flesh which was also her flesh.

'But – oh, well, then, yes.' She drew the covers protectively around her but she could not tell him to go away. He was fully dressed. He kicked off his shoes, one, two, and climbed in beside her. He brought a wet and muddy breath of outdoors with him. His socks were damp.

'I'm covered with earth,' he said. 'I don't know how we'll explain to Maggie about the sheets. Please, Melanie, would you mind holding me until I feel better?'

It was an honest and simple request. So she held him until his teeth stopped chattering. She did not know what to think. The encounter was of a piece with the unreality of the day but somehow it seemed more ordinary in the night, as if it had happened many times before. The brass buttons of his fire-man's jacket dug into her ribs.

'Where have you been?' she asked at last.

'In the pleasure gardens.'

'What were you doing there, for heaven's sake, in the middle of the night?'

'I went to a burying.'

'Whose?' she said, momentarily prepared for a death.

'It was the swan.'

'What's this?'

'The swan. Rest in peace. The swan.'

'You buried,' she repeated, to get it clear in her own mind, 'the swan.'

'Yes, I did.' His voice was curiously light and weightless. 'First of all, I dismembered it down in the work-room. I went downstairs and chopped it up with Maggie's little axe we chop the firewood with. I chopped it into small pieces. It was easy.'

'Oh, Finn, you never did.'

'I did so.'

Their whispering ceased for a while. The curtains heaved in a night wind. Now her eyes were accustomed to the dark, she could make out his face on the pillow beside her in vague outline, but nothing more.

'Finn, the enormity of it!'

'It is a gesture.'

They fell into another pit of silence and eventually surfaced from it.

'All by yourself!' she marvelled, picturing him in the work-room which was so full of the sense of Uncle Philip, surrounded by severed limbs and watching masks.

'Well, you see, Francie is out playing his fiddle. There is an all-night Irish party in Kilburn. Or else Francie would have come with me, I suppose. And so I had to come in to you, because Francie is out. I had, you see, to have someone because I felt so bad when I got home.' He moved comfortably. 'It is much better, now. Dear God, I thought I'd never be easy again. I was burning and freezing at the same time. It was like dying.'

There was enough room for both of them in the bed if they stayed close together.

'There is a bit of a moon,' he said. 'I've left feathers all along the road. I saw a man walking his dog and panicked and hid in a hedge. Who would want to walk a dog at this time of night? He must be off his head.'

'But why did you break up the swan?'

'I was lying in my bed and suddenly I thought I'd do it. I don't know why. It came to me, I'll kill his swan for him. I had a swallow from Francie's bottle to give me courage.'

'He'll murder you,' she said. He did not answer. Victoria chuckled in her sleep. Melanie repeated, 'He'll murder you,' and thought: 'Of course, he wants me to say that.'

'We'll put our cards on the table, me and him.'

'Oh, you are foolish!'

'Keep your voice down. You'll wake the child.'

'I think you are not right in the head where Uncle Philip is concerned.'

'Don't nag me,' he said, as though they had been married a long time. 'Don't nag me when I've had such a night of it. God preserve me from the perils and dangers of the night.'

The bed moved. She reared away instinctively because she thought he was trying to touch her and then, with a shock, realised that he was making the sign of the cross. She did not know what to make of this at all. He must have been through a great ordeal. It must have been like the wedding-dress night. In the pleasure garden, Finn had walked in the forests of the night where nothing was safe. 'I have been in that place, too,' she thought. She could have cried for them both.

'I buried the swan near the queen,' he said conversationally in this dimensionless voice he now had. 'Do you think that was kind of me? I suppose I thought they'd be company for one another.'

'Well,' she said, 'it is as good a place as any.'

'I'm not really sure why I went to the pleasure garden when

I could have put the bits of swan in the dustbin. But somehow it seemed best of all to bury it in the pleasure garden. Do you know, though, I was almost delirious in the pleasure garden? I was that bad, Melanie . . . the stone lioness was tracking me. I was sure of it. I heard her growl. And the queen was upright on her pedestal. That gave me a turn, I must say. I saw her from a distance but she must have seen me coming and gone and lay down again quickly. She was lying down, all right, when I got up to her. The bitch. Also, very faintly, was a sound of someone playing a concertina. That troubled me more than anything.'

'What music was he playing?' she asked.

'You're making fun of me,' he said reproachfully.

'No.'

'And I took this spade with me, to dig a grave for the swan, and I kept dropping the spade. It kept slipping out of my fingers as if it didn't want to go with me. And the swan's neck refused to be chopped up; the axe bounced off it. It kept sticking itself out of my raincoat when I buttoned it up to hide it and it kept peering around while I was carrying it, along with all the bits of the swan and the spade as well. I had my arms full, I can tell you. It must have looked, to a passer-by, as if I was indecently exposing myself, when the swan's neck stuck out. I was embarrassed with myself and kept feeling to see if my fly was done up.'

He went on and on talking. He was talking as freely as he used to do. More freely.

'You must have had a time of it, poor Finn.' It had been a bad day for them both. She felt that somehow their experience ran parallel. She understood his frenzy. 'Poor Finn.'

'Ah, but it was a pleasure to destroy the swan.'

'I wish that you hadn't.'

'It covered you,' said Finn. 'It rode you. I did it partly for your sake, because it rode you.'

'It didn't hurt me.'

'Besides, Philip Flower loved it so.'

'What will happen?'

'I can't tell,' he said. 'Only surmise.'

They were peaceful in bed as two married people who had lain in bed easily together all their lives. It seemed the most normal thing in the world to be sharing a pillow with Finn, but, when she closed her eyes again, Melanie was inside the white igloo of the swan's wings. The swan was too big, too potent, to all at once stop being.

'It was a ludicrous thing, the swan,' she said. 'But so much work went into it.'

'He put himself into it. That is why it had to go. Oh, I'm weary.'

'Go to sleep, then.'

'It will flop through the window to haunt me.'

'No, it won't, stupid.'

'You are sharp with me,' he protested.

'That's because I'm sensible.'

'Maybe.'

'Take your socks off, Finn. They're wet. You'll catch cold.'

There was a small earthquake in the bed as he obeyed her.

'The grass was wet and got over the top of my shoes and wet my socks. It was very long, the grass. It seems longer at night. Why is that?'

'I don't know. I've noticed that, too.'

Then they settled down to sleep together. He snored, as was only to be expected, considering that he breathed through his mouth, but Melanie soon got used to it. She began to dream.

She dreamed she was Jonathon. She had been so uncertain of herself all day that it was almost a relief to find she was, in fact, Jonathon. She saw the world the same but different through bottle glasses and felt her knees all bare under the hem of the short grey trousers and above the itching pressure of the gartered knee-socks and heard insistently the call of the sea. 'I must go down to the seas again.' The pull was very strong, like the undertow of a wave. The world went obscure and myopic; she was bat-blind Jonathon sleepless in his little iron bed in his whitewashed grotto high up in the cliffside of the house and the sea was beating at the foot of the wall, where the backyard ought to be. He listened to the singing waters and the screeching gulls until he could bear to lie down no longer and got up.

Of course, he was wearing his white pyjamas with the design of racing cars, a little faded from the wash, with the laundry mark of the old laundry in the country still on the collar. He put on his shoes and also his grey flannel jacket with the school badge on the left breast, to protect himself against the salty bite in the air. He took his glasses from the chair by the bed. Carefully, he opened the door into the passage.

Caught in a skylight, the moon winked at him intermittently through clouds which raced across it. Jonathon crept cautiously downstairs. He began to flicker; as in a faultily projected film, Melanie found herself superimposed upon him, the two shapes stealing downstairs on the same feet; and part of these Siamese twins started as they passed all the closed doors, imagining an inquisitive eye behind the keyhole of each of them. But Jonathon did not care and soon the image of Melanie disappeared. He went through the shop where the moonlight gleamed on polished wood and the parakeet was solid silver, down into the work-room, where it was broad day, as he had guessed.

Daylight filled the work-room from the open curtain of the stage and Finn's painted seashore sparkled and all the little waves had white caps. The sky was blue and the sun shining. It was a beautiful day. Jonathon watched the painted water melt and transmute. It swirled and splashed on the sandy shore, where grains of mica glittered, and, far out, the dolphins frisked merrily, somersaulting in the water. When they saw him, they cried out: 'Hello, Jonathon! Jonathon is here at last!' in high-pitched, adenoidal voices. He had always known dolphins could talk. He had read it in a book from the library. The sand crunched under his feet with a noise of munched cornflakes. He walked by the sea, a fresh breeze buffeting his spectacles. The stage had gone but he did not look back to see where or how.

He came upon a small rowing boat, beached on the sand, with a pair of oars ready in the rowlocks. He dragged it down to the water's edge, pushed it out until it floated and climbed on. Standing in the bows, he scanned the horizon beneath his hand to make sure the ship was there. The ship was ready to sail away. With a gentle plashing, he made for the ship. As he neared it, a rope ladder tumbled down the side. He heard a preliminary whistle; they were preparing to pipe him aboard his vessel, as was only proper. His glasses misted over with spray. Impatiently he took them off and threw them into the water for he did not need them anymore. They sank, leaving a trace of bubbles on the surface, which soon dissolved.

Melanie woke. The room was a blurred, short-sighted haze and her hands hurt as if she had been rowing. She shook the dazzle out of her eyes. She was Melanie, at last. Her hands relaxed. It was morning. Victoria sat on the floor beside the bed, gazing at her inquisitively. Somehow she had crawled from her tall cot. Her nightgown was all rucked up and her peachy backside settled on the bare boards.

'Come to bed with me before you get your death, half-naked like that, Victoria.'

'Why is *he* in bed with you?'

Melanie had forgotten Finn. She turned to look at him. He slept with his cheek on his dirty hand, his jacket up round his ears. He looked, sleeping, sweet and childish. He was still snoring.

'He was poorly,' said Melanie at random, 'in the night.'

'I see, I see,' said Victoria, parroting a grown-up, satisfied. Melanie invited her to bed again.

'I want Auntie Marg'rit!' said Victoria and pulled off her nightdress defiantly. Bare as a fish, she frisked around the room, carolling: 'Auntie Mar'grit! Auntie Mar'grit!'

'Oh, do be quiet, Victoria!'

Finn surged up in bed, blearily. 'For God's sake, will you shut up that child, Melanie!'

They might have been married for years and Victoria their baby. Melanie had a prophetic vision as Finn sat beside her in his outrageous jacket, unclean in the clean sheets, yawning so that she saw the ribbed red cathedral of his mouth and all the yellowed teeth like discoloured choirboys. She knew they would get married one day and live together all their lives and there would always be pervasive squalor and dirt and mess and shabbiness, always, forever and forever. And babies crying and washing to be done and toast burning all the rest of her life. And never any glamour or romance or charm. Nothing fancy. Only mess and babies with red hair. She revolted.

'No!' she cried so loudly that Victoria stopped short and began to bawl, outraged by her vehemence. 'No, I don't want you, Finn!'

'Come off it,' said Finn with a touch of his old insouciance. 'I haven't had you yet.'

'That is just what I mean,' she said despairingly. 'You are always so . . . grubby.'

He tossed a packet of chewing-gum to Victoria.

'Chew on that,' he advised her. His squint was particularly bad this morning. He tugged at Melanie's hair affectionately. He knew it, too. They were tied together, whether they wanted it or not; he was only biding his time. He tugged her hair harder when she made no response.

'What is the matter? What's biting you, pet?'

'Is "pet" an Irish endearment?' she asked, sidetracked.

'Oh, it's quite common all over the British Isles, I should think. What's wrong, though? Didn't you sleep?'

With a depressed sense of the inevitability of it all, she slumped against his shoulder while Victoria choked herself on bubble gum. She might have been going to bed with Finn for years. She wished in a corner of her mind he could show some surprise or appreciation but he put his arm round her, instead, with straightforward tenderness.

'I had,' she said slowly, reluctantly, 'the strangest dream.'

'Did you, now?'

'I dreamt I was Jonathon . . .' The dream was clear in her mind, ominous, meaningful. She thought the bed rocked like

a boat but it was Finn scratching his armpit. He had no shame
She would have to get used to that.

'What did you dream, pet?'

'That Jonathon sailed away. It was very strong. As if I wa
he.'

'But only a dream.'

'Yes,' she said doubtfully.

'Once,' he volunteered, 'I dreamed I was dead and went t
heaven. Which was like a fun-fair, with slot machines and
pin-tables.'

'And was it a portent or omen?'

'I don't know. Perhaps. A bee stung me next day.'

'What?'

'That is why my eyes are crooked. It was in the orphanag
with all the nuns, after my mother died. I expect that's why
dreamed of going to heaven. But it was a seven year old'
heaven, with candy floss, and I forgot my mother, God res
her, the minute I started playing the football machine.'

He took out a crumpled packet of cigarettes and lit one fo
himself.

'And about the bee . . .'

'I was playing by myself in the garden because they were a
praying. I picked a rose and a bee flew out. It was angry. I had
disturbed it when it was minding its own business, fertilising
It stung my right eye. I was lucky not to lose the sight of it.'

'Oh, dear,' she said. 'Did it hurt?'

'I forget. They were very nice and gave me lots of jell
babies and clove balls and pictures of religious things while
was convalescing. Is there anything in here I can use for ar
ashtray?'

'No.'

'Oh. Well, I'll have to use my shoe.'

'It is time to get up,' she said and pushed aside the covers. He lay watching her, smoking. His squint seemed less extreme now she knew what had caused it. She thought of small, red Finn trustfully reaching for the rose and then his eyes exploding with pain, while the nuns were on their knees thinking about Calvary.

'I am so sorry about the squint,' she said.

'I am used to it; I wouldn't know myself without it.'

She unbuttoned her pyjama jacket and had a momentary tremor of unease as she slipped it off; then thought, 'Well, he has seen me without my clothes on, often enough.' Anyway, he did not seem to notice her nakedness but lay and smoked and tapped the cigarette ash into his shoe under the bed. She put on her blue sweater and began to dress Victoria. There was a yacht embroidered on the unused pocket of Victoria's nightgown.

'But I can't help feeling,' she said, 'that the dream of mine had a significance. I hope Jonathon is all right. Oh, Finn, I do hope he is all right.'

He did not answer.

'Finn?'

His face was terror-stricken.

'Jesus,' he said. 'I killed the swan last night, didn't I. I must have been drunk out of my mind.'

9

She splashed the shreds of the absurd night out of her eyes with cold water. The well-iced shock of water did her good as it took her breath away; it impinged on her, it was palpable. Water is water. You can't argue with water. There it is. Her face dripping, she raised her head from the coughing tap and saw that Uncle Philip's teeth were gone. The glass was there, the cloudy water was there, fragments of decaying food dislodged from the crevices between the teeth still formed a white sediment at the bottom of the glass, but the cheesy plastic grimace itself was somewhere else again. So Uncle Philip was up and about, already, although it was so early. It was quite early. The Disney fish sported more zestfully on the plastic curtain because Uncle Philip's teeth were not there. There was a white hair in the crack in the basin and the towel was clammy with damp. Had he washed and spruced and gone off by himself somewhere? Was this a possibility? She examined it as she cleaned her teeth, spat white and rinsed.

There was a new rack specially screwed up for the children's three newcoming toothbrushes. She saw, with some relief that Jonathon's still flaunted its splayed and shaggy head in spite of the dream. If he was gone for good, he would probably have taken his toothbrush. Though (she swallowed a gob of toothpaste, peppermint ice, in her dismay) not necessarily. But, her face washed in good, real water, she was prepared to laugh at her dream. Clean and in her right mind, she hardly expected to find Finn in her bed when she went back to the room and, at first, she could not see him. She thought: 'Thank heavens, I am back to normal.'

Victoria, partially dressed, had clambered back into her cot and glowered through the bars, clutching a couple with either hand. The pink female fold smiled longwise between her squatting, satiny thighs.

'My, you are indecent, Victoria.'

Victoria continued to scowl and took no notice of her.

'Bad Finn's still in bed.'

He really had been and still was. Burrowed deep, his hunched form made a small tumulus or burial mound in the Salisbury Plain of the bed. She drew back the covers. He was curled up succinctly, like a whiting on a plate, served with its tail in its mouth. He should have been garnished with sprigs of parsley and lemon butterflies.

'Finn? Finn!'

'I'm gathering my strength,' he said. His eye were tight shut.

'Uncle Philip's teeth aren't in the bathroom.'

'All the better to eat me with. They're in his mouth, of course.'

'Perhaps he's off making a trip?'

'So likely, so likely. He's up bright and early to rage round after me.'

'I thought you wanted to face up to him.'

'Ah, but I've come to my senses, now.'

'Perhaps he's taken a day's holiday?'

'If all my perhapses came home to roost, I'd be feeding the pig in my Galway smallholding this very minute.'

Flocks of brown-feathered perhapses flapped ragged, witless wings against the windows. She could hear their clucking and squawking. But this one sad, wet hen fluttered inside the house. A miracle. Aunt Margaret's hair waved a red flag of joy. Uncle Philip had taken Jonathon off into the violet dawn to a gathering of model boat enthusiasts on a man-made lake in the Home Counties.

'Oh, dear,' said Melanie, who would have liked to touch Jonathon to make certain it was only a dream. But the ex-pedition sounded so unlikely it must be true. There was an element of ordeal about it that Uncle Philip would like. And there was such festivity in the kitchen that all her doubts were soon forgotten. The very bacon bounced and crackled in the pan for joy because Uncle Philip was not there. Toast caught fire and burned with a merry flame and it was not disaster, as he would have made it, but a joke.

'You could have slept late,' chalked Aunt Margaret. She was not in her best clothes and her stockings were sieves for holes but somehow she was beautiful and she smiled without strain and her movements were assured and sweet, not jerky as a hungry midwinter sparrow under Philip Flower's stare. They sat around the table and mopped up eggyolk with breadcrusts. Uncle Philip's ominous chair stood empty, the shell of a threat, the Siege Perilous.

'Sod it,' said Finn. 'I'm going to sit in his chair.'

Aunt Margaret's hand flew to her aghast mouth.

'Don't fret, Maggie. It can't engulf me.'

He sat at the head of the table like the Lord of Misrule, feeding the dog marmalade sandwiches, which it appeared to relish. Soon it seemed quite normal for Finn to be seated there.

'Finn is Daddy,' said Victoria with fat satisfaction.

'Not yet,' said Finn. 'But we'll christen the first one Proximity.'

Melanie choked on a mouthful. Waiting outside, possibly on the landing, stood a chattering troupe of squinting, red-haired children jostling for admission to her belly. Francie struck her briskly on the back and soon she recovered sufficiently to finish her breakfast. It would have been a pity not to have appreciated the breakfast, which was lavish. Bacon and eggs and mushrooms and tomatoes and fried bread and cold potatoes fried up in bacon fat. Aunt Margaret must have fried up everything friable in the larder. There were also tinned beans, which Francie particularly liked. Rusty tomato sauce stains appeared on his tie, which today was a celebration satin, painted with small birds. Somebody must have given it to him. They took a long time over breakfast and all ate a great deal, even Aunt Margaret. In Uncle Philip's chair, Finn seemed taller and of more consequence than usual.

'Don't,' he said, 'let's open the shop today.'

The chair gave him authority. They all stared at him.

'You see,' he went on, lighting a 'Sweet Afton' cigarette with a grandiloquent gesture, 'I broke up his swan last night.'

Silence thickened like the thickening, cooling grease on their plates.

Almost with admiration, Francie breathed: 'You mad bugger.'

Aunt Margaret, bereft of beauty, clutched Victoria to her breast as if she were a shield or talisman. Victoria squirmed and wriggled.

'So we won't open the shop today. We'll have a party. We'll have a wake for the swan. With music and dancing. No, not dancing.'

'You broke up his swan,' said Francie in awe. His lips opened on all his teeth like a broken wall. He laughed hugely, rolling in his chair, and cried out again and again: 'He done it! Finn done it! Good on Finn! Good man!' He leaned over the table, scattering crockery and upsetting the marmalade jar, grabbed Finn's hand and wrung it and laughed until the tears came seeping down his rough cheeks.

Aunt Margaret gradually softened amid the laughter. The sun came out in her face. For the first time since Melanie had known her, she seemed to be examining the possibility of her own tomorrow, where she could come and go as she pleased and wear what clothes she wanted and maybe even part her locked lips and speak. Or sing. In fact, she opened her mouth, forgetting she was dumb; her lips quivered and closed again on a smile.

Then they all washed up together, giggling and splashing water at one another. It was a soap-sud carnival. The bubbles floated in the air and burst with wet, opalescent pops and Victoria rolled about the floor chasing them as they vanished. While they were drying up the cups, Finn thoughtfully took Uncle Philip's very own mug from its hook on the dresser. It was so pretty, with its rosebud lettering. He weighed it in his hand.

'Jesus, Mary and Joseph,' he said, 'I come of age today.'

He raised his arm, took aim and flung the mug at the

cuckoo clock. The little door spurted open. The cuckoo came out and chanted fourteen o'clock, fifteen o'clock, sixteen o'clock. Melanie had never seen the brothers laugh so much. Francie sagged, a partially demolished tower, hooting and hic-coughing over the sink. Finn rolled on the floor, holding his stomach. Victoria caught the infection and went berserk, nearly tumbling off Aunt Margaret's lap with mirth. Melanie did not think it was very funny although she was glad to see the death throes of the cuckoo clock. The stuffed cuckoo belted out thirty-one calls and then jerked back into the clock. The door slammed to behind it with a dithering shud-der. The ticking stopped.

'There goes the time,' said Finn, wiping his eyes.

The day stretched before them with nothing to do. It was like the first day of the holidays and, in fact, this was just what it was. Outside, it was a fine winter's day. The edges of build-ings stood out clear and shadowless and there was no smoke in the air. The little backyard garden tried to pretend it was spring, on tiptoe to put out its leaves. Finn opened the kitchen window and leant over the sill, taking deep breaths. Melanie had never seen this window opened before.

'I can smell the sea,' he said. 'It must have come up from Brighton to Victoria on a day excursion.'

'Oh, Finn,' said Melanie, troubled. 'Can you really smell the sea?' For she remembered her dream and the waves swill-ing against the walls of the ground floor.

'Well, no,' he admitted. 'I am just being exuberant. Do you know, I'm going to wash.'

And he did. He washed himself with beautiful thorough-ness in innumerable kettles of hot water and he even washed his hair and asked Aunt Margaret to trim it for him with her pinking shears. When he was clean, he dazzled Melanie; he looked made of ivory and red gold, a small, precious statuette, a chessman. He went to his room and grubbed about for a fresh shirt and came downstairs splendid in a white one with a pleated front, a dress shirt, but a little too big for him.

'I didn't have one of my own clean so I borrowed from Philip.'

'I'm sure he'd never grudge you,' said Francie.

Aunt Margaret did not even look apprehensive. She caressed his shoulder lightly and chalked: 'Nothing will be the same, now.'

What did that mean? But there was no time to wonder. They all went to put on their best clothes, because Finn was clean. In her room (where Finn's shape was still impressed on the unmade bed) Melanie took out her pretty green frock and paused with it hanging from her hand. She could not bear to think of Aunt Margaret taking the ghastly grey dress from her wardrobe and putting it on, not today. She would give her her own dress. She had plenty more; and, even if she had not, she could live off the fat of fifteen (nearly sixteen) years of nice clothes. As an afterthought, she took, also, the red morocco box that had held her confirmation pearls. Give one, give all. Perhaps it would be good to strip off her possessions, anyway, just as perhaps it would be best to cut out her memory and her dreams or to wash them away in cold water.

She knocked on Aunt Margaret's bedroom door down the landing and her aunt opened it. She was wearing a white cotton slip. There was goose flesh from the cold on her upper arms.

'I want . . .' said Melanie and stopped, not knowing how to

give away the dress. Her aunt raised her red eyebrows anxiously and motioned her into the room. Melanie had never been inside it before and entered with a queer terror.

There was a cupboard in the wall and a safe set deep into the plaster beside it, not at the foot of the bed, as she had imagined. The bed was very broad and did, indeed, slump down on one side which, by the striped pyjamas folded on the patchwork coverlet, was Uncle Philip's side. The patchwork quilt was very old, faded and homely, out of place in the aggressively bare room. She guessed it belonged to Aunt Margaret and had come from Ireland with her a long time ago. Beside the bed was a plain, wooden, upright chair with an alarm clock on it. The alarm clock had very clear black figures and a metal bell on top that promised to wake you with a snarl. There was nothing else on the chair. From the ceiling hung an electric bulb in a pink plastic lampshade and on the floor was a square of plain brown carpet, so worn the warp showed through. The mantelpiece was quite bare except for a photograph. It was the same photograph of her mother's wedding that had stood on Melanie's parents' mantelpiece before she tore it up.

'Oh,' said Melanie. There was her mother in white and her father and her father's family and Uncle Philip. The photograph was in a narrow brass frame. Melanie sat down on the bed.

'The house is haunted,' she said. Aunt Margaret scribbled on a pad: 'What do you mean?'

'The photograph. It gave me a shock. I shall be all right in a minute.'

'You poor thing. It must have upset you.' Aunt Margaret swept the photograph off the mantelpiece, hiding it.

Aunt Margaret's cotton slip or shift had broad shoulder straps and came high up on her bosom but you could still see the deep salt-cellars at the base of her throat. In her slip, she looked like a refugee camp child, all limbs and eyes. She had already changed into her good stockings. The cupboard door swung open revealing the dress, grey and upright as Lot's wife after she looked back. Melanie conceived a superstitious dread of the grey dress. If Aunt Margaret put it on, nothing would go right; the figures in the photograph might come alive, Uncle Philip might come home early with a machine-gun.

'Here,' she said, pushing her own dress towards her aunt. 'I thought green would suit you because of your hair.'

'For me?' wrote Aunt Margaret. 'To borrow?'

'To keep, if you like.'

Melanie helped her aunt like a lady's maid, setting the dress fairly on the shoulders and adjusting the hang of the skirt and zipping up the back. Her aunt stood stock still and let Melanie dress her. She looked beatified. An angel could have entered holding a long, white lily, with a special message from God, and it would not have been surprising.

'Where is your comb, Aunt Margaret?'

On a shelf in the cupboard next to a tangle of hairpins. Melanie picked everything up and began to arrange Aunt Margaret's hair, making her sit down on the chair and putting a cloth over her shoulders in a proper manner.

'However does she manage to do her hair without a mirror?' she thought.

And it seemed especially hard that her aunt could not see herself in the dark green dress, against which her hair took on a rich, fresh ruddiness and her skin seemed whiter than foam. Her hair was silken and slippery as Victoria's five-year-old hair and it kept escaping from the pins and slithering out of Melanie's fingers and it took a long time to coil it up and secure it becomingly on top of her aunt's head. And then she thought: 'No. Today shall be different.' And she pulled out all the pins again and let the hair fall down like a shower of sparks. A firework display, but it was way past the fifth of November. Red and green, red on green, Christmas colours, like the holly which bears a berry as red as any blood. Melanie stepped back to look at the result.

'Goodness,' she thought. 'Am I as thin as that?' For the dark green dress fitted her aunt perfectly, taking the awkwardness from her perpendiculars and giving her a Gothic kind of grace. A blurring thumb might have pressed, dark green, on her jutting hipbones. And then, such pyrotechnic hair. Melanie felt like the sympathetic friend in a Hollywood film who has finally persuaded the plain stenographer to take off her glasses and have herself a facial. It was as simple as that. Aunt Margaret was lovely, young and lovely, and she chuckled and preened, such a happy bird flaunting new-grown plumage.

'The dress does suit you,' said Melanie. 'Oh, it does. Please have it, from me; I have so much.' Or had.

Aunt Margaret found her speech at last and wrote: 'I'll borrow it from you just for today. While Philip is gone. I can't take it from you.'

'No. Have it for always. And these.' The pearls. And Aunt Margaret cried and would not take them. Melanie slid them round her neck and would not take 'No' for an answer. Let it all go, let it all go.

'I was going to put on my silver,' wrote Aunt Margaret, fallen tears blurring the writing on the pad.

'It is not right, for today.'

'I'll have the pearls for a lend, Melanie!'

Melanie shrugged. She wanted to give them away outright and have done with it, even if her mother watched somewhere in the room from a frame. She felt young and tough and brave, giving away her relics. And the pearls nestled so sweetly, cuddling up to her aunt's flesh, which had the same sheen on it as they. She hoped her aunt would grow so attached to the pearls during the day that she would think they had always been her own.

What shall you wear, Melanie?'

'Trousers,' said Melanie.

'You look leggy,' said Finn. 'What nice legs you have.'

'I haven't worn trousers for ages.'

'Because of Philip.'

'And he's not here.'

'Quite right.'

Francie sat in the kitchen with his fiddle in one hand and a half-empty bottle of whisky in the other.

'Jesus,' he said to Finn, 'you made free with the Scotch last night!'

'It was Christmas, after all,' said Finn. 'Besides, I was thirsty in the middle of the night.'

'I can see that,' said Francie half derisively. 'You must have been drunk as a lord, waving your little hatchet.'

He began to tune up. Aunt Margaret pushed open the kitchen door, carrying her flute, wearing Melanie's dress and pearls and her own glorious hair. Francie lowered his bow.

'That's my girl,' he said. 'That's pretty.'

'I remember you like that,' said Finn. 'In Ireland. When mother was alive.'

Their shared past sprang up between them, tangible, their

years together, their own old home, their parents. The woman in the brothers' bedroom, their mother. What was her name? How had she talked to them and showed them how she loved them and what family names, little names, did she have for them? How had she died? Did they get their red hair from her or what colour had her hair been? And how had she worn it? All Melanie knew of her was her guarded face and the feel of her dead eyelids, transmitted to her fingertips from Francie through Finn. Melanie wanted all their past, every bit of it, to share. She wanted to know when Francie had started to play the fiddle and who had first given Finn a set of paints. And how had Aunt Margaret met Uncle Philip; what doomsday had that been? And their father, who was he? Everything, family jokes and their parents' love-letters before they were married (if their parents had exchanged love-letters) and cut locks of treasured hair and clippings of birth announcements from yellowed old local newspapers. She felt she would die if she could not know everything.

'What was your mother like?' she said to Finn, as a beginning.

'Like a mother.'

He was drinking Scotch again. Soon he would become sentimental. But he was not grinning at her; she was glad his satyr's grin was safe on the face of the devil in the painting, never to embarrass her any more. Francie and Aunt Margaret began to play jigs and reels. Francie tapped his foot.

'Give us a bit of step-dancing, then, Finn,' said Francie.

'My dancing days are over.'

'Never.'

'Oh, yes, they are. I fell from a great height and I chopped up a swan so I'll never dance again. Besides, I'm almost a family man, now.' And he pulled Melanie's hair, which tumbled loose because it was a holiday.

'You're joking,' she said doubtfully. He hugged her. She could not get used to his smell of soap.

'Fate has thrown us into each other's arms,' he said.

'You're drunk.'

'I expect I will be, presently.'

'You are quite your old self.'

'No. Let's not exaggerate.'

And he was straining to be happy. It was not spontaneous, he was trying too hard. Melanie was sorry for him and moved closer to him. They sat together on the table. Francie's whisky was almost done.

Victoria had become over-excited, in her floral smock and a pink bow in her hair. She kept up a high-pitched yowl, leaping around the kitchen from lap to lap and grabbing at their clothes. But nobody cared. They were making too much noise to hear her, Francie and Aunt Margaret leaning together, played as one musician, rocking the kitchen, six-eight, nine-eight, twelve-eight, 'Rolling in the Barrel', 'In the Tap Room', 'The Earl's Chair', 'The Morning Dew', 'Kitty Gone A-Milking', 'Galway Rambler', 'A Trip to Athlone', 'The Pipe on the Hob', tune after tune after tune. The dog sat on the rug, beating its tail in time. Every now and then, Finn played spoons until they fell from his hands. He and Melanie sat on the table and occasionally he fondled her. She did not stop him because she did not quite know how and she was not sure if she wanted him to stop. When the pubs opened, Finn went out and returned clinking many bottles of Guinness, though Melanie did not know where he had got the money.

'I got Guinness to prove we're Irish,' he said.

Francie and Finn pressed Melanie to drink a few mouthfuls of the treacly stuff. Francie was extremely animated, like a boy, and Aunt Margaret seemed younger than Melanie, because more carefree. 'When you're sick, is it tea you want?', 'The Rakes of Mallow', 'Off she goes'. Jigs and reels, one, two, off they go.

'It is far nicer without Uncle Philip,' said Melanie, beginning to enjoy herself.

'When he comes back, I shall hit him,' said Finn. 'Francie will distract his attention while I hit him. Then we shall all walk out on him together, while he grovels on the floor. That'll fix him! It will be easy. I never thought it would be so easy.'

Melanie's dress on Aunt Margaret was the colour of pine forests. She was on the top branch of a happy tree, playing the flute with Francie, and Victoria tumbled on the floor. Downstairs, the shop lay in its Christmas Eve disorder, and, below that, the work-room was still littered with shed feathers, but the kitchen brimmed over with joy. ('Soldier's Joy', 'Huish the Cat from Under the Table', 'Rakish Paddy'; there was no end to the tunes they knew.) Bottle tops and empty bottles scattered over the floor. The air grew thick and blue with cigarette smoke. When they were hungry, they ate cold goose and cold stuffing and cheese and bread and mincepies and the music went on. Finn unwisely gave Guinness to Victoria and suddenly she sank down and out on the rug, with her head between the dog's paws. The room took on a debauched and abandoned look.

'I shall respect your youth and innocence, Melanie,' said Finn. 'Never fear that.'

'Then why did you kiss me in the pleasure gardens when I didn't like it?'

'You didn't know you didn't like it until I did it,' he said.

She thought: 'Well, he's certainly half seas over, now.'

'Look at me,' he said, turning her round to face him.

'Why?'

'Look at me.'

They looked at each other. Was he trying to mesmerise her? As in the pleasure gardens, she saw herself in the black pupils of his squint. 'My face in thine eye, thine in mine appears, And true plaine hearts doe in the faces rest.' John Donne, 1572–1632, alias Jack Donne, alias the Dean of St Paul's. In the school poetry book, between extracts from Shakespeare and 'The Rape of the Lock' by Alexander Pope. How all the young girls loved John Donne. And John Donne thought souls mingled as the eyestrings twist together, tangling like the puppet strings on the night of the fall. She sat in Finn's face; there she was, mirrored twice.

'I'm not going to be rushed,' she said desperately.

He leant forward and put a finger on her lips.

'Sh.'

The music had ceased while they looked at each other. The fiddle and flute were cast down on the floor. Francie and Aunt Margaret embraced. It was a lover's embrace, annihilating the world, as if taking place at midnight on the crest of a hill, with a tearing wind beating the branches above them. The brother and sister kneeled. The room was full of peace. The cigarette smoke shimmered and dissolved. The wise dog and his portrait gazed at them uncensoriously.

'Come away.' said Finn. 'We are not wanted here.'

Melanie was wide-eyed and grave. She let him draw her outside and he closed the door behind them. Away from the kitchen, it was cold. Finn's white shirt loomed like an iceberg.

216

He took his fireman's jacket from the rack and buttoned it up. He was quite sober. Perhaps he had only been pretending to be drunk.

'It is incest,' whispered Melanie. 'Like the Kings and Queens of Ancient Egypt.'

'Yes,' said Finn.

'I never guessed,' she said.

'No,' said Finn.

'I thought she was fondest of you, because you were the youngest.'

'Will you just shut up?' said Finn.

They went upstairs to his bedroom. She was glad she was wearing Mrs Rundle's sweater, knitted by her homemaking hands with wool from fubsy sheep who ate common grass and went 'baa, baa' predictably. She sat on Finn's bed. She was hushed and silent. He lay on Francie's bed, smoking.

'They are lovers. They have always been lovers. Do you understand?'

'Yes,' she said, in a very small voice.

'They are everything to each other. That is why we have stayed here, since Francie and Maggie . . .' he stopped.

'But she is much older,' said Melanie. 'Surely she is much older.'

'Do you think that matters?'

'I suppose not,' she said after a moment.

'Are you shocked, a nice girl like you?'

She thought for a moment.

'I have never encountered it before,' she said. 'Not incest. Not in my family.'

Francie and Aunt Margaret locked together in the most primeval of passions, down on the floor near the gas stove among the empty stout bottles with the dirty plates from dinner still on the table, crumbs of cheese, picked goose bones, and, on the wall, the cuckoo clock which did not work anymore.

'And Uncle Philip . . .'

'He's a cuckold,' said Finn grimly. 'By his own brother-in-law, whom he never would have suspected.'

'I gave Aunt Margaret my pearls,' said Melanie.

'Do you want them back?'

'No. I love her.' It was true. As she spoke, she felt the love, warm and understanding, inside her. And she loved Francie, too, there was no helping it. 'Pearls are the tears of fishes,' she added, inconsequently.

'What's that?'

'The tears of fishes. Pearls. You wouldn't think fish could cry. I remembered, suddenly.'

'That is our secret,' said Finn, dismissing weeping fish. 'You know our heart's core, now, the thing that makes us different from other people, Francie and Maggie and I.' He stamped his cigarette out on the floor.

The early-coming night settled over the rooftops and the lights came on in the houses across the way, those strange houses where people had no secrets. Melanie sat on Finn's bed and he on Francie's and the secret filled up all the space between them and around them. It was a hieratic and ancient presence. Incest, invoked downstairs on the worn rug, invoked upstairs in the quiet bedroom.

'I hope Victoria does not wake up.' said Melanie.

In spite of the dusk, she could see a charred stick in the fire-place, all that was left of the Christmas Eve rite. She found herself gazing at it as if it were the most significant object she had ever seen, as if it might start talking to her of past and present and future and a grand concept of them all as a whole in which incest had an explicable place. But it was only a charred stick.

It was about half past five (tea-time on a winter afternoon, the most British time of the day and year) when they heard the first crash.

'Oh, no,' said Finn, dropping a cigarette. 'No!'

Another crash and a woman's scream riding high and clear to the top of the pitch of sound and then falling away. And after that a roaring voice. They could hear it plainly where they sat, it was so loud.

'You filth! You dirt!'

Melanie leapt the gap between the beds into Finn's arms, burying her head in his jacket and saying: 'Save me, save me.' The dropped cigarette smouldered on the sheet.

'I thought it would be me he would kill,' said Finn. 'And so did he, we always thought that of each other. But we were wrong.'

For Uncle Philip had come home and found his wife in her brother's arms. This was the final point to which time flowed; this the finishing-post of the steeple-chase in which they ran in red colours.

'Keep me safe,' said Melanie, holding Finn's coat as if she were drowning.

'All right,' said Finn, absently. 'Don't go on, all right.'

The crashing went on, and shrieks.

'He is smashing the crockery,' said Finn in amazement. Astonishment made marble of him. He did not seem to be able to move.

'Save me,' said Melanie.

The bedroom door burst open and Aunt Margaret ran in in a red veil of dishevelled hair, the pretty green dress ripped half off her shoulders, holding a wailing Victoria. It was a storm in the room. The rug lifted off the floor in the gale she brought with her.

'Get out,' she said. 'Now.' She could speak. Catastrophe had freed her tongue. Her voice was thin but true. 'Get out while there is time. I'll keep the baby safe. Whatever happens, she'll be safe.'

'Where is Francie?'

'All right. But we must stay and finish our business with Philip.' With her voice, she had found her strength, a frail but constant courage like spun silk. Struck dumb on her wedding day, she found her old voice again the day she was freed.

'Maggie, dearest Maggie—'

'Look after the girl. Go now. Philip is gathering wood and lighting it. He is going to set the house on fire.'

'Kiss me,' said Finn, over the top of Melanie's head. 'God knows what is going to happen.'

She kissed his mouth. Melanie, ever afterwards, remembered the stately formality with which they kissed, like fellow generals saluting each other the night before a great battle where one of them is like to die and, later, it seemed to her that she saw them framed in fire, but she knew she imagined this. Her aunt was a goddess of fire; her eyes burned and her hair flickered about her. She and Finn drew apart slowly. She put her hand on Melanie's head for a moment and then ran out. So Melanie never had a chance to say good-bye to Victoria. The noise from downstairs increased in volume. Now furniture was being broken up. Melanie smelled smoke but it was Finn's forgotten cigarette burning the blanket. Finn took the picture of his mother from the mantelpiece and put it in his pocket.

'Time to be gone,' he said.

There was a barricade of smashed, piled chairs at the foot of the stairs, on the kitchen landing. Philip Flower pulled the table through the door to add to it. The floral tablecloth still flapped disconsolately around its legs and the remains of their meal tumbled to the floor as he heaved and tugged. 'Trap them like rats and burn them out!' he shouted with insane glee. And it was glee. They were all to burn and gleefully he would watch them. The blood showed through his eyes. He still wore his overcoat and broad-brimmed, familiar hat. He was too big and wicked to be true, thought Melanie, while from the kitchen came a crackling and a smell of woodsmoke.

As they stood uncertainly on the stairs, the white dog came hurtling out of the dining-room, scrambled over the barricade and sped past them up the stairs, panting, its flanks throbbing. Did it or did it not carry a basket of flowers in its mouth? But it was gone too quickly for Melanie to be sure. Philip Flower upturned the table behind the chairs, saw Finn, yelped with hatred and flung himself on the barricade, which was now quite sizeable. As he struggled to pull himself up, he gabbled: 'Let me get my hands on you, Finn Jowle, you're all in it together, you took turn and turn about to do her—'

'Liar,' said Finn. He took Melanie's hand and they stumbled back up the stairs.

'The skylight,' said Finn, who was pale but calm, as if all this had been rehearsed somewhere a long time ago. 'We'll go on the roof.'

The crackling noise was now all around them. Uncle Philip might have been roasting a herd of pigs.

'With all that wood in the basement, the place will go up in no time. We must hurry.'

One of the sinister doors of Bluebeard's castle sprang open as they went by. Francie came out, carrying an iron bar.

'Good luck,' said Finn.

'Oh, take care!' said Melanie.

'God bless you,' said Francie. He was in his shirtsleeves. There were black rings of sweat under his arms. He went downstairs and they went up.

Finn hoisted Melanie through the skylight and swung up himself, onto the high and windy roof, with the first stars and the chimney pots. They rested for a while.

> *Sally go round the stars,*
> *Sally go round the moon,*
> *Sally go round the chimney pot*
> *On a Sunday afternoon.*
> *Wheeeeeeee!*

When she was a very small girl, her father recited this to Melanie, and, when he came to the 'Wheeeeeeee!' bit, seized her round the waist and whirled her up in the air. She and Finn sat whirled among the chimney pots and held hands.

Melanie thought: 'Now we have shared all this, we can never be like other people. We can only be like ourselves and one another. We have only each other, now.'

She said aloud: 'I have already lost everything, once.'

'So have I,' said Finn.

'But then I had my brother and sister left to me. Where is Jonathon?'

'I don't know. If you've got your breath back, Melanie, we

must go on. There is a fire escape on the next house and we can get across the roof easily.'

It was the deserted jeweller's. The rusty metal treads clanged beneath their feet. The rooms above the shop were empty but might soon be full of fire. In a few seconds, they stood knee-high in the grass of the neglected garden. It was full of discarded tins, jam-jars, rubbish thrown over the wall.

'We must ring the brigade. 999. Fire. Ambulance,' said Finn. 'Police. Help for us.'

The house burnt like a giant chrysanthemum, all golden.

'But then,' said Finn, almost to himself, 'I expect somebody has rung 999 already.'

Windows opened around them on all sides and anxious heads poked out, chorusing agitation. It was night. The house jetted flames. A man standing in the alley a few feet away from them said lugubriously: 'There can be nothing left alive in there.'

'Do you think they are all burnt up?' Melanie said to Finn.

'I think Francie and Maggie and the baby are safe. And the dog is an old dog and knows many tricks.'

'You don't think so. You only hope so. And the poor talking bird . . .'

'Poor Joey,' said Finn. 'Philip bought him.'

They watched the flames.

'My jacket,' said Finn with a choked half laugh, half sob. 'It is ironic under the circumstances, a fireman's jacket.'

'I often wondered where you got it.'

'Just at a jumble sale.'

'Oh.'

A floor caved in inside the house with a gush of fire. All burning, everything burning, toys and puppets and masks and chairs and tables and carpets and Mrs Rundle's christmas card with all her love and lightshades bursting open with fire and the bathroom geyser melting and the bathroom plastic curtains dripping to nothing as the fire licked them over. Edward Bear burning, with her pyjamas in his stomach.

'All my paintings.' said Finn faintly. 'Such as they were.'

'Even Edward Bear,' she said.

'What?'

'My bear. He's gone. Everything is gone.'

'Nothing is left but us.'

At night, in the garden, they faced each other in a wild surmise.